BEYOND THE INFERNO

ALEX L MORETTI

BEYOND THE INFERNO

A Novelisation of The Divine Comedy:
A Lover's Quest To Save Mankind

Cover illustration by Chloë B Martin

ISBN: 979-8-6517-8524-7

For my darling daughters, for whom my love knows no bounds.

CONTENTS

INFERNO

I am man and are we not seeds of Adam, open to temptation and sin just for we are lacking in spiritual strength? Yet to succumb is to condemn ourselves to eternal separation from Him; banished to that dark and desolate place where there is nothing but torture and pain.

THE DARK WOOD

As a man I am mostly unremarkable yet in this precise moment know I partake in an event truly extraordinary. It is ominous, perhaps, that today marks the crucifixion of our blessed Mother's son upon the gibbet at the gates of Jerusalem. Just shy of one million moons have passed since that onerous day and although I know I am not to suffer the same torment as he, believe that I, too, find myself as in death. Yet this is most confusing for, certainly, I am alive! In truth, I know not why I have been plunged into this bleak wilderness nor what it is I shall find, but I suspect it is the afterlife, for the living do not reside here I am sure of it.

In solitude and from within the depths of my soul I yearn for it to be Paradise, for I seek deliverance. To know I am arrived in the celestial spheres would bring great comfort, for is it not man's fervent desire to attain salvation? Indeed, to find myself in the realm of darkness would be to accept eternal separation from the Creator and I am unprepared to contemplate such a ruinous truth. Thus, just as I pray for eternal life, I pray for light in these shadows of foreboding. Yet I fear this darkness. Am I to be denied? Exiled thus?

Banished to a cataclysmic afterlife of eternal death, to the very core of the Underworld where the Black Emperor reigns? I fear this is what He has ordained, although why I cannot think. This is not my time, for most assuredly I am not dead. Indeed, my heart beats strong, as the Roman drums of war.

In this moment I know dread. I am not blind yet cannot see the path ahead, for in stumbling and lurching about this desolate wasteland I look up to find myself in a forest which has an impenetrable darkness, as black as the ebony trees within. I have lost one of my senses for the blackness is such to be blinded, eyes gouged and tossed aside, for they are no use to me here. Tree roots ripple at the decaying soil as undulating waves, such that they wish me to falter and stumble, and they are victorious. I stagger directionless, reeling and pitching, drawn in as a spinning whirlpool sucks me deeper and stronger, as if Charybdis drags me into his very bowels. As ebony, so dense it may sink in water, I too plunge to the depths of the abyss, hauled into the forest with a force more powerful than the Mighty himself, but I cannot escape. A scream echoes as I am pulled to the core of the terrifying entangled maze, determined to avoid it and all the bedlam that resides within for I fear this is a gateway to the Underworld. Yet struggle is futile as the violent maelstrom drags me in further, the solid arms and fists of trees which, as I, breathe with life, force me deeper into the black void. For this is The Dark Wood. That desolate and hideous place of which we have heard and of which we are all afraid.

I cannot find my way through the tangled forest, for I am blinded by the darkness. Battling through the labyrinth, I cry out in terror, for trees attack me; whipping, lashing as whistling rapiers, slashing and slicing. Abandoned cobwebs, thick and oily, veil my eyes and mask my mouth as bats swoop and screech about me. Confusion and desperation contaminate my mind, for I thought I was searching for Paradise, but it is not here. Anxiety reigns, for although I am cast adrift unto this grim and fetid wilderness where I fear the dead reside, I am not. I breathe and I feel and I sense for I am mortal man. I am alive!

I do not sleep, I am not gone; departed. I am here as surely as God himself exists, albeit not in this place. For the wood is dark. It is bleak and is devoid of air, for my lungs ache as I breathe ether most foul. I shall not attain salvation here for He is not present, only chaos and mayhem. There is to be no warm embrace in The Dark Wood, no soft glow of His love, nor shall I know the radiant light of bliss. For my journey is just beginning and the gates to Hell await, for I believe this place to be a portal. I do not doubt my destination, for the path of Light, that which leads to Paradise, does not exist here. I know that to follow the path of righteousness and reach the glorious radiance that is Heaven is to find God. Yet here is only darkness.

Am I not to attain salvation? For what is salvation if not to triumph in the rapturous bliss of Divine light? I confess I am fearful He is not present, for here there is no light, just the darkness of foreboding. It appears that I, as this place, am forsaken, for here it is empty, rancid and grim and if this is my denouement, it shall not lead me to the light of redemption. And if I am denied, cast adrift to a place furthest from the warmth of His love, shall a life without deliverance offer nothing but ice and all the coldness, muteness and numbness of eternal death? It shall be a castigation most cruel for, indeed, what is eternal separation from Him if not absolute rejection?

But what is this that catches my eye at the forest canopy? A shard of gold in this blackness; the dawn sun caressing a hilltop yonder? There is light above so I must muster every effort to battle through this entangled abyss to that place, to make my way unto that refulgence, for what is light if not God? His love illuminates, so guided by that radiance, I shall seek a path through the darkness out of this desolate, abandoned wood and pray it will lead me from this fearsome wilderness into salvation. For, in my heart, I believe that skyward light to be Heaven.

Yet this is to be a hardship indeed and I am to be tested. For, as I emerge from the blackness of the forest, I have heard a frightening noise. A raging beast, snarling, grunting, salivating. I am rooted to the spot; paralysed. I feel its breath upon my neck for it snorts so close the hairs on my head are blown with the potent force of its rank exhalation. I am to show strength, for if this is a trial I shall demonstrate to God that I have faith, that I trust in Him to deliver me from such evil. Yet I fear it is not one evil that stands before me. It is three. And they are ominous. For these dark, monstrous beasts of a black, bleak night have revealed themselves unto me in the shadows of the shard of light.

I am cautious for my instinct is survival and I have no doubt these are brutes, gruesome behemoths. A lion, a leopard and a she-wolf appear before me, albeit I can barely see them. Yet they are not as they seem, for instinctively I know them to be carnal sins incarnate; lust, pride and avarice in physical being. They are vile. For what is sin if not vile? And these sins are the vilest of them all, for they are the greatest. They tempt me to submit, they insist upon it; that I surrender unto them, that I relinquish my faith in the Divine, for they wish me to return to the black valley of error and force me back into the depths of The Dark Wood. I fear they intend to plunge me ever deeper into the darkness furthest from that ray of light, for they do not wish me to escape and attain salvation. I am in danger! For I am alive in a place abundant with menace, threat and enticement such that with each step I may weaken and yield; that I may submit. For I am man and are we not seeds of Adam, open to temptation and sin just for we are lacking in spiritual strength?

I cannot move towards the golden light, for these gargantuan beasts who live in the shadows, block my path. They encircle me, padding the earth, grunting, nudging, snorting, writhing, and momentarily I am enthralled by thoughts of these vile sins. I confess I am tempted, for does not man have carnal desires that need satisfying? Are we not conceited and smug, beholden to arrogance? And are we not wanting and covetous, rapacious in desire, in greed? In truth, there is nothing here to distract me; nothing to divert my thoughts and God has forsaken this place so He will not be witness to my wrongdoing. I admit I am curious; tempted, for I am man and these sins entice me. Without God man is weak. And God has abandoned me here in this place and I fear that without Him I may be seduced.

Something in the distance appears vaguely unto me although how, in this blanket of black, I do not know. It is a man and one whom I recognise, praise be! For this is the departed Virgil, a fellow poet renowned for his sage and judicious words, for who is Virgil if not wisdom? He has sought me here, I am certain of it. Did God send him to release me from this hell, this torture? I believe it to be so, for the beasts have been driven away by his virtuous presence and I am safe. I may hope after all, that God watches over me here, for His embrace shall offer protection.

Virgil is calm; serene. He is a being most rational and exceptional, for he has an intelligence and reasoning which has remained unmatched amongst earthly mankind. He radiates tranquillity so I may hope that he guides me to do the same. Indeed, if he can help me to emerge from the bleakness and danger herein and steer me towards the light, away from all that is dark, God will have presented me with a gift most precious. For this man is insight and dignity combined and it is my intention to savour every crumb of wisdom he imparts. It is no surprise that he wears the laurel wreath, for this Roman has been lauded as a paragon of human and artistic knowledge, a masterful poet crowned by the Protector of Arts, Apollo himself. In truth, he is most impressive and I am captivated.

I reach out in welcome embrace but my arms pass through him, for they fail to find physical form. At my confusion he tells me he is merely a shade, a soul, for he is not of the living. He reminds me that upon death, man's

7

spirit and flesh are disconnected and, having been judged by God, his soul is cast into the afterlife. Indeed, it is only upon the Last Judgement, that final day of humanity when the dead are resurrected and all humankind are judged, shall those blessed spirits deemed worthy of eternal life in the spheres of Heaven undergo a reunification of body and soul. He tells me I shall not be witness to such glory within this terrestrial realm. So, he confirms it is thus; we are indeed far from the celestial Paradise.

He gestures for me to follow, for it is his intention to lead me from the wood out of the darkness into the new dawn. We walk silently and, in quiet contemplation, I call upon the Three Muses for I wish to relay the story of my meeting with the Beasts of Hell but find I have not retained any memory of it. The sublime goddesses of art and poetry inform my conscious mind and Virgil heeds without alarm as I tell how the vicious monsters deliberately obstructed my path to the hilltop, for it was their intention to entice me to stray, to force me back to The Dark Wood, to the depths of the blackness furthest away from the light.

He listens intently and replies that Fortuna favours me, for the she-wolf is salacious, violent and brutal. I believe him and give thanks for my lucky escape, for a dismal death would be her intent, torn limb from limb by this crazed, salivating temptress. He reveals that she will not survive long in this place for a powerful creature, a magnificent hound, will chase her away from this ominous forest back to the depths of Hell. I confess I am not reassured, for she is a wily monster with the cunning of all things female. Until that moment, he tells me, we are to navigate a different path, for our task is to ascend the hill to meet the light.

Our journey will be perilous and treacherous he warns, for to reach the celestial heavens of Paradise from whence the light emerges, we must first pass through Hell, a dismal place of eternal punishment, and then negotiate the realm of lesser castigation; Purgatory. These sound like wretched cities indeed and with all my heart I wish to avoid them for

I am alive where all are dead and I fear those within may not know this and carry me with them to the depths of eternal despair. He tells me we are to venture through the afterlife towards the mouth of Hell, whereupon I fear we shall likely be devoured by every demon and devil and eternally damned, cursed soul that resides within. But what else can I do, for I seek the golden light that is Heaven, for I desire salvation and only God may bestow it upon me.

I confess that courage deserts me, for is it not thus that no living soul before me has journeyed into the darkness? That mortal man, as I, is a stranger to these foreboding shadows of misery? I fear hopelessness shall reign in my heart, for dread and despair will drag me to an unearthly kingdom of woe and pain, for I am not Aeneas, hero of Troy, zealously championed to victory by the gods and goddesses of ancient Greece and Rome. I fear I am not worthy such that God has presented me with not magnificent deities of the classic civilisations, merely a virtuous poet in a blue tunic, so I am anxious the place of eternal punishment shall overcome and I will not survive. Yet, I seek the light and there is no other path, for until the she-wolf is dispatched, I need to venture through these two places of depravity and misery.

I am admonished for my despair and Virgil reminds of the need to have a stronger faith that God will deliver me from this place, for without it, and burdened by the invisible weight of fear, I will succumb to sin, that which shall entice me at each circle of Hell and cause me to drift away from God into eternal damnation. This journey is not for the fainthearted, he cautions, yet understands that he too is on a mission, called upon to attend herein and act as my guide. He is a sage being and so, to distract me as we walk amongst this bleak and barren terrain, relays the tale of how he found himself to be here. For he had received a message from an angel in Heaven who, having witnessed my stumbling plight in the depths of the murky wood took pity and sought him out with a compassionate and tearful entreaty. This angel, it transpires, was my beloved; my soul, my heart. For it was Beatrice, my own muse, the too-early departed, the cherished and blessed, and I find myself relieved to tears to know that she is safe in Heaven and still loves me.

He tells me that she, with three holy women including the Virgin Mary, watch over me from above and I am reassured to know this as my companion and I continue ever closer towards the cesspit that is Hell. I am much obliged to Virgil, for his wisdom and serenity has informed my emotions such that but for his presence and intercedence, in confusion and desperation I would have succumbed to sin and all that was depraved in The Dark Wood. I am most fortunate that his strength, prudence and judiciousness remained steadfast, for I have avoided a fate most unimaginable; that of a life cast adrift from God to the furthest place away from His love, for Virgil overcame the she-wolf that I would not retreat back into the forest. But I fear I am in need of more than prudence at this moment, for we have arrived at our destination; the place all men dread. For it is the entrance to Hell, whence no man returns.

VESTIBULE OF HELL

The dark corridor to the city of woe is a place most foul, for it is cankerous. The grim stench invades my craw as brimstone, sulphur and all that is rank in this fetid world curls through the air as the gnarled fingers of a winding fog strangling at my throat. We stand at the opening to a cave, and though I have not yet passed through the shadowy entrance, already I know this place to be horror and suffering and all that is misery. For I have read the words written upon the arch and they fill me with dread such that they command: *all hope abandon, ye who enter here.* I know when I walk through this gate I shall pass into eternal pain. Yet all I have is one hope and I am unable to abandon it, however much the devils and demons demand it. For in seeking salvation, I seek God. Thus, I must descend through the darkness to reach the light that is God's love, that which I have seen upon the hilltop yonder and that which, in his wisdom, Virgil confirms is the celestial Paradise.

I look to him for strength, for now we have begun our journey, we must complete it. There is to be no turning back, for our destination is the place of eternal damnation and to enter through the gates of Hell is to commit to a quest. But where will it end? In evolution? Salvation? In truth, it is most likely death, for though I am not as wise as Virgil, I am not so naïve to know this place is perilous. From within, I hear the perpetual screams of the damned souls and know they endure eternal suffering such that my mortal ears have never before known the howling cries of agony and torment, the harrowing wails of misery and grief they emit therein.

In this arena most foul I need to demonstrate faith, for to trust God is to love God and He will love me by delivering salvation if I trust in Him. So it happens, that my companion and I step forward from the vestibule and pass through the opening into the darkness that is Hell. This place is as uninviting as those hostile words above, for indeed it is the city of pain where lost souls endure eternal suffering. Again, I am submerged into blackness. Not even a lone star lights our way and it is cold, damp and bleak, as The Dark Wood, although this is a place more vile, more depraved, more terrifying. For this is the realm of the cursed dead, who reside here in perpetual woe as they sustain punishments no living man could endure.

I cannot believe the scene I behold. I am stunned into silence for I am utterly appalled at the desperate sight unravelling before my eyes. Virgil attempts communication with me but I cannot tear myself from the view. Nor can I hear him above the sorrowful wails, the angry screams, the deep, hoarse voices tumultuous as they reach an ear-splitting crescendo. This soundtrack, I suspect, repeats itself for all eternity. At first, the emission of a quiet groan, then another and one more until, ten-thousand-fold, they are joined by shrieks and howls and moans, some piercing, some low, but all loud and deafening, a shrill, thunderous, voluble symphony; a cacophony of the sounds of sorrow. Virgil speaks, for he can see by my tears I am appalled by the hideous exhibition of suffering I witness. He informs me I need to prepare myself for sights more grotesque than this, for I am to pass through all the torments of Hell to understand sin in all its guises, for not to do so would be to deny myself salvation.

Have I so displeased God? Did my earthly actions offend Him such that I am to be punished, castigated, tortured? Or does He cast me here that I may redeem myself within the darkness? Am I to locate my spiritual soul in order that I may be cleansed and purified and thus find my way back to the path of righteousness and truth? Whatever His reason, I do not intend to create my eternal downfall, for to attain salvation and reside in Heaven is the only outcome I seek knowing, beyond doubt, that what I witness is beyond any threshold of mortal suffering.

It is impossible for me to hear what Virgil is saying but he mouths the words *The Uncommitted* and gestures to the naked souls herein. I know these neutrals to be those who forsook God on Earth, for they were too cowardly to commit to a decision for moral good or, indeed, evil and have thus been denied entry to both Heaven and Hell. Hence, they are destined to reside on the banks of the fetid River Acheron, the Ante Hell, for they are only *of* Hell, not *within* it and they suffer in perpetuity because of it. But why am I here, alongside them? For I am as committed to God as Mary unto Jesus. My allegiance is with Him and I am aggrieved that He may think otherwise and unite me with this errant yet pitiful tribe.

I look at them again for they howl; groaning and wailing in their torment. Hornets and wasps diligently sting their cursed souls for there is to be no peace for the wicked here, not even the comfort of sleep. These yellowjackets mobilise to swarm as ferocious, venomous beasts targeting their whimpering prey, engorged with toxic spite, primed for brutal torture as a noxious pestilence. Virgil points to the floor whereupon I see a carpet of pus, of blood and tears which cascade from the bodies of these pitiful souls. Their faces, contorted in agony, emit screams, shrieks and moans for, as well as pain and misery, they demonstrate sorrow and shame, their suffering and distress as audible as it is visible. Feasting upon this cankerous slush are worms and slugs and maggots in a sickening vision of physical and spiritual stagnation. And now I know that to find salvation is to find eternal peace, for to live in perpetual misery and torment such as this is a punishment I, as mortal man, am incapable of enduring. It is apparent to me I must escape this place, for a more cruel apocalyptic world, a more harrowing and disturbed scene, I cannot imagine. Yet I am not to turn back for I have committed to this quest so the only course available unto me is to cross the river towards the chaos of Hell itself, for I partake in the unavoidable journey.

We move away from this cesspit and head for the lake of black water. As I stand on the bank of the Acheron it is to Charon I must look, for he is the ferryman of dead souls and only he may move me closer towards my destination. It appears there is to be a crossing imminently, for upon the shore yonder is a crowd of tormented souls, one thousand, maybe two, newly dead and awaiting transportation to the true depths of Hell. Virgil and I thus join them, for our destination is as theirs. Already I am despairing, quietly weeping. A boat approaches in the dark, the sound of gentle waves breaking upon its bow a welcome relief from the moans of sorrow and misery, albeit I remain terrified of what lurks on the other side of the water.

Upon the boat stands Charon, he who we know ferries the souls of the Damned; a demon devoid of compassion, consideration or pity. For he is a soul most brutal; abundant with judgement, menace and corruption. A scourge; malignant, vile and repugnant. For how cruel is a man who collects payment from the dead, prising coins from their very eyes and mouths as he leads them towards the furnace of Hell, who hits out with his oar at their already broken souls as they wail and curse at their misfortune? Battered by the storms and rains, the winds and snows have destroyed his naked body and razed any love or compassion he may have held within. His weather-beaten outer is as haggard and decaying as his inner, for the ravages of Hell have eaten at his skin and entered his heart. He groans in despair, barks and snarls in anger and I am desperate to avoid him, yet he is the ferryman thus encounter is inevitable. The boat touches the bank and he roars at the souls gathered here that they shall never know Heaven, only perpetual darkness and suffering, torture and misery, for to enter his boat is to enter into the realms of fire and ice. For he drags them to Hell.

His words torment me and I am petrified such that I may barely breathe. I look to Virgil but my eyes land instead upon the queuing throng, now grown in quantity such that one cannot fathom how sin has undone so many, how death has affected so many. I lurch back, for I am unprepared for the savagery Charon describes and am most reluctant to board, yet the hoard of damned souls plunge into the boat, tumbling in as falling leaves with zealous enthusiasm, despite their bitter tears and wails of anguish. Virgil sees the confusion upon my face and tells me these wretched sinners crave eternal misery such that their desire for justice to prevail outweighs their fear of suffering to come. As Hell is that place where God's will is meted out, they desire residence there. But, the Uncommitted, he continues, shall not be accepted into the dark realms of deep Hell, only the banks of Ante Hell, for they have no hope of eternal death, just eternal torment, knowing their unwillingness to commit in life has caused neither Heaven or Hell to commit to invitation upon death.

But what is this? He refuses me entry? How can it be, for I am not to attain salvation if I cannot make my way towards the light! To journey through Hell is my only route, for the she-wolf still roams The Dark Wood and thus the straightforward path is blocked. Yet it appears that Charon can see I am not of the dead, that I do not share the cursed soul of the Damned who have cause to reside within the toxic bosom of Hell in all perpetuity and he gestures for me to move away, for he will not carry me across the river. This is good news Virgil tells me, for Charon recognises that I am mortal man, of the living, and should not be in these parts with the sorrow-laden miscreant sinners. Yet, understanding the critical nature of my unavoidable journey, he ventures into conversation with the sadistic ferryman.

Thanks be to Virgil's intercedence; that he stands steadfast at my side and that in this precise moment judiciously performs his role as my guide, to see me safely through Hell towards the light of Heaven. I know not what he has said but I am most grateful for, once again, the sage words of this wise and dignified man have saved me. It appears he has managed to tame Charon and persuade him my journey has been preordained by God Himself, that Divine will commands it, that under the watchful eye of Mother Mary, I must complete a challenge most demanding. For I am to witness the punishments of Hell, explore the damage that sin may do yet not succumb to enticement, temptation and seduction. For if I do this successfully, I will purify my soul and be led out of Hell towards salvation.

An assignment, then. This is the first I have heard it spoken thus, that I understand the reason for my siting in this putrid abyss. Yet I must question what has caused God to be displeased with me. For I am no sinner, no transgressor. I have not succumbed to avarice and corruption nor have I violated or betrayed. Well, perhaps a little, but I believe myself to be mostly morally virtuous, a loyal enough servant of the scriptures. Indeed, have I not earnestly endeavoured to remain upon the earthly path of Truth, albeit there has been the odd temptation to stray? But this is just a human weakness, surely? For, I have said, I am a seed of Adam. I am afraid, I confess, for we know that to err is human and all I seek is Divine forgiveness. Yet I know forgiveness shall not be granted here for it is the Devil, Hell's monarch, who reigns in this place.

Praise be! Out of the corner of my eye I glimpse an angel! Yet Virgil tells me that it, too, is a neutral, banished from the celestial Paradise, such that during the War in Heaven when Lucifer rebelled and was cast by God to Hell in his fall from grace, these holy messengers failed to commit allegiance to either. Heaven thus exiled them, driving the unaligned angels away from the highest Paradise that it could retain its magnificent radiance; its perfect beauty. Hell rejected them also, such that their sin did not warrant the evils of the Underworld should triumph eternally over their souls. And thus, it seems, I am not to be protected by God's messengers, for they only reside here such that they too, as the pitiful souls of the Uncommitted, have been rejected by Heaven and Hell.

So, my champion, Virgil, has convinced Charon that he is to ferry me across the river into Hell proper and he agrees without paying any heed or attention other than angrily waving me on to the boat. It dips slightly as I board, which interests the other passengers for now they know me to be of the living, but Charon continues to ignore me so I am unlikely to catch his eye, black and lifeless as a chunk of coal such that it is. I am grateful, for he is vicious with his oar and assaults these wretched souls most violently.

My heart breaks, for it is indeed a sorry sight and I am forced to look away, for I cannot help them even if I so desired. But, in truth, they do not appear to retreat or recoil; rather they accept their destiny willingly, for Virgil tells me these souls do not fear God, such that they desire His justice and glory to triumph. If it is His will, that they shall endure eternal pain and never know eternal life and joy, they accept their residence here such that He has bestowed this justice upon them. Indeed, barely have we cast off from the bank than another band of cursed souls break from the queue to congregate at the river's edge, quite willing to endure the hardships of Hell for they, too, seek freedom in eternal justice.

And now a storm. Am I never to be free of danger in this place? For a tumultuous earthquake shakes the shoreline, a frenzied wind and fire rise up from the abyss. The river swells, torrential rain lashes in a fearsome tempest and I fear my life is over, for the boat is close to capsizing. Indeed, I feel my knees give beneath me and I collapse with a final breath, screaming, panicked, terrified yet reassured that the face of my brother, Virgil, is the last I see before I finally depart this life. But I am not dead, for a booming crack of thunder awakens me from my faint. I have reached the other side of the river so presume it was the storm that cast me here, more likely Virgil has carried me from the boat, for I awaken in his arms yet in a place so high I conclude it must be Heaven. But it is not. For my view is of a bottomless valley, a desolate and barren subterranea looming down to dizzying depths. For Virgil tells me I am looking at Limbo. The first circle of Hell.

1ST CIRCLE OF HELL - LIMBO

Away from the swamp of vomit and pus at the banks of the Acheron, we are at a place of rocks and dry earth but must descend, for we are at a precipice and there is no way forward other than down. Unusually, Virgil is hesitant and, too, his complexion is much paled. My emotions are informed by him so I am unnerved, for if he shows fear, this surely is a place most foul and dangerous. Again, I hear screams and howling of the wretched souls therein, albeit I am blinded by the darkness so may not yet see the faces hidden in the depths of the valley. The wails are lower in tone yet still reach a roaring crescendo as they echo within the cavernous basin. We cautiously make our way down the steep path, for to stumble and fall into the pit from such a height would end in certain death for a mortal man such as I. And thus, it is with much trepidation I follow my guide, yet listen intently to his discourse, for over the hours we traverse, descending deeper and further into its centre, he explains that we approach Limbo, the primary circle of the Underworld, that he is of this place and has only been granted leave to assist me on my journey.

I am shocked, for I did not realise that Virgil resides in Hell but he explains that Limbo is merely a painless border on the outer edge of the abyss. It is reserved solely for the faithful and virtuous who, just by unfortunate circumstance, may not enjoy the eternal bliss of Heaven, for without express acknowledgement of the theological virtues of faith, hope and love, they are deemed morally incomplete and are thus damned. I am confused and need clarification, for surely virtue and faith is all that is required to gain entry to Paradise? He elucidates that for the Faithful, merely having been denied a baptism or failing to repent their sins prevents them an afterlife in the celestial spheres. For the virtuous, as he, born before the coming of Christ thus denying the existence of doctrine, albeit in ignorance, they too, are eternally banished herein. His hesitancy is not borne out of fear he assures me, rather disappointment and regret that he returns to this place.

There is no happiness or sadness in Limbo, he clarifies, rather its peaceful environs and bountiful gardens allow for contemplation and reflection. For although there is no joy, just as there is no suffering, there is honour. Yet, he concedes, residents here accept they are waiting, drifting and stagnating in a pointless, stultifying, listless and futile existence, for until the day of Final Judgement, when the souls of the dead are resurrected and reunited with their flesh, they are the indeterminables. Indeed, only then will they learn their theological fate; whether they rise, sky-bound, saved, to enjoy eternal bliss in the celestial Paradise, or if they are to be perpetually damned in the cesspit of Hell. I listen again to the howling and realise it is not the violent screaming of the Uncommitted, rather crying, sighing, a plaintive sorrowful lament. I confess I am most moved and, not for the first time, I know I am weeping.

What injustice is this? That God forsakes the virtuous who, by the timing of their birth, did not know of Christ so may not enter the kingdom of Heaven? Or those faithful, including innocent babes who, having been deprived a baptism are thus denied access to the gates of Paradise, lost to eternity in the circle of Hell that is Limbo? This seems most unjust, for these virtuous pagans are condemned to Hell and are punished by eternal separation from God and the heavens although not by conscious wrongdoing. They are not sinners for they did not reject Christ but were merely ignorant of his teachings, only for he was not in existence during their earthly lifetime. Are these not very different things? Does not Heaven possess a Limbo where these souls may reside instead? I am angry but Virgil tolerates it with good enough grace for, he says, it is not as The Dark Wood, nor the place where the Uncommitted reside on a carpet of pus and maggots, for there is no torment here, no pain or suffering. Indeed, I see ahead in the distance it is thus and the conditions are ripe for contemplation but, still, it must rankle. I am irked on his behalf but he remains unperturbed and unduly accepting.

I ponder and reflect in this moment as I look yonder to the vast expanse of meadow. I have Virgil at my side and he gives me immeasurable strength, for he is wisdom beyond five thousand scholars. Yet I cannot be certain he will remain as my companion, for what if he should prefer the tranquil, yet unyielding, gardens of Limbo to the torment and suffering of the Underworld? And if he leaves me, who may I turn to for moral guidance, for inspiration and courage in the depths of the inhumane depravity I am set to witness? I cannot traverse this vile and fetid sewer unaccompanied for, alone, I will not have the strength to deny myself when temptation casts its net, yet my challenge here is to reject enticement in all its forms. Indeed, the consequences of not doing so, as I have witnessed in the rank, malodorous hole where reside the Uncommitted, are too terrible for mortal man to contemplate; nay, to endure. I thus pray, that with Mother Mary's blessing, Virgil remains steadfast by my side; pray that God wills it, for should I weaken and yield to sin or, indeed, terror, I shall be eternally undone.

We emerge from the darkness into the meadow whereupon souls are gathered, conversing, roaming, drifting. Unlike the Uncommitted, these shades are clothed and there is a dignity and serenity to this place for, as Virgil says, these faithless but virtuous shades do not endure torture or suffering. We continue our discourse, for Virgil can see I am moved and disconcerted. I ask if God releases these souls to Heaven for, surely, He can see the injustice in such a punishment for as much as they are without faith, they are without sin. They did not succumb to temptation nor willingly deny Him. Virgil tells me that indeed there was a time known as the Harrowing of Hell, that moment between Christ's death and the resurrection, when he descended into Limbo to collect righteous souls that they could triumph in the celestial heavens. I am flabbergasted when Virgil tells me he was witness to this himself when notables such as Noah and Moses were released, albeit despairingly, others including himself, remain here. For eternity.

We continue across the field upon which an empty sun sighs, breathing just enough life to the trees and flowers herein, when we chance upon a group of men, known unto Virgil but not to me. They are introduced as Homer, Ovid, Horace and Lucan, acknowledged as the greatest poets of antiquity. I am enthralled as I witness them greet their old friend and recite verses from each other's epic works, yet I feel this is a tired conversation they have endured a thousand times before, for there is little joy. Indeed, it is the same as we pass through the citadel walls when I am introduced to more wise souls, this time of theology, philosophy and astronomy. We converse briefly, albeit they discourse at a level of sagacity and intelligence I find myself unable to match, so I remain silent, my contentment exalted in this brief moment such that I am in awe of their scholastic astuteness, which more than satiates my intellectual cravings. Yet, do I hear true? They deem the greater punishment is to be denied a beatific vision in the Kingdom that is Heaven? For in accepting they are forbidden sight of the blessed Father in His home of angels, for as faithless pagans they shall not witness the Almighty God in Paradise, they judge this theological loss affects them far worse than their siting in this nefarious realm?

I confess I remain confused at their status within the sewer of Hell and it is my fervent desire that upon the Final Judgement, these souls shall be resurrected, reunited with their flesh, that they may ascend to enjoy salvation and eternal life in the celestial heavens. Yet I know not God's will and may not presume to. Whilst they are deep in contemplative conversation and without them noticing, Virgil takes my arm and quietly escorts me away from this serenity towards a new darkness, where no light shines.

We continue downwards, for Hell is a subterranean underworld spiralling to unfathomable depths, a black, damp, cavernous funnel into which we must journey. He tells me of the topography here such that there are nine concentric rings, ever decreasing circles, within which are an increasing number of sinners, for the intensity of noise, dirt, stench and squalor become intentionally more overpowering the closer we reach to the core. These circles are connected by a dim corridor of stairs, bridges, ramparts, causeways and rivers, all of which need navigating with extreme caution, for there is peril at every step such that there are demons and devils, behemoths and serpents hiding within the shadows. Indeed, living man would surely die should he slip and plummet to the bottomless depths of the basin. Or, should he be pushed.

After considerable effort we successfully traverse the first deathly slopes and narrow passages, for he has brought me safely to the second circle of Hell, albeit we stand at a cliff edge. Still vast for, as Limbo, I cannot see to the other side, yet I can tell the misery herein is one thousand times that just past, for already I know here reside sinners who are judged most harshly and punished even worse.

I watch in awe as a monstrous beast, a huge snorting

creature with a tail as long as the Jordan, stands at the rocky threshold to accept an endless line of malefactors. Upon taking confession, for he listens impatiently as each wretched soul reveals his sins he, Minos, consigns them to their rightful sentence thus; he coils his enormous tail around his trunk by way of indication of the circle of Hell the sinner is to attend, for they will need to accept the eternal punishment therein. The infernal judge works to the law of Contrapasso, dictating that for every sin there is to be an equal and fitting punishment, and it is he who assigns these torments in Hell for, once, he was the King of Crete and his golden crown, which he wears today, demonstrates his authority in this cavernous abyss. He metes infernal justice most willingly and the sinners obediently follow his direction for, if they do not, he snatches them with his tail and hurls them into the bottomless pit himself.

He is a foul, grotesque creature and I know I would not wish to deny or offend him, for he is bestial and therefore lacking intellect, unable to apply reasoning such that one may not expect him to employ logic or sympathy. Yet, I tell myself this is what he does as he guards the entrance to the second circle and doles out punishment. He has caught me staring. I hold my breath for, like Charon the ferryman, he knows I am not of this place, that I am of the living, not a criminal to be punished in Damnation for all eternity. He warns me not to advance, for to do so is to confess to sin but, in order to attain salvation, I must go forward. With a few words Virgil is able to convince him that it is my destiny to pass through the second circle, for God has willed it and thus, reluctantly, this monstrous beast grants us passage and we rush past him into the core of the ring. How I wish we had not.

2ND CIRCLE OF HELL - LUST

This is a dark place indeed with eternal wind, rain and storm, and immediately it snatches me. I look for a solid beam or a tree, a rock, any object to cling to, to root me, for the hurricane carries me off my feet and I am transported back and forth, rolling through the air as this violent tempest lashes and takes hold. I am caught in the stormy blast of Hell and am whirled and whipped and carried and dropped in perpetual motion. Torrential rain seeps into my skin and I am swept helplessly about this desolate place. All I seek is a moment of calm, of quiet serenity that I may gather my thoughts, perhaps rest or sleep, but this is denied me as the thunderous, violent squall is never ending and takes me with it in every direction. For this is the realm of the Lustful, those so damned for they are adulterous carnal sinners of the flesh, and for this lechery, they shall never know peace.

I am delivered abruptly unto Virgil who has barely noticed my absence such that for him it was merely momentary and we witness the exhausting scene unfolding before us. A crescendo of moans and screams, groans and shrieks may be heard above the tempest, for these lascivious libertines shall never enjoy respite such that they are condemned to unending torment in this storm. For this they are exhausted and endlessly weeping. It is a pitiful sight, I confess.

For distraction, I shout at Virgil above the storm to ask if he recognises any of the faces herein. He does and points them out to me. There is the Queen Cleopatra and her lover Mark Antony; also Paris, who abducted the beautiful Helen of Troy and claimed her as his mistress. Hereto are Tristan and Iseult, slain for they drank a magic potion intended for her husband and thus became lovers. Shot with a poisoned arrow, a wounded Tristan embraced Iseult so tightly they died in a lover's clench, to spend eternity wrapped in each other's arms. Finally, the perverted Semiramis of Babylon, so immoral she legalised the vice of incest that she may lay with her own brother. He tells me these naked, adulterous sinners could not control their lustful desires upon Earth and thus their fiery passions have condemned them to a life of perpetual agitated motion, for does not the desire for carnal pleasure make one eminently restless?

In truth I am saddened, for I have known love and when it takes hold there is little one can do to reject its overwhelming force and is not lust just excessive love? Do the adulterous whirl and drift herein the second circle solely for they could not deny their hearts? Or, for not controlling their desires, they allowed passion to dominate free will? It appears so and yet a life of eternal death, of perpetual motion in the thrashing, howling tempest seems a punishment most harsh, for surrendering to love seems not such a crime when it is a force so sweet and tender. Virgil sighs and encourages me to enter into conversation with a carnal letch to better understand this sin and I am fortunate that a pair of young lovers, intertwined and clearly still desirous of one another, answer the plea I thought was lost on the wind.

The woman has recognised that I am of the living and

steers their tumbling, storm ravaged bodies towards us. She introduces herself as Francesca da Rimini and relays their story thus: that she was a married woman, albeit her husband was old and deformed. His younger brother, Paolo, the handsome blade she caresses here, a man most sweet and gentle, had stolen her heart. Upon them enjoying the Arthurian tale of Lancelot and Guinevere they recognised their own secret love in the story and shared but one tender embrace; a trembling lovers' kiss. Upon hearing the news, her husband arranged to have the young lovers slain, leaving them doomed to spend eternity in the second circle of Hell writhing in cataclysmic storms and infernal winds. But she does not appear to mind, for the love that seized her has not left and she is bound to her lover in perpetuity. Overcome with emotion at their sad plight for, in truth, I am quite heartbroken at the romantic story of these eternal lovers, we three - Paolo, Francesca and myself - stand weeping. In this moment I find myself reminded of my beautiful Beatrice, as I am at any talk of love and, breathless, collapse in a faint at Virgil's feet.

3RD CIRCLE OF HELL - GLUTTONY

Again, I awake away from the place where I fell. I know not who or what is moving me without my knowledge, for Virgil tells me I am now in the third circle of Hell, that where the souls of the Gluttonous are punished. How I wish I was not, for the rain of the violent tempest from the previous remains although it is not clear as before. Instead it is discoloured; dirty, brown, of disgusting muck, a pyroclastic flow of filth, a volcanic eruption of sewage. And what is this smell most vile? It is of excrement and grime, for I believe the rain to consist of the shit of the Devil himself. How can this be, for it is repellent, repulsive? My nostrils are contaminated with this stench most foul and my eyes water, for I retch as Satan's rain drops upon me, soiling, polluting, staining my skin which crawls at the thought of the filth and parasites within.

But I am distracted from the putrid vapours of all that is rotten by a being most strange which waits ahead. Another dreaded beast to block my path, yet this is a sight most rare indeed. For the slathering creature, part lupine part canine, has a neck as wide as the Nile for it supports three heads.

28

Yet, more removed from the gospel Trinity it could not be. Baying and howling, salivating and grunting, it bears sharpened teeth, for its aim is prevention and, as the beasts of The Dark Wood, I fear he may split me limb from limb. For he protects the cavernous third circle, refusing to let mortal man enter nor sinner escape, for this is the final vestibule of Lower Hell and to enter is to submit to eternal suffering and pain.

The creature must be confused, I am certain, for we two are of each; one, living man and the other, sinner for, in truth, Virgil is of this place, but we may not convey our plight to him in words, for he is a bestial grotesque and therefore incapable of reasoning. Virgil tells me this is Cerberus, the demon Hound of Hades, guardian of the gates to the Underworld and he is a menace, a terrifying force, for with his fangs and claws he tears and rips at the sinners herein.

I wonder in this moment if he is the vicious hound Virgil talked of at the forest, the one who would see off the repugnant she-wolf, for he is a devilish monster that all creatures would fear. I am stumped for I know not how we shall pass him such that he guards this place ferociously. In the darkness Virgil spots some clean earth and, gathering it in his hands, shapes it into a lump and throws it at the cur who leaps upon it as a thirsty babe to a breast. Indeed, it proves as gluttonous as those greedy insatiables it despises. In the moment it is distracted, we rush past into the core of the circle. How I wish we had not.

For the sight is most vile and pans out beyond my mortal vision. Fat, naked bodies writhe in the foul earth. Grotesque obese forms thrash in a stinking mass of sewage, for we are now with the voracious Gluttonous and their punishment is to endure eternity swimming and squirming in their own excrement, being force-fed this repellent filth, choking upon dung and muck and all that is rank and fetid. For, as they over-indulged on Earth, denying sustenance to the poor and needy, so shall they be indulged in Hell. This rancid and grim stench, of which they must be used for they do not retch as I, seeps into my skin and the odour contaminates it. The Gluttonous, as the other sinners, cry and scream and yell out in distress but here, their open mouths are filled with both the sewage they lay in and raindrops tainted with excrement and waste. This fetid deluge will never wash their sins clean, for it is as polluted as their very souls.

I am repulsed beyond words, moved again to tears and need to flee this circle despite knowing a more harrowing scene awaits. But we are thwarted by a soul who says he knows me! I confess I cannot think of one person in this place with whom I may be acquainted but he is most insistent. He introduces himself as Ciacco and I confirm, with relief, he is a stranger, for it was just my accent he recognised. He, too, is of Florence so we discuss the politics of his earthly life (of which he is surprisingly well informed) and I am shocked to learn that many names which are familiar to me already reside in Hell, in deeper, darker circles than he. He prophesises that my beloved Florence will become a cesspit of sin, one which will lead to a political divide and the ultimate destruction of our beloved homestead. He repeats his name and asks me to remember it although why I cannot imagine, for I do not see this gluttonous oaf leaving the third circle any time soon. Yet, I cannot deny, I am much affected by his suffering.

Virgil gestures that it is time to leave, to make our way out of this circle and descend even deeper to the next. We continue along the dank, malodourous and dark expanse, leaving behind the howls and groans of despair and I ask Virgil about the punishment of sin, for to endure eternal death swimming in filth is an idea, a sentence, too distasteful to contemplate. He replies cryptically that upon the Last Judgement, when God judges all of humankind on Earth's final day, when he resurrects the dead, He will bring perfection to all creation and, so too, to all punishments. Am I to believe that as the Harrowing of Hell, the errant hoards will be released unto the celestial heavens? For they are not of Limbo, that painless border reserved for the virtuous pagans or the unfortunate faithful. Rather they are the malcontents, corruptives, outlaws; the faithless. The sinners. Will they find their way unto Paradise upon the Last Day or are they to remain in Hell in perpetuity, knowing that they are to suffer here in eternity whilst the blessed souls are reunited with their flesh and ascend to the heavenly spheres? He does not answer, for we finally approach the edge of the circle but the question remains; if Divine will is that earthly man follows a path of righteousness to attain eternal salvation, must he forfeit eternal salvation if he inadvertently strays from that path of Truth?

4TH CIRCLE OF HELL - AVARICE

Tracing a downward spiral we continue our gruelling descent into the rank darkness, moving further away from the light at the hilltop, for we plunge ever deeper into the pit. Finally, we enter into the threshold of the cavernous fourth circle and, indeed, the first we rest eyes upon is a demon leaping wildly, so I know God is not near. Virgil tells me his name is Plutus who, on catching sight of us, screams something undecipherable and makes to lunge. I am unnerved but Virgil is already upon him, muttering in his ear, and he falls to the floor in an instant, for he has been told of my ecclesiastical quest; that God on high has willed it and that the Virgin Mother watches over me from the heavens. I am relieved to see there is no demonic power here and we are able to pass, albeit gingerly, into the core with no further torment from him.

There is a calamitous noise which pains my ears. Banging, crashing, thudding; a cacophony of sound. I know not what it is although I suspect a quarry of sorts, for there is industry here. As I have come to expect there are the requisite howling screams and moans polluting my ears and infusing my mind to the point of madness. I smell an odour most unpleasant for, amongst the stench of sulphur and fetid air, is the stink of stale bodies, aged sweat, of those who have toiled and laboured. For these are the dishevelled, the unclean.

Despite the darkness I notice immediately this pit is different for, not just are there thousands more souls within, it is surrounded by a deep ditch, the height of ten men or more. The ring is formed of two arcs wherein, condemned to eternal strain and exertion, are two groups of beleaguered souls: the Avaricious and the Prodigals. In perpetual motion and suffering immense pain and intense discomfort, these sweaty, naked adversaries struggle to roll impossibly heavy stones along their arcs towards the approaching group. Bones are shattered, bodies are ruined for they are broken. Shoulders and palms are worn to flesh; backs, chests and thighs scratched, bruised, torn and crushed as harrowing cries of anguish and despair echo around the circle. Meeting at one end the grimy, sticky bodies of these wretched souls clash and crash violently, smashing their large rocks together whereupon the Avaricious shout aggressively to the Prodigals "Why do you squander?" The Prodigals, shaking their fists, reply "Why do you hoard?" At this point, wearily they turn and, with much effort, push the heavy stones back along their arcs that the same exhausting performance may repeat at the other end, both groups angrily berating and cursing each other, ready to begin the ritual joust again. And again.

It is a sad and pathetic scene I witness, for this gruelling, endless, monotonous yet violently strenuous act would drive anyone to distraction. Yet they work back and forth in perpetual pain and discomfort, for the rocks weigh heavy and they have no tools to help in this dangerous and operose task. These shades are dirty for they sweat. There is filth and muck and stench in the air and they are unwashed. I cannot see their faces such does the grime cover every inch of their naked beings albeit they do not look upon me. They cry out in misery for they suffer the torment of eternal labour, of arduous and demanding toil, of backbreaking and gruelling effort. Some are weak and small, others enormous, for in pushing these weights for eternity, they have developed muscles worthy of Hercules himself but do not enjoy any glory as he. It is a wretched vista. A pointless, relentless and unrewarding exercise that brings nothing but torment and frustration to the captive souls herein this circle of slog and despair.

I observe most of the men within are shaven headed and I wonder to Virgil if they were members of the clergy upon Earth. He confirms they were and that amongst this group of sinners reside mainly clerics, cardinals and a pope or two; the prelates. I am not surprised, for I have long suspected immorality and corruption within the Church, thus playfully enquire as to whether he recognises any of the souls herein. I have looked hard upon their faces to see if I may know them but, in truth, the grime is caked on and I am unable to identify even one.

Virgil explains that the labours of this circle purposefully render them unrecognisable, for their sin is considered so wicked these once lucky souls are immersed in dirt and are thus unidentifiable. For, it transpires, that due to her lack of sight, the blindfolded goddess Fortuna inadvertently favoured a few amongst the many with immeasurable riches. Upon realising her error it was her fervent hope they would divide these riches amongst their fellow men, which they did not; the Avaricious preferring to save and the Prodigals preferring to spend. However, the sinners here share one trait - that they were not prudent with their fortunes upon Earth and did not share what they had with the impoverished to reduce their hardship and suffering. Thus, they must endure perpetual punishment herein the fourth ring because of it. It seems to me that not all the gold in the world may save these uncharitable reprobates now, for they are doomed to spend eternity pushing these weights to and fro for absolutely no reward. Financial, spiritual or otherwise.

5TH CIRCLE OF HELL – WRATH

We leave the greasy, filthy souls behind as Virgil continues ahead, scrabbling and descending ever deeper into the cavernous depths of the valley towards the fifth circle, leading us to even greater misery. In truth I am mystified to know what we may discover here but Virgil instructs me to be patient, for we have an arduous journey ahead before we reach our destination. After many hours fumbling in the darkness, trudging, slipping, meandering downwards into oily damp squalor, as ever accompanied by the soundtrack of misery and pain, we arrive at another river.

This is a murky expanse indeed; black, thick and slimy, a carpet of dark mist hovering above it, releasing putrid gases and fetid vapours. Virgil tells me this is the Styx, the primary river of the Underworld of which we have all heard. Upon the bank is a scene most upsetting, for thousands of filthy, naked souls, covered in mud and dirt hit out, striking and gnawing at each other, punching and fighting, screaming and moaning.

Virgil explains that these are the violent Wrathful, those

who were consumed with rage, hate and anger during their time upon Earth and thus, in death, are forced to fight for their lives in perpetuity. It is a hellish scene indeed and one which saddens me greatly, for this disturbing afterlife presents a punishment most sadistic. That one man may abuse another thus, for I see them assaulting, punching and kicking, tearing at hair, gouging out eyes and biting chunks of flesh in an horrific display of brutality is, I confess, alarmingly savage. They suffer in a continuous, eternal loop of barbarity, sound-tracked by a crescendo of agonised wails and horrified screams. I hear my own cries, for my heart is tormented such that it is close to breaking. I am as much moved as I am horrified, dismayed as I am disgusted, sickened as I am appalled. I look to my feet, for yet again I feel a tide of tears erupting forth from my eyes for, in truth, I cannot bear to witness such violent pain as this.

Immersed within the Styx yet invisible to my eye, hidden by the rising putrid mist of the river, are more naked souls, incalculable in number, whom Virgil has had need to point out to me. I am told these are the Sullen; those, who, despite the light and miracle of God's creation on Earth, sulked and moped and muttered and pouted. But there is no light or wonder for them here, no glorious spectacles of love, light and colour, for they choke and splutter as they frantically recite hymns, retching and gurgling just under the surface of the swamp, gasping for rancid air, desperate not to drown yet barely managing to keep their heads above the polluted, grimy filth that is the Black River. And they suffer thus in eternity.

In truth I cannot tell which is the worse punishment - to bite and thrash out at the body of a wretched soul while he reciprocates by pummelling and assaulting you worse, or to be in a perpetual state of drowning, desperate to stop all that is rancid and grim from the boggy swamp of the fetid Styx entering into your mouth, gasping as it fills your lungs, choking and suffocating, not quite fatal but, equally, struggling and fumbling with no respite or sweetness of breath. I confess it is most pitiful, that which I witness.

Upon the bank opposite is a tall, crumbling tower. As the skies above, its walls are black for it is blanketed in soot and ash. Its peak is aflame albeit no one seems unduly concerned. I turn to Virgil for I don't think he has noticed but he has already motioned to the boatman, Phlegyas, an angry, violent soul for, without his help, we may not cross the quagmire and it is crucial we do, for our destination is Dis, the sixth circle, ever deeper into the bowels of Hell. Naked but for a filthy rag at his hips, this bearded roughneck is disinclined to give us crossing for he can see I am of the living. Yet Virgil does not indulge his censures, rebukes him thus and steps aboard. He gestures for me to do the same and I scramble on such that it rocks and dips with the weight of my mortal mass. It is only small and albeit we three are the sole passengers, there is little room to manoeuvre and I fear the vessel may tip.

Phlegyas moves quickly, for he is strong and deftly steers us to the opposite bank with ease. I am alarmed when, before we reach the shore, my ankle is grabbed by a soul from within the river, almost capsizing the boat. I am furious to see it is Filippo Argenti, a miserable hostile known unto me and for whom I feel nothing but hatred. For, upon Earth, he harassed and beleaguered me most aggressively albeit I could not fathom why and, for his sullen state, had always refused to enlighten me. He is covered in debris and grime from this mire in which he is submerged and is a pathetic sight indeed. Lifting himself up onto the boat he tries to board and demands to be told why I am at Dis, for he knows I am of the living and it is not my time to be in this place. I am not set to indulge him and do not wish to enter into discourse so answer curtly that I am not here to stay and angrily push him back into the quagmire. But, he is a shade and my foot has no effect, thus Phlegyas obliges with his oar. Argenti is incandescent with rage but, in the moment, this is of no concern to me.

Virgil can see I am agitated so, in a fit of pique, I yell out that I curse the man and wish only bad things for him. Much to my surprise he replies that before we reach the opposite bank my wish will be fulfilled, for this Sullen is arrogance and all that is ego and, despite having been cast to the circle of anger, remains furious with God and the world. I care not that Argenti's soul is tortured and, in truth, when a group of Wrathful dive in from the shore and drag him away to rip his body apart in front of my eyes, as Virgil predicted, I feel almost gleeful. I confess this revenge sits easy with me and, because of it, for the first time in this place feel a little stronger.

I await for Virgil to admonish me, for I realise this is behaviour most disingenuous, but Argenti infuriates me and I am glad for his cursed end. Most unexpectedly, Virgil rests his hands upon my shoulders and instead of berating, praises me for my actions, for it seems he, too, senses a change in me, a maturity, a strength perhaps; an understanding that through lack of pity for this miscreant, I discover myself. It is my fervent wish that if God secretly observes me from the heavenly heights, he is compelled to feel the same.

We cross the river and disembark, for we have reached the black walls of Dis, that place of eternal torture, suffering and woe, for this is the entrance to Hell proper; the brutal and forsaken Underworld. Rising up from behind the gates is a fortress of flames, a burning fortification, for the city within glows red. It could be fire. It might be blood. Or the broken hearts of those that reside within; likely all three. Already I know it to be a ghastly place; a sordid, shocking, sickening and evil realm. Gathered alongside us upon the bank are thousands of naked souls, cursed and damned, moaning and howling, sobbing and weeping, for all queue to cross this threshold into despair.

I am not minded to enter for the piercing, anguished screams are as torture to my mind. I am unable to imagine what suffering lies beyond those walls for these howls and wails are unfamiliar to my mortal ears. Yet, I know I must pass through unto this realm of Hell, for to not do so would be to fail in my quest and, upon my day of judgement, I shall not attain the salvation I so desire but be cast to this or another place by Minos and his angry tail, for weakness will have prevailed.

A crowd of demons swarms angrily towards us, screeching and crying out, affronted that one of the living dares to attempt entry to the sixth circle, the gateway to the citadel of Dis. Virgil steps forward and begins his entreaty, to explain the reason for my presence to these despicable guardians of the gate. He pleads; imploring, increasingly beseeching but they refuse to enter into parlay. For these are the Fallen Angels, those who sided with Lucifer in the War of the Heavens, adversaries of virtue and enemies of God. They do not fear Him, for the Black Emperor reigns here and so it is with arrogance and glee they castigate and rebuke my righteous Virgil, cackling, mocking, scorning. Alarmingly, he is unsuccessful and the gate is slammed shut by the enraged demons.

He is not angry but I am embarrassed to see he is ashamed, for he returns to me head bowed, humiliated, contrite, utterly wretched, for he has failed to secure my transit. I confess to panic for I know not how we may progress our voyage now that we are denied passage into Dis, for we cannot turn back to retrace our steps. Virgil strives to reassure me but his words, usually smooth and strong, for he is an orator most eloquent, are spoken in a stutter; hesitant and incoherent. I am unable to decipher his message so, to distract him, ask instead how many virtuous souls have travelled this deep into Hell before us, such that I may know if they were denied entry as we.

He admits it is rare but asserts such a phenomenon has occurred albeit neither, as I, was mortal man, for he recounts the tales of the apostle Paul and Aeneas of Troy and declares that he, himself, completed a mission for the sorceress Erichtho, purveyor of the blackest magical arts. I am intrigued as he tells me she had conjured a spell to cast him to the vilest, cruellest pit of all; Judecca, in the circle of traitors, that deepest and darkest place furthest from God in the heavens, for she had not the courage to enter it herself and remove the wretched soul she sought. I am reassured that at least he is familiar with the terrain we navigate, but confess I am unsure as to whether we shall be successful from hereon in, although he weakly tries to convince me otherwise.

He is distracted, for he seems to search for something and I follow his gaze to the top of the fiery tower upon which a hideous sight unfolds. For there, hang three creatures, each blood-soaked and crazed, dangling inverted, suspended from the blackened turrets. They are half-woman, half-serpent with snakes for hair, who cackle, screech and wail as they scratch at their breasts with talons long and sharp. Virgil identifies them as The Furies, the infernal goddesses of vengeance, whereupon they gleefully exclaim that Medusa is venturing towards us to turn specifically me, to stone! As I, Virgil is distraught and warns me to avert my eyes, for to meet her gaze is to signal certain demise. His hands shield them from any wayward glance she may throw in my direction and, not needing to be told twice, I scrunch my eyes tight and pray that I survive the encounter such that I may return to earthly life to seek the path of Truth and attain salvation.

In the distance, yet fast and furious, I hear the winds of a hurricane, for a flying beast approaches. I am unnerved for I suspect this to be Medusa yet Virgil instructs me to open my eyes and rest them upon the sight, for God has sent a messenger from Heaven. Indeed, he is huge and I look upon him in awe as with a single motion the glorious angel sweeps aside thousands of sinning souls. With a second wave of his magnificent wings, the city gates burst open whereupon he severely admonishes the insolent demons for resisting the will of God, which is to secure my safe passage through Hell. I am most taken with this heavenly sight for, indeed, I am reminded that God is here and, through His angel, protects and watches over me. I scamper after Virgil who is already marching through the gates but am met with a sight and smell most gruesome, for in this vast landscape there is an undeniable stench of burning flesh in the air. It is dark yet there is a red light, dimly glowing, illuminating the terrain just enough that I may observe the scene unfolding before me. And it is a most dreadful sight.

6TH CIRCLE OF HELL - HERESY

The heat is unbearable. I cannot breathe for my lungs are scorched with each inhalation. Sweat drips as a tempest dousing and every forward step is impeded by an invisible barrier of solid hotness. But this is nothing compared to the punishment I witness. Pain and suffering abound here for, buried within the ground, is a labyrinth of open tombs wherein rage the roaring flames of ferocious fires. Captive within these burning braziers, these vaults of bonfires, are wretched, accursed souls who cry out in terror and anguish, screaming and wailing, for their grisly and painful torment is repugnant. Indeed, the truth is that in death they are being burned alive and I am appalled. These shades are the blazing dead, imprisoned within the cemetery of Dis, their tombs afire, suffering the violent cruelty that is searing crackling heat; skin and bodies melting, scorched and charred from the roaring fires in which they roast. Agonised screams echo in the cavernous abyss, the soundtrack a cacophony of pain, anguish and torture. It is a confrontation most dire and I am nauseous, utterly despairing.

I confess this torment is more than I may bear and

despite that Virgil explains these are the Heretics who committed one of the worst sins of Hell, for they denied God on Earth, I am not consoled. Their punishment is to eternally burn in intense fire and suffer all the pain and agony that fire brings. Yet this is an inferno. I know flames to be cleansing, to purify, but this is a torment too much surely, even for the dead? I avert my weeping eyes from this grotesque sight but not before Virgil announces there are thousands of sinners herein, shadowy souls suffering in this Hell that burns and I must endeavour to witness the pain, torment and sorrow, for I need to know the punishment of sin in all its guises.

He sees from my tears I cannot endure this pitiful torture and motions that I may move forward. I am relieved, for the sight of these leprous, deformed souls is harrowing for they are hideous. It is vulgar, perverse even, to look upon their suffering, for their charred features, now distorted and misshapen, demonstrate a pain beyond endurance. They are as Icarus, skin and flesh melting as the wax between his feathers, but they shall not feel the beautiful relief of the chilled Icarian waves as he, such that he could plummet from the torture of fire to a cool oceanic death. I pity them and their misery; their agonizing torment, for they endure this horror in perpetuity. A gruesome reminder that to follow God is to take the right path, for on their journey through earthly life, they succumbed to distraction, enticed by the wicked sin that is the denial of God, thus their route to the afterlife took a wayward diversion to this nefarious place.

We pass along the open tombs of the burning dead for there are thousands upon thousands of rows, all ablaze with sinners crying out and screaming in distress, the symphony of wails rising as the fierce, untamed flames. Virgil talks of the violations that sent the heretics to this blazing cesspit while the fetid smell of charred flesh pollutes my nostrils, yet I am unconcerned with irreverent heresies for I remain overcome with the pain, suffering and misery I witness. I confess it pierces my heart such that these entombed sinners affect my emotions thus and we continue to walk through the labyrinth, hiding eyes yet taking care not to inadvertently stumble and fall into an unlidded vault. In truth, it is a torment no mortal man could endure yet I am amazed at the quantity of shades herein this burning cemetery, open tombs laid out in strips as harvest crops in a field, as far as my mortal vision may see.

Virgil gestures to the area in which we stand and says these are followers of the heretic Epicurus who denied immortality of the soul. With this blasphemous ideology he thereby rejected God's doctrine, believing instead that upon death the soul and body die as one. I ask after the significance of the open graves for none are sealed here and he tells me that all will remain open until the day of the Last Judgement. Thereafter, they will be sealed shut for eternity. It is as I suspected then; that the souls enduring perpetual punishment in Hell will remain here, in eternal death and torment, to suffer the indignity of an afterlife forever separated from God, never to be reunited with their own flesh, even on Earth's last day.

I glance quickly inside the tombs as we walk along for, although aghast, I am interested to see if there is anyone known to me amongst them. Suddenly, a stray voice calls out and asks for me specifically, for he can tell by my accent I am a fellow Florentine. I cannot bear to look, for to see a man with burning flesh, skin melting and dripping is a sight most grim and it devastates me. I hide behind Virgil who pushes me forward and forces me to speak to the man, Farinata, for he already stands in his enflamed tomb. He is a man full of contempt for the Church, for I know him to have the rare distinction of being entombed, posthumously declared a heretic, exhumed, then excommunicated. Indeed, his disinterred body was unceremoniously burned upon a pyre with all his possessions and, thus, he replays his death on Earth in perpetuity in Hell. I glimpse, but do not study, and we enter into discourse, for Farinata is a politico and wishes to discuss opinions and views of the Florentine establishment. Yet before we begin in earnest, we are interrupted by another soul, one who *is* known to me. It is Cavalcante, my good friend Guido's father!

Whimpering pitifully from within his burning grave, for indeed he suffers greatly, he demands to know where his beloved poet son is for, knowing me to be alive, he cannot imagine why Guido has not accompanied me to this place to share mortal man's greatest honour. I know not how to respond for I am on a most specific and personal journey and the quest is not Guido's, thus I gabble some words, which I concede are ambiguous, but I do not wish to appear rude to Farinata whose conversation has been interrupted. Cavalcante mistakes this and my momentary pause to mean his cherished son is dead and, before I am able to correct this awful wrongdoing, wails in despair and sinks back into his burning tomb, whimpering. I am utterly appalled - ashamed and full of contrition at my lack of compassion - for now his suffering, thanks to my insensitive tongue, is twofold. I admonish myself at my brazen disregard for his physical and emotional misery, for this wretched, fragile soul is now quite broken.

Farinata is most insistent we continue our discourse but, in truth, we do not share the same politics and I no longer have the appetite for intellectual conversation. Yet, I suspect from our brief discussion that shades here may see only the future, not the present, and Farinata confirms it is thus. Indeed, he states, part of their punishment is to be unaware of current events, only those impending, and it is for this reason he desires word of our homestead. My conscience is again pricked with guilt for I realise Cavalcante cannot know the news of today, that his son, Guido, is very much alive and well on Earth, thus I implore Farinata to reassure him, that he may be comforted.

Naturally I am keen to understand what Farinata may know of me and my future and he declares baldly that I shall be banished from my beloved Florence! In this instant I am called upon by Virgil who is eager to move to the next circle despite that I have not finished my parlay. I am perplexed, for Farinata has spoken of my exile and I need him to expand for he did not relay timings nor how long the banishment will last, nor indeed the reasons behind such a shameful disgrace. Virgil refuses to answer but confirms that we shall soon meet a lady, an all-seeing, all-knowing divine and virtuous woman who will provide a proper account of the event and sufficient details to quell my fears. Am I to hope it is my beloved Beatrice? I pray it is for she remains in my heart and thought of her brings me great comfort in this dismal place of misery and woe.

It takes a few hours in the searing heat and stench but we finally make our way through the maze of enflamed tombs and head towards the outer edge of the gargantuan circle. We continue to descend in a downward spiral, blindly clambering down steps and across ledges and bridges in the heat and darkness until we reach a fork in the filthy path. Virgil turns left into an alley but I know not why, for the stench is vile and overpowering.

We are upon the rim of the seventh but cannot proceed for we are overwhelmed by a smell most foul. We rest near the tomb of St Anastasius and wait for our noses to acclimatise to the rank odour. This infamous saint was another heretic who denied the divinity of Christ so I am not surprised to find him here, for we remain in the sixth circle, albeit on the periphery. It is clear there are more burning tombs ahead and the quantity must be significant for the stench that streams up from the abyss reeks most fetid, for something is aflame.

While we sit Virgil tells me he shall use this opportunity to explain the structure of the last three circles of Hell and the divisions within, for they are complex. These punish the more serious sins of violence, fraud and treason. I cannot begin to fathom what dreadful sights I may bear witness to from hereon in, for already I have seen more depravity and misery, suffering and pain than any mortal man may imagine. He reminds me we have negotiated six of the nine circles thus far, those devoted to the sins of excess and overindulgence. He tells me we are to enter the seventh, the second of Dis, known as the circle of the Violent. This is divided into three rings, one outer, one middle and one inner, for they punish violence against one's neighbour, against oneself and against God.

I am despairing at the thought of the harrowing scenes which may unfold, yet intrigued enough to ask him to provide more detail. He obliges, announcing that murderers, plunderers and robbers reside in the first sub-circle; those committing sin against their neighbours. Violence against oneself is the ring reserved for suicides and squanderers and, those who commit violence against God, the blasphemers and usurers, occupy the final, inner ring. However, he warns, there is a category of sin more evil than violence even, and that sin is fraud. It is those fraudulent sinners for whom the last two circles of Hell are reserved, for in breaking the trust of a man, he warns, we directly oppose the great virtue of love, and what is God if not love? Thus, the eighth circle punishes sins that cut off the bond of love that nature forges, that is those who committed fraud against people who trusted them. These include flatterers, hypocrites, panderers, sorcerers and falsifiers. Worst of all are the sinners who committed betrayal and it is these who are punished in the ninth and final circle of Hell, the very seat of Dis. For these treacherous souls violated bonds of particularly special trust, including loyalty to family, homeland, political party and, most brazenly, Benefactor.

I know Virgil to be the wisest of all men and thus I ask him to clarify a puzzle which has perplexed me throughout our journey, for not all sinners receive the same degree of punishment. I understand the law of Contrapasso applies here, yet all have sinned against God in that they have acted contrary to Divine will, so why does He distinguish between the severity of penalty? For He does not in Heaven, where we are told all are considered equally blessed in the eyes of the Lord. Does He play at Nemesis, passing retribution for the sake of it?

I sense Virgil is a little frustrated but he gently reminds me of the book of Aristotle named Nicomachean Ethics. This neatly divides sin into three categories; fraud, violence and lack of self-control, known as incontinence. In God's eyes, he continues, the least offensive of these sins is incontinence and it is these we have seen demonstrated in the previous circles including the excesses of gluttony, avarice, lust and wrath. As God's vengeance is merciful, He deems them deserving of lesser punishments. I confess, to my mind, eternally writhing in one's own excrement or whirling in a violent tempest with no respite, or biting and fighting without rest, or roasting alive in scorching tombs, most harsh outcomes for lesser sins.

Virgil explains that rationality plays its part, for sins falling under the category of incontinence are directed by desire not reasoning. Heresy, that wicked sin punished by eternal torture in the flaming tombs, is directed not by desire but a rational thought process, however irrational it may prove to be. Thus, it cannot be classified as a lack of self-control as the other, lesser, sins he argues. Therefore, he concludes, God's vengeance is more determined; more violent. It torments me, I will not lie, to ponder upon the unforgiving punishments reserved for the most wicked of sinners if their severity is to exceed those I have already witnessed, for it is clear the closer I journey to the core of Hell, the more sadistic, cruel and barbaric the punishments become. In truth, it already exceeds that which mortal man may endure but, despite my increasing dismay, I have to trust that God knows what He does with me.

Virgil stirs, for he says we need to make haste while there is a slither of red light that can help us navigate the steep passage ahead. We rise from our seats at the tomb of St Anastasius and make our way down the corridor, that of the stinking, foul odour. Using our togas to protect our noses, we inch our way down the dark, narrow alley, a seemingly endlessly winding slope, descending ever deeper into the scorching chasm that sits at the depths of the cavernous abyss, for we are searching for the first ring of the seventh circle. My heart sinks as I recall this is reserved for the Violent, for I understand the punishments must exceed those nefarious and brutal abuses I have witnessed thus far. And indeed, they do.

7TH CIRCLE OF HELL - VIOLENCE

We continue our descent, passing across stone bridges and wooden moats, pushing through gates and ramparts. Finally, Virgil leads me to a rocky ravine whereupon we meet an onerous brute, the monstrous half-man, half-bull that is Minotaur. I know not why but Virgil incites him to rage by shouting that we are only here to watch him suffer in torment and he responds by furiously biting himself! It is a ruse only, a distraction, for whilst he is engaged in this most peculiar and masochistic task, we break for the embankment. I can see Virgil appears confused, for he looks about uncertainly. He tells me, puzzled, that the rock formation today is not of his last travels here when the vile sorceress and purveyor of the dark arts sent him on a most dangerous errand, and he is bemused.

In this moment he recalls that during the Harrowing of Hell when Christ released members of the virtuous and good from Limbo, the Universe shook with pleasure whereupon an earthquake caused rocks from the cliff face to cascade down, thus forming the dangerously rocky path and ravine we now unexpectedly stand upon. With effort and difficulty, we manage to circumvent the misplaced stones and boulders and arrive at a place most foul. How I wish we had not, for it is the Phlegethon, a bubbling river of boiling blood wherein burn murderers, plunderers and robbers. Indeed, these perpetrators of violence against neighbours find themselves submerged in the scorching liquid.

Their spine-tingling shrieks, as primal screams, resonate two-fold for they suffer inordinate pain such that their bodies roast from within but, also, at any attempt to raise their burning souls out of the blazing river, find themselves under attack by the centaurs who patrol the bank. These creatures, half-man half-horse, stomp angrily, aiming their arrows most keenly upon any sinner who dares attempt release from the boiling liquid by rising beyond the agreed height pre-determined by the magnitude of their sin. The howls and wails suggest they hit their targets with much frequency. Blood curdling screams echo in perpetuity as these malefactors roast alive in abject pain within the scorching, scalding, apocalyptic mess that is the river of boiling blood, for as their attempts at respite in the cool air are thwarted by the vicious armed guards patrolling the shoreline, they return to the blazing, bubbling waters, submerged, burning and choking once again.

We have been spotted and, roaring an ululating war cry, the centaurs charge over to us, bows akimbo, as they threaten us with death. My knees weaken but Virgil boldly places himself in front of me and holds steadfast as he demands to parlay with Chiron, the chieftain. While Chiron approaches, Virgil whispers the names of the centaurs and describes the violent crimes committed which have caused their banishment unto this place. I am horrified to hear that one, Nessus, attempted rape upon the beautiful Deianira and in doing so, indirectly caused the death of her husband, Hercules. Chiron is a stallion, a true warrior indeed, yet he is most curious, for he has observed that I move each rock I touch underfoot, as only a living soul could.

Virgil confirms that I am not dead, indeed I am mortal man here on a mission from Heaven. He is reverence and humility at this news and when Virgil asks him to provide a guide, for the rocks here are most treacherous and we need to navigate away from the river of boiling blood, Chiron immediately agrees. Nessus steps forward and we are told that not only will he guide us but he will protect us also. In truth I fear for my safety, for have I not just heard he is a rapist and murderer most foul? Yet, with no way to negotiate the ravines of this hazardous valley without him, we acquiesce. Virgil allows himself to be hoisted by Nessus' muscular arms but I, less elegant and more reluctant than he, clumsily clamber upon the centaur's back whereupon he begins a slow walk towards the edge of the ring.

Surprisingly, we keep close to the riverbank but Nessus is not scared of the boiling blood. He does not slip on the loose rocks or stones underfoot, albeit chippings swept by my toga spill into the red-hot liquid, spraying out fiery bursts. He attempts to entertain us by relaying tales of the sinners we witness writhing in agony within this bloody river of pyroclastic liquid, for their bodies roast and their skin is scorched and blistering. It is a sight most foul and I am utterly appalled. Harrowing screams and agonised shrieks thwart my concentration, as does the stench of burning flesh and, so hideous the distraction, his words are lost to me.

He points to the river, for its depth changes commensurate with the degree of sin an earthly soul has committed. It is deepest when we approach the tyrannical forms of Atilla, the invader Pyrrhus and Rinier of Cornetto, the brigand who robbed pilgrims on their journey to Rome. Indeed, their bodies are completely submerged. We continue on until we meet a point in the shallows where we may cross in relative safety. Nessus deposits us on the opposite bank whereupon he turns to retrace his steps across the bubbling blood and begin his travails home. I watch, impressed, for he has an equine elegance about him which is surprisingly graceful, given he is an onerous brute.

Before he has taken but a few strides, Virgil has marched into a forest. There is no path for us to survey, no tracks exist, for no mortal man but I has put foot to soil here, so I trust that Virgil follows his instincts or is guided by God. This forest is not of The Dark Wood such that I was blinded by the density of the blackness, for I can see the vegetation within quite easily. It is a monstrous maze of dead tree trunks, a labyrinth of twisted branches and boughs, of brittle twigs and dry bushes. All, quite dead. The leaves are not green, rather black, and the branches are knotty and gnarled. They are devoid of fleshy fruits or colourful blossom and instead bear poisonous thorns.

I have not Virgil's knowledge but we are both poets and because of this I know we are in the homeland of The Harpies. These human birds of prey are foul creatures indeed, for what else may I call them? Half-woman, half-avian with claws sharp and talons long to rip the flesh of their succulent victims, these are soul snatchers; agents of punishment instructed by Hades to abduct and torture the guilty as they make their way through the barren forest to the core of Hell and they gleefully do his bidding.

Virgil imparts that we are in the second ring of the seventh circle but there was no need, for I am well aware. From within the trees come all the sounds of suffering and woe; groaning and wailing, sobbing and howling. He suggests that I break off a branch to discover the source of the pain which I do, for I wonder if he knows there is something magical in the sap. How I wish I had not, for the violent shriek, the anguished scream that is released, reveals to me that the trees conceal the souls of sinners and, in this moment, the forest comes to life in a symphony of agony, a crescendo of the misery and pains of torture. Indeed my action was akin to ripping the arm off a man, tearing the womb from a woman, snatching the laughter from a child, for it was not sap that trickled down the bark, rather blood and the trees rise up in furious protest against me. And thus

I find we are in the Forest of Suicides, a monstrous maze of suffering, specially reserved for those sinners who denied God by abusing both the body and free will He granted them upon the living Earth. These architects of violence against self are condemned to reside imprisoned within the twisted, gnarled trees for eternity such that as they did not respect their bodies in life, so they are condemned to eternal suffering in death without any chance to revert to human form. Indeed, they shall not know their flesh again.

The tree-soul whom I had violated speaks up. His name is Pietro and he admonishes me severely between howls of anguish, for I have clearly inflicted untold pain upon him. He castigates me, a fellow man, a brother, for committing him to additional suffering, for every day, he tells me, his punishment causes torment, misery and sorrow. I am completely aggrieved yet at a loss to understand why Virgil instructed me thus, for I believe he knew the consequences of me pulling at that branch.

To my surprise and utter indignation, Virgil aligns himself with Pietro and I am embarrassed into contrition for he insists I make a declaration of apology! I cannot do this for I am overcome with guilt at the pain I have caused and ask Virgil to manage the conversation for, in truth, the blame lies with him for encouraging me to violate the tree. He asks Pietro how the sinners herein came to mould as one with the forest and if they might ever be set free for, without doubt, they are arboreal, no longer of humankind and, thus, one must question how they may achieve separation on the day of Final Judgement.

It transpires that when Minos and his tail judge and cast sinners unto the forest, they are rooted here as saplings. Birds and Harpies peck and claw at the sprouting tree-souls, wounding and harming them, for they feel pain as any human would. Indeed, for a branch to be snapped (as I did to Pietro) is akin to dismemberment. I am full of self-loathing at this news for I consider myself a decent, moral man and did not plan to maim him, to cause him to suffer thus. I am troubled by Virgil's intentions, for clearly, he knew the consequence of my actions. Does he indirectly accuse me of something and want me in pain for it; tormented? I am much perplexed, for I thought we were kin and expected better of him.

A downcast Pietro continues. We are informed that the tree-souls will never be free, for upon the day of the Last Judgement, when the dead are resurrected, these suicides will not resume human form. They shall never retrieve their natural flesh, for their skin will be hung on the branches within this forest of nightmares as an eternal reminder of the bodies they rejected on Earth. He recounts his own story whereupon we hear he was the private counsellor to Frederick, Emperor of Rome and King of Sicily. So beloved and trusted was he by the emperor that the other courtiers became envious and he was plunged into wicked rumour, such was their jealousy. So shameful were the words spread that he took his own life to rid himself of the embarrassment and disgrace.

It is a sad tale indeed and, if one were to point the finger, the guilt would belong to the envious hoard would it not? To hurl a dejected and heartbroken Pietro to the seventh circle only that for want of removing the torment he wilfully abandoned the living, seems most undeserved for what, if anything, has happened to those who sinned against him? I confess I do not know where to find justice in this story. In this moment Pietro pleads with me to clear his name upon my return to the earthly world. I shall try, of course, but in this instant, I continue to wallow in remorse and my own disgrace, but will endeavour to do thus, for I owe him this gesture of compassion.

Suddenly, and to break the awkwardness, a great commotion is unfolding as two naked souls run towards us, chased by a pack of hounds. One cries out for death while the other teases his friend although he himself is the slower of the two. For his lack of concentration, he stumbles and falls into a thorny bush whereupon the dogs begin to rip at his body and, snarling and biting, they tear him limb from limb. Shrieking, weeping and wailing, agonised howls echo about us, but not from the young shade under attack, rather the bush he has landed in. For it has suffered immense damage in the tussle and all its branches are broken. The bush endures significant pain but, tragically, there is nothing we may do to relieve him from it.

I try to distract him by asking his name but he answers only that he is of Florence and begins to relay the story of his own suicide. We oblige him, listening, while I collect the dead leaves, twigs and branches so discarded and scattered when the bush was accosted by the runner. I return them to him as gently as I can, for he is a fellow Florentine and I am happy to show him a kindness as he relays his sorry tale. Virgil gestures that we need to move on and we bid the bush a sad goodbye.

We continue walking, always descending and approach the third ring of Hell's seventh circle where I immediately notice its landscape is vastly different to those we have experienced thus far. For this is a dry, arid terrain, flat as the salt marshes, sandy, barren and sweltering as the desert under a midday sun; an island in this otherwise forested geography. I confess I am relieved for the punishment here cannot be severe, for what harm may sand do to a soul? But, I tell myself, we are not yet *in* the third ring, only at the periphery and as we approach, the wails and screams of those cursed souls within sound yet ever louder until, as we enter, they reach an ear-splitting crescendo. And what a harshness is the reality herein.

Against the backdrop of howls and cries of anguish, Virgil reminds me that this third ring is divided into a further three hoops for here reside the sinners who have committed violence against God in all its forms. There are naked shades within; a hoard of many thousands who either walk, lay or crouch on the sand, but I should not have rested easy for, indeed, they are being punished most severely and suffer much because of it. The sand is burning hot, scorching the skin of these wretched sinners, blistering and peeling wherever it touches. Fireballs rain down upon these souls like meteors, as enormous burning snowflakes in a torturous blizzard, and the sand onto which they land bursts into flame, causing those blaspheming sinners laying upon it, swimming within it, to sizzle and scream out in pain. Indeed, they suffer most cruelly and the sight is grotesque.

They use their hands to beat out the flames as a dance of fire but I am not entertained, for their misery is immense. I am witnessing the end of the world surely? Apocalyptic flagellation by flame, by the fiery rain that drops upon their souls, scalding their skin, all for they have committed violence against God and their life in death will be to burn, for eternity, from above and below, as from the heavens and hell. It is a hideous punishment for it is a merciless torture indeed. I spot a giant in the distance writhing in the burning sand, angrily fighting off scorching red rain which ignites the ground as it lands. He is enraged, relentlessly cursing God in a booming voice which carries in the air and I am compelled to ask if Virgil knows of him. Virgil identifies him as Capaneus, one of the seven kings who besieged Thebes; a blasphemer who defied God's might, inviting Him to throw each and every thunderbolt in his possession towards him. Arrogance and hubris combined, he is most insistent that his soul shall never be broken by the torments of Hell and defiantly rages on in the burning sand, even now rejecting God. There is no hope of salvation, for his denial of God is eternal, as is his torturous punishment, thus I am not inclined to offer him pity.

We move on and Virgil gestures for me to walk closer to the edge of the Forest of Suicides where the desert sand is less hot, for it will burn and blister the soles of my feet if I continue to walk upon it in earnest. We come upon a welcome stream which flows out of the woods and I ask if we may rest for I wish to relieve my feet in it for a few moments. Virgil looks at me surprised, so I turn to the water. I realise it is likely the end of the Phlegethon, the river of scorching blood wherein boil the murderers, plunderers and robbers, for it is red, albeit no longer hot. Virgil explains the importance of this narrow stream for it emanates from the same source as all waters in Hell. He talks of The Old Man of Crete, a colossal statue which sits on Mount Ida. Formed mainly of clay but also gold and silver, brass and iron, it has weathered substantially over time. It has many cracks and from each of these flow the statue's tears. These tears trickle down the side of the mountain and flow from the earthly, living world into the depths of the abyss whereupon they form the four rivers of Hell; the Acheron, the Styx, the Phlegethon and Cocytus, the pool at the bottom of Hell I have no wish to see.

To my mind there is a fifth river in the Underworld and I ask Virgil about this. He concedes that there is, although being situated in that place called Purgatory, it is not technically of Hell. The Lethe is the river of forgetfulness, he explains, providing purification only for those sinners deemed worthy of absolution, for it enables them to resurface with no memory of their previous wrongs. Indeed, he continues, in order to repent one must purify the mind by forgetting the past, forgetting all sins. But he does not expand further. He gestures for me to keep walking and reminds me to stay close to the forest edge where the sand is not as hot and we continue along in silence as I ponder the river that removes all recollections of sin, that which cleanses the spiritual soul.

We follow the path of the red stream for an hour or so and when I turn back, am surprised to see the Forest of Suicides is no more, for we have left it far behind. Dodging the burning sand, we cross the stream and enter the second hoop of the third ring whereupon we meet a band of naked Sodomites, those sinners who were violent against nature. These cursed souls suffer the onslaught of a perilous tempest, for their punishment is to spend eternity engulfed by an inescapable typhoon of pyroclastic fury; of red rain which lashes down in a blazing torrent, as a cascading waterfall of lava, causing howls and screams of agony and misery. I am witnessing more flogging by flame and the pitiful souls suffer greatly, for there is no shelter in this barren land; not one tree, one bush nor one canopy.

From the stream materialises a mist which rises and envelopes us such that it provides a shield against the deluge of flaming raindrops. Yet the Sodomites are not so fortunate for the suffering here is immense, an apocalyptic abhorrence. Their day of reckoning has surely come and it is now for just as they committed violence against nature upon living Earth, so does nature commit violence against them in Hell. Thus, their life in death is to suffer a torturous burning of their bodies, from above and below, for the scorching sands lie here too. They stare at us most wilfully, for we are new to the group and they are curious, for the mist blankets us as a shroud of gauze. Suddenly, my tunic is roughly grabbed by a man who declares he knows me!

His outstretched arms did not stop me from gazing at his face, for although it was burned and charred, I recognised him immediately as the philosopher and scholar, Brunetto Latini. I would know this man in an instant for he is my friend, my mentor, my father. Indeed, he became that upon the death of my beloved papa and I owe him much. He is exhausted and, overcome with pity, I beg of him to rest that we may converse about times past but he tells me that to do so, even for an instant, would add another hundred years to his eternal punishment and, although dead, he would most surely burn alive in the fiery storm. He points ahead where the riverbank splits into two levels and gestures for Virgil and me to take the lower, for the misty shield will protect us. Yet as a sinner, he informs us, he must take the higher for his punishment is eternal and thus his body must always know the agony of red rain. We continue in conversation but it is most awkward for we are separated and our words become lost in the mêlée of anguished screams and moans, pained howls and wails.

He asks why I am in Hell for he sees I am not dead and

is baffled. I begin by relaying the story of my journey here which, in truth, only began yesterday; that upon finding myself lost and stumbling in The Dark Wood, Virgil was sent unto me by my beloved Beatrice in Heaven and it is he who escorts me through the circles of Hell, for I am on a mission. He shows surprise and asks for explanation, so I reply that I am to witness the punishment of sin in all its forms that I may better understand earthly man's best recourse is to follow the path of truth and righteousness, for only through virtue and faith may one attain salvation.

Latini, as Virgil, appears most impressed with my precise response and says he believes me to be blessed, for a spiritual journey such as this is a rarity indeed. He senses God has placed much faith in me and is comforted. Yet, he becomes distressed as he tells me his greatest sorrow is that he is not alive today for, to accompany me, to encourage me on my momentous adventure would be his greatest desire, for he remembers me fondly as a son. But, the harsh truth is that he may not, for he failed himself and God, and is to remain burning in the second hoop for eternity.

We begin to reminisce but he quickly becomes agitated, for he recalls the hoards at Fiesole, neighbours of Florence, whom he accused of neither respecting nor appreciating our intellectual endeavours. I am warned to avoid them should I stumble upon them in this place for all here are tainted by wickedness. He is charged now and coiled as a spring so I decide it best to move on for fear he will garner too much attention from the other souls. Yet, first, I insist upon him that I will continue to miss him and thus lavish him with praise and gratitude. I do this by reciting what I have learned from him during our very short meeting; that it is through endeavour and not soul that man earns immortality and that man must be prepared for any opportunity Fortuna throws his way. I have been furiously scribing during our conversation for if, or when, I encounter the treasured beauty that is Beatrice, I wish to show her I am even more learned than when we last met.

Latini pulls me close and speaks to me in earnest, for he believes I am to be rewarded for my heroic actions and wills me to value and revere his last great poem, Tesoro, an encyclopaedic summary of the day's knowledge, even that I may borrow from it! I brush off the first but assure him that I will ensure his works are honoured, for he was my maestro, my friend, my father. I can see that Virgil is pleased and I am relieved, for the incident with the tree-soul Pietro still plays heavy on my mind. I am moved, just before we leave, to ask Latini of the other Sodomite souls who reside here but he is suddenly distracted and appears reluctant to talk. He hurriedly throws out three names and then declares, that having seen new smoke rising from the sands can tell that unsavouries approach. With that, he disappears from view under the fiery torrent, moving faster than the arrows off a centaur's bow.

We remain on the lower path, for the burning rain continues to lash down upon the upper level, scorching, singeing and blistering all whom it touches. In the distance I can hear the babbling of water, for the stream is getting wider. The unsavouries who Latini mentioned have come into view and draw closer. They are a group of three men, also Sodomites and can tell by my clothes I am of Florence, as are they. I confess that for the hideous burns on their faces they are unidentifiable to me, but when they speak their names I recognise them, for they are of my time! In truth I feel great pity for they endure much suffering, tortured by this flagellating, fiery rain disfiguring their faces, deforming their bodies such that they emit sobs and moans in a chorus of anguish. I cannot imagine how they tolerate the pain, for their skin drips, melting as wax down a candle before my very eyes.

I judge them to be not unsavoury, especially when they ask if the character traits for which our countrymen are most renowned - valour and courtesy - still apply. I admit that regrettably they do not, for they have been overtaken by acts of excess and arrogance. We sigh collectively, saddened that our once honourable city is now reigned by corruption and avarice. I am again asked why I find myself in Hell albeit I am not dead but, for once, I wish that a more original question be thrown my way. I focus instead on reassuring the trio that I and my fellow compatriots feel desperately for their plight and shall do what we can to honour them. They take comfort from this pledge and continue their painful course along the upper level. It is a pitiful sight, I will not lie.

Virgil and I change tact and, moving across the scorching sands, realise we have reached the end point of the Phlegethon, for we are upon a cascading waterfall, thunderous and roaring such that we are deafened. We peer into the cavernous ravine filled with dark, murky spray but are confused, for we have run out of path to walk. I look into Virgil's eyes, for we cannot talk above the crashing noise of the gushing water and he gestures for me to remove the cord belt from around my waist. I do so but cannot imagine that he expects us to enter the ravine, the abyss, yet I suspect he does, for he contorts the rope into a lasso and throws it down. I hear grunting, snorting, snarling and expect a raging beast, a monstrous brute to appear before me, such does the terrifying sound remind me of the lion, the leopard and the she-wolf. But those behemoths were nothing in comparison to the fiend that is presented before us as it clambers out of the gorge from the surface of the water.

To put the three beasts of The Dark Wood into one could still not describe the grotesque, thrusting, malevolent force that has come from the depths of this chasm, and I find myself quite paralysed at the thought of what he will do to us. Yet Virgil seems most relaxed, for what reason I cannot possibly fathom for the creature is of a mythical beast in form and stature, the very effigy of everything that is sinister, terrifying and monstrous. Virgil tells me he represents fraud, for his human face belies him such that his very presence and stench taints the already fetid air. Indeed, he emits a fishy odour most nauseating. The winged creature has the head of a man, the body of a serpent, two hairy paws and a poison-tipped tail that thrashes most menacingly, as a furious scorpion. Virgil bids that we approach it for he wishes to parlay. On seeing I have no intention of getting close to the hideous beast, Virgil pushes me away towards the edge of the void where inhabit a small group of stragglers, sinners who were violent against art; the Usurers, those unscrupulous money lenders who lived off the toil of others.

These poor souls crouch or sit on the scorching sand squirming under the rain of fire, desperate to avoid the crackling of the flames burning from above and below, for this searing heat is as a firestorm. They flick their hands into the flames for, as the Uncommitted upon the banks of the Acheron, they are bitten and stung by insects which lay hidden in the sand. They seek relief in the fire and when it does not come, weep tears to bathe their injured fingers only for the biting and stinging to resume, this time by airborne hornets. In truth it is a wretched sight and I am moved to tears, for their cries are harrowing such that they endure eternal agony, as the endlessly burning flames scorch and blister their skin, which suffers further injury from the poisonous insects. It is abundantly clear these corrupt souls will know no respite and, for this, I find my heart weeping.

From the coloured purses around their necks bearing family crests and emblems I recognise these to be Florentines well known for their practice of usury, and it is for the greed in money lending they suffer here in perpetuity. They are not friendly. Indeed, they fear I am to take the seat of their friend upon whose soul they wait to join them in this sweltering circle and galvanise to set upon me. So, dancing across the boiling sands, I hastily return to Virgil at the waterfall.

I am utterly incredulous for he informs me he has persuaded the vile, salivating beast, Geryon, to transport us to the eighth circle. I begin my objection but he is uninterested, for the truth is there is no other way down. With much hesitation and awkwardness, I clamber onto its serpentine back. Virgil, by contrast, climbs elegantly and effortlessly, positioning himself behind me to protect me from its venomous tail for I am alive and therefore mortal, thus there is danger for me here. Geryon wobbles, stumbles, reverses clumsily and then, with no terra firma beneath his hairy paws, I find we are in flight!

I sit astride a dragon, I am certain, for he dips and curls, swerves and glides. It is more graceful than I could have imagined and I caution a look down into the watery pit hoping I will not faint. I wish I had not, for it is not just the dizzying distance down that bothers me, but the pitiful sounds of the tormented and afflicted sinners within. Their souls suffer punishments most brutal for their howls and screams tell me this is a cruel apocalyptic place. We circle downward slowly and, in doing so, we descend beyond the waterfall into the ravine, that which is the sadistic and merciless eighth circle.

8TH CIRCLE OF HELL – FRAUD

Geryon sets us down surprisingly gently and we scrabble off his back whereupon he disappears back into the thunderous spray of water. We now enter the true depths of Hell, for this is the eighth circle, that bleak and violent afterlife called Malebolge. I am reminded of the bottomless ditch at the fourth circle wherein reside the wretched Avaricious and Prodigals endlessly pushing their heavy stones, for this enormous bowl is encompassed by a great corridor coiling down around the interior wall. At the very centre sits a huge hollow from which rise putrid vapours and foggy mists of rotting air and this is surrounded by a spiralling ditch of pockets, bolgas and pouches, all accessed from the crumbling corridor by a series of perilous bridges and causeways, and from where emit all the sounds of misery and woe.

Virgil tells me that residing within each of the pouches are sets of sinners condemned to eternal suffering, for they receive punishments for acts of fraud, of which there are many guises. It is dark, hot, bleak and loud. There is danger in the air, for this is every level of sinister and I am reluctant to enter. I am fearful for there is a fetid smell of all that is rank and decaying and, the noise! I cannot escape these infernal howls and agonised screams, the cries and the harrowing shrieks of pain and torture such that they invade my ears, for already I know barbarism is at work here.

We enter into the circle and cross the threshold to the outer corridor walking in an anti-clockwise direction. Drawn by the screeching within, we look downwards to our left and peer into the first pouch. If only we had not. It is brimming with naked bodies running from one side to the other, yelling and squealing in torment. For they are being beaten most violently by crazed, horned demons wielding axes and cudgels, sticks and whips, who stand and tease from the ledges and bridges above. I am aghast for there is no respite for these accursed souls, for the violent assailants are positioned at both ends of the pouch, also above on wooden bridges, thus assault comes from all angles. Just as the poor exhausted shades reach one side of the pit, the demons set upon them with their instruments of torture, forcing them to race to the safety of the wall opposite whereupon they are viciously assaulted once more by the cackling, enraged fiends. This charade is relentless and the exhausted, sweaty, naked souls, of which there are thousands, rush back and forth in the enormous pouch, screaming out in pain and anguish, for they suffer a perpetual beating from these wicked and sadistic tyrants, the crew of the Damned.

I make eye contact with one of the souls who I guess to be from Bologna and, although he initially tries to avoid my gaze, knows that I wish to converse. In the mêlée I shout down and ask what sin he has committed, for to spend eternity in perpetual motion and torturous pain from violent thrashings is a dire punishment indeed. He is ashamed but confesses to pandering his nubile sister into performing sexual deeds for a nobleman and is thus doomed to a life of eternal death. For this, I learn, is the pouch of the Panderers, that of the Pimps. Also residing here, he continues quickly, are the Seducers; those who deceived women for their own advantage. Indeed, I espy herein the magnificent specimen Jason of the Argonauts, for did he not impregnate Hypsipyle of Lemnos, then forsake her and his unborn child to make his quest for the Golden Fleece and, in turn, abandon Medea once she had helped him to steal it?

Virgil has seen enough and gestures at me to move forward for we are to descend down the spiralling corridor to the second ditch whereupon a foul stench besieges us such that I am quite repulsed. I see soon enough that this pouch contains human excrement in which are immersed the Flatterers for, literally, in flattering they speak shit. They wail and yell and scream and, as they do, their breath turns to mould which encroaches upon and encrusts their naked bodies. They fight amongst themselves most brutally and it is all we can do to keep clean, such that the filth is splayed and splattered, but we do so by remaining at the top edge of the bridge. Virgil observes a sinner amongst the Flatterers, a young girl named Thais and he beckons her. She was, she admits, a prostitute, yet she declares her only sin was to give excessive but false thanks and praise to her client as he paid for her services. For this minor lapse she is condemned and damned to eternal death. Indeed, is this not a punishment most harsh? I am appalled.

Continuing along the outer corridor we reach the third bolga where reside the Simoniacs, those wicked clergy who traded absolution and other ecclesiastical favours for money. I have long felt the Church to be corrupt and I am right, for this pouch is full to bursting! To my mind these sinners fornicate for gold and silver so no punishment is too harsh yet, what a punishment they must endure. For they are buried inverted, head first in this dry barren landscape with their bare legs and feet protruding out of the rocky ground. There is no air, for their heads and lungs remain underground, and ferocious flames rage and whirl around the soles of their feet above, thus burning, scorching and charring with each touch. So, for these corrupt sinners, it is punishment by eternal suffocation and immolation, for they writhe and flail, but it is to no avail as they cannot breathe, nor escape the roaring flames. I wonder if my nostrils shall ever be rid of the stench of melting flesh albeit my ears are glad of the respite, for all screams here are muffled by the decomposing earth wherein are buried the heads and torsos of those who emit them.

It is a sad sight although they are not undeserving of their suffering, and Virgil and I continue along the dark corridor, peering down to observe them but with little pity. Just before we reach the next bolga we notice one set of feet markedly redder than any other and I ask Virgil if he knows who they belong to, for they have captured my eye and I am fascinated. He has no mind and suggests I investigate. I cannot approach the soul directly for there is flame aplenty and the heat scorches, so I shout down from the ledge.

With a muted voice he introduces himself as Pope Nicholas III and assumes I am Pope Boniface come to take my rightful place in Hell. Affronted, I assure him most candidly that I am not and ask what dreadful deed he has committed to end up inverted in this penultimate circle of Hell. He tells me he took the purse of the Church but, he weakly justifies, only to serve his own family. I consider these men of the cloth wicked copulaters, for they may as well perform coitus with diamonds and rubies and I tell him so. Virgil seems most amused at this description for he chuckles, scoops me up in his arms and carries me to the fourth pouch!

We look into the enormous ditch, dark and hot, and I am relieved to see just a line of naked souls trudging slowly as if in religious procession. If this is the extent of their punishment they cannot have sinned so much degree although for them to reside, condemned for eternity in the eighth circle suggests otherwise. I am confused at the insignificance of this punishment so take a second look. I am amazed! Indeed, I am appalled, shocked and horrified in unison. For their heads have been reversed at the shoulders

- brutally twisted, dislocated and repositioned - so these poor afflicted souls are compelled to walk with a backward gait! They are mournful, sorrowful and weep silent tears which fall down their spines onto their buttocks. Do they shed tears in repentance or for their deformity? For clearly their bodies are distorted. This is a sight most upsetting for the procession contains thousands upon thousands of despairing souls and, again, haunted by their harrowing cries of woe I, as they, am moved to shed tears.

I ask Virgil what sin these men can possibly have committed, such that the dislocation of their heads is a grotesque and, for me, one of the cruelest punishments I have witnessed thus far, for it has affected me greatly. He informs me they practiced the art of divination, that they sought to predict future events and, in doing so, denied the will of God. Among them are astrologers, sorcerers and magicians and, he explains, that by reversing their heads they are deprived of the power to see before them, into the future; denied any chance of prediction. I wish most fervently that God could undo the deformity for I believe a punishment so severe is a wrong in itself. Yet, I know for these poor souls the paths of righteousness and truth can never be located, for they may only see what they leave behind.

Virgil does not think as I and reproaches my grief and compassion, for I am to remember these offenders resisted God's will and in doing so rejected Divine law. He insists on pointing out the sinners he recognises amongst the trudging hoards, including King Amphiaraus, the famous soothsayer who foresaw his own death at the War of Thebes so went missing before the battle began and, also, Manto the witch, a particularly bizarre sight, as her long hair now hangs down her front, covering her naked breasts. He wishes to move on, for already we are of the second night and I have thus been alive in this funnel of woe for two days witnessing the torment, suffering, pain and misery of Hell. I know, then, that to avoid an afterlife in this cesspit will be my earthly mission, for the punishments these sinning souls endure is more than anything I may bear.

We are at the fifth pouch whereupon we are plunged into darkness, another blanket of black, and can barely make out the enormous pit within, filled to the brim with boiling, bubbling tar, albeit we can hear the agonised, harrowing wails of suffering from the accursed souls submerged in this scorching, pyroclastic quicksand. From nowhere, a blackened demon races towards us, shrieking and cackling and I fear I am to faint again, for we are likely to end up in this scalding gurgling liquid if we collide. Just as he is upon us I realise he has not spotted us in the dark, for he is too busy tormenting the naked shade upon his shoulder who he suddenly flings into the pit of scorching glutinous mass. He calls his demonic crew over who rejoice at this poor wretch's suffering and, any time he rises to the surface for air, use their pitchforks, barbs and hooks to batter him, skewer him, tear him apart, pushing and forcing him back underneath, all the while dancing, crowing, screeching in delight as they watch his skin burning, blistering, peeling; disintegrating.

They are as cooks stirring a giant cauldron of stew such that they are devoid of compassion for this most violent act. I am aggrieved, shocked and terrified and run to hide behind a rock for safety. I cannot imagine what crime must have been committed to meet such a grisly end for, even in Hell, to suffer thus in perpetuity is a monstrosity too much. I turn to whisper to Virgil, to ask him what dreadful sin is punished within but he has gone! I spot him, steadfast as ever, defiantly approaching the demons, for he wishes to negotiate our crossing. I am incredulous that he displays stupidity at such a time! He reaches the unruly group and requests they lower their weapons for he is unarmed. They refuse, naturally, for they are impudent devils. He tells them he wishes to discuss a route out of the circle so they call upon their leader, Malacoda, an enormous, fierce, yet nimble-winged demon.

They are shocked and more than a little curious to hear that a living soul is present this far into Hell and Virgil is asked to explain the reason for my being here, for they see I am not dead and all are truly flummoxed. He tells them that it is the will of God in Heaven but beyond that, does not progress, for he is poked and prodded into silence by these insolent imps, the crew of the Damned. Malacoda agrees that we may pass and deigns to provide us with an escort of ten demons on condition they continue their torturing along the way. I would rather none, for I do not trust them one inch and fear I will be next for the tar pit, but Virgil accepts his offer, for the chief has also advised the main bridge between the sixth and seventh pouch is damaged. I know he fears that without escorts to navigate we may not find an alternative route, but I am willing to gamble, for these rabid demons unsettle me greatly.

We begin our journey with this motley crew in tow and again I ask Virgil what sin could justify such a cruel punishment as to boil alive in a pit of tar. He tells me this is the pouch of the Barrators, corrupt politicians. He does not need to elaborate further, for the corrupt deserve everything they get to my mind. I whisper my concerns about the impudent demons but he says their wanton violence and crowing is just for show, to scare not us but the sinners herein. I confess I am not entirely convinced. We follow the ten-strong group of rowdy imps along the dark and spiralling corridor but all the while I glimpse down at the surface of the boiling tar to see if there is any soul within that I may converse with. Naturally, they do not show themselves often, for to do so is to get clubbed, pierced and battered unless they can escape such a beating by diving quickly back under once they have taken air.

I spot a sinner who is being tortured outside the pit upon a ledge and decide he would make a suitable study, so approach. But the demons are already upon him, stabbing, poking, whipping. I am tormented by guilt as I do not wish to get involved, for they are nasty, violent mischief makers and I do not trust them not to turn on us. Virgil thus takes charge and, in an attempt to stop this poor soul's suffering, immediately calls out and asks where he is from. He provides a lot of information to answer this one question for, in seeking a moment's respite from this torrent of violence, plays for time. He tells us not his name, rather that he is from Navarre (of Spain), that his father was a wastrel, that he was thus adopted by King Thibault and that his sin was to swindle money from the city's coffers. Having imparted these details, a demon, as a wild boar in his appearance, sets upon him and splits his middles open with his tusk! I am utterly appalled. He does not die but surely will, as another makes haste to disembowel him!

Virgil quickly interrupts to ask if he knows of any Italians residing in this pouch of swindlers whereupon the Navarro nods and points to a soul submerged in the tarry pit. He tells us he is Friar Gomito, a clergyman with many masters, all from whom he managed to pilfer money or gold and that if we so wish, will summon him from the tar should the demons concede to forego his punishment. Sensing a trick, the demons rush forward but it is too late, for the disembowelled Spaniard dives back into the basin where, for the moment, he is free of the violent stabbings and whippings, albeit treads tar frantically to avoid total submergence in the boiling, blistering liquid which scalds and burns his naked body as he cries out in agony.

Incensed, the battling demons remonstrate angrily with each other and, not taking care, inadvertently plunge into the cavernous pit, immersed in the molten lava, flailing, thrashing about, desperate to save themselves from total submersion. While they struggle to scramble out, for it takes considerable effort given their wings, now covered in the sticky tar have become heavy and cumbersome, Virgil and I use the distraction to make our own escape. We are not entirely sure of the route, for we know the main bridge out to be damaged, but this is no matter as survival is the driving force behind our flight. The demonic group is furious that the swindler was able to outwit them, absolutely raging and are howling and screeching their dissent as they clamber out back onto the ledge.

I confess I am nervous, for when they realise we, too, have outsmarted them, their already frayed tempers will likely be fuelled to exploding, provoked into violent action. They cannot return to Malacoda and admit their grave lapses and errors of today, so I am certain the ten will seek us out to impart a special justice. From the shadows I suddenly hear the flap of wings and clatter of talons for, as I suspected, we are being chased by the flying devils and, as predicted, they are incandescent. They are as a pack of wolves, snarling, salivating, baying, for they are rampant and quite uncontrolled. I cannot faint, such that I wish to, for to do so would be tantamount to surrender to this rabid crew, but the hairs on the back of my neck stand proud for I am terrified as at no other time in my life.

Sensing the danger, Virgil scoops me up in his arms and runs towards the cavernous incline that leads to the sixth pouch. He flings himself off the verge into the darkness whereupon he slides down the sloping corridor with me on his lap like we are two brothers on a wooden sled enjoying a snowy hill, but I am neither carefree or jubilant. The demons are furious such that they yell and curse at the top of the ledge, hurling their various weapons at us as we realise, thankfully, that they are unable to navigate beyond the fifth pouch and cross the border into the sixth, for they are as much captives there as the Swindlers they torment.

We are back at the winding corridor, stumbling in the dark, retching on an odour of rotting meat and burning skin, of putrid air and rank earth and look down into the next ditch wherein another procession takes place. These men are clothed in hoods and capes, as a monk's habit but of shimmering gold. They cry out in pain, sobbing and weeping but remain still, or so I thought until I realise they move forward with tiny steps, no more than the width of a head of corn with each pace. It is a sight to behold, for it may as well be a parade of gilded snails and tortoises for the lack of distance they cover.

Virgil and I discuss their plight for this does not appear to be a severe punishment until he tells me the capes are lined with lead. This incumbrance, for lead is the heaviest of all metals, weighs them down from head to toe and now I can see their heads are bowed, shoulders hunched, knees caving, for to bear the burden of this load is almost impossible and the only means to do so is to trudge, face down, with the tiniest of movements. I ask Virgil what sins have been committed by these souls and he replies that we are in the pouch of the Hypocrites. As ever, I am keen to see if I know any of the souls residing within but am interrupted by a gilded sinner who recognises my accent.

Overhanging the ledge that I may call down, we enter into conversation, for it transpires he is most eager to confirm that I am alive, as he suspects, albeit he is mightily confused to find mortal man in Hell amongst the dead. I reply in the affirmative and ask him about the sins and punishments related to this pouch. They are indeed Hypocrites he states, for they all performed acts of supreme selfishness having insisted others practice ultimate judiciousness. I am about to ask for examples when I see the most extraordinary, but macabre, sight ahead, for a naked sinner is crucified to the ground!

This poor soul is awake and screaming, writhing and spitting, for he is furious, utterly incandescent and, one imagines, he suffers significant pain for each time he moves, the flesh surrounding the nails driven into his extremities (five inches to his wrists and seven to his heels) must rip and tear in a swell of pure agony. Not only does he lie nailed to the earth but suffers further indignity as the procession of heavily weighted Hypocrites passes slowly over his body, for they are disinclined to break the line and divert around him. He endures this torture and ignominy for eternity, for this is Caiaphas, a high priest of Pontius Pilate who called for Christ's crucifixion. In doing so, he committed the sin of hypocrisy by preaching prudence yet not practicing it himself.

I am stunned, not just for the depravity of the idea but more so because this punishment is personal, tailored, is it not? We ask the robed friars to point a way out, for we are keen to navigate safely and avoid further encounter with any stray demons, for we need to continue on our unavoidable journey. They tell us that although the bridge is broken the canyon remains passable, for there are rocks and rubble aplenty either side. This is not what Malacoda advised, so I am glad to be rid of the lying devil as is Virgil who tells the group of his treachery. The friars laugh, I imagine the first time since their placement here, and openly call him a fool, such that he deigned to trust the reliably untrustworthy demons. I see that poor Virgil is quietly seething, for he is humiliated by his own naivety.

We descend the dark, dank spiralling corridor and come to the damaged bridge whereupon we realise it would be foolhardy to risk a crossing given the perilous depth of the canyon below. As the Hypocrites correctly stated there are rocks to each flank and, although it looks treacherous, it is likely possible we may reach the other side if we navigate them with supreme caution. I can see that Virgil is already assessing the most appropriate route and, within a minute or two, he's off! I scramble to follow him but lose my footing and fall hard, having taken only one step forward, for I am of the living and the stones give way beneath me. Virgil backtracks and pulls me up, this time remaining at my side for he can tell I am shaken and have lost my nerve.

Many times I wish to give up and turn back, for the danger for mortal man such as I is that should I slip and plummet into the nadirs of the funnel, I shall perish. Yet, Virgil reassures me and we slowly move forward, downward, traversing the terrain as best we can manage. As we walk together he earnestly states that our immediate endeavours require the best of man. I am somewhat affronted I confess, for does he suggest that rather than endure and struggle as I do, I seek instead to lay on a bed of feathers or, rather, relax under the canopy of the oak tree with a flagon of wine? This infuriates me indeed, for am I not showing bravery in the face of adversity? Does he consider me lacking in spirit? Does he accuse me of laziness? He is my friend but I confess, at times, I find him a little condescending and pious; ironic given his earthly ignorance of Christ.

After an hour or two, possibly three, having safely navigated the rocky landslide, we clamber up the last of the rubble and find ourselves back in the dank winding corridor looking down into the enormous bowl of the eighth circle. Putrid vapours and foggy mists of rotting air continue to rise from the core, screams and shrieks, moans and howling also polluting the atmosphere. We move to approach the seventh pouch, that of the Thieves. A voice calls out from within but it is too dark and deep and I cannot locate its owner, even from the bridge. Virgil gestures to a jutting ledge and suggests we may get a better look into the pocket and converse with the soul from there, so we carefully negotiate the incline.

It is difficult to see with any accuracy, for there is little illumination, but the multitudinous sinners within are naked; bodies glistening and wet. They run and scream, trip and slip, yelling out in disgust, for it appears they are in a pit of serpents, so numerous they have formed a carpet of grease, a floor of slime and gunge. They have scales and scuta of varying shapes and sizes, their bony plates of different materials and sharpness; some glass, some horn, some steel. The snake pit is reptilian and this place, I believe, not entirely of God's creation, rather a mythological kingdom in the realms of phantasmagoria. It is a vile pestilence indeed, as a plague from the Book of Exodus, for these serpents, some as wide as Charon's oar, coil their slimy bodies around the limbs of these desperate souls then bite down hard, sinking venomous fangs between their victims' shoulders.

I watch aghast as a wretched sinner erupts into screams of agony whereupon he combusts, bursting into flames before he falls as a heap of ash on the ground. To my amazement, the body rises up from the ashes, reinvents back into human form whereupon it queues on the carpet of serpents, with thousands more sinners, to relive the experience again. In perpetuity. They are as the phoenix but far removed from that gilded bird who represents, as it does, exceptional man in his highest form, all colours of the rainbow and heavenly life, for these shades are all wanton thieves and are being punished most savagely for their wicked misdemeanours.

I speak to the soul newly risen, another Tuscan and I find he is Vanni Fucci, an associate from my earthly life! I know him to be a man filled with anger so am surprised to find him here when to rot with the Wrathful on the bank of the Styx would have been more fitting. But, he has been found guilty of theft, of stealing holy relics from the Church and this is the sin he has been judged on. He is angry, nay ashamed, that I have discovered him thus and mocks me, for he tells that the Whites, the party of politics to which I show allegiance, will fail at the next election. This man is a fool, for he has been found wanting such that three pockets of the inferno could accommodate him without ado, for is this prediction not worthy of the fourth pouch whereupon his head would be reversed on his shoulders with the other soothsayers? Aloud, I sardonically congratulate Florence on its capacity to produce sinners of his calibre, and Virgil and I move on through the seventh bolga, watching with incredulity as more souls within disappear inside the coiled form of a serpent, then fall as ashes upon a nest from which they are reborn.

Humiliated and demonstrating a blasphemy most obscene (with his fingers), Fucci attempts to flee albeit serpents are wrapped around his legs and feet. I confess I am not upset for he deserves the justice meted, such that we reap what we sow. We remain in the seventh ditch whereupon somehow, he has disentangled himself and escaped from the serpent. From nowhere, an angry centaur thrashing and stomping, crashes onto the scene looking for Fucci, who has now disappeared. Virgil tells me this centaur is Cacus, easily identifiable for he has a dragon on his back which obligingly burns anything blocking their path. He explains that whereas the vicious centaurs at the first ring watch over the sinners of violence in the boiling river of blood, Cacus is a thief, for he stole cattle direct from Hercules, whereupon Hercules administered 100 blows with a cudgel and thus killed him. He resides in this pouch reserved for thieves albeit he still demonstrates anger, wrath and violence in all its forms.

He is a vicious beast and I am keen to avoid him so we move along the corridor, still at the seventh pouch and I cannot believe what I am witness to next. For two souls huddle together just beneath us and a huge, six-footed serpent - as a centipede - slides alongside them. The serpent wraps himself around one of the souls and, squeezing and constricting with his six legs and clenching the unfortunate's head in its jaw, does not release until they fuse into one. Before our very eyes, the serpent becomes half-man and the man becomes half-serpent, forming one new, alien creature. I am astounded, for this is most surreal. Indeed, it is horrific and quite unearthly; truly unimaginable. Yet, minutes later and before I have time to recover, another serpent rises and immediately plunges his fangs into the neighbouring soul's stomach! Their eyes meet, despite the serpent is at his torso, yet the soul does not cry out in pain, he merely yawns in an action I find utterly mystifying.

Each holding an unblinking gaze, there follows many seconds of intense staring, deep into the other's eyes. Their bodies begin to smoke and I expect the third soul to combust as before. Yet this does not happen for the smoke is merely a screen, a fog behind which an extraordinary transformation takes place. For the serpent's tail divides in two and legs begin to grow. At the same moment, the sinner's two legs merge into one and a tail can be seen to appear. The shade's skin grows hard while the serpent's grows soft, the serpent's torso sprouts limbs whilst the shade's disappear and his hair drops to the floor as the serpent grows a mane, resplendent and thick. The serpent, with his new legs stands up, proud and tall and a face begins to form, ears protruding. The man, having lost his legs, falls to the ground whereupon his ears disappear back into his head which has a face no more. In a final grotesque, the man's tongue splits and forks while the serpent's fuses into one. With mine own eyes I have witnessed a man become a snake and a snake become a man. The man, now a serpent, slithers off with a hiss and a backward scowl.

I am rooted to the spot, for a more monstrous, pitiful, outlandish yet fantastical occurrence I cannot begin to fathom. Indeed, this is a vision so freakish in its nature that my own sight begins to fail me, for I no longer see with clarity and precision. Or perhaps I am tired, lacking in sleep for, in truth, I am drained, exhausted from the non-stop trek, the bizarre apparitions I have witnessed and, wearily, I ask Virgil if we may move on, for conversation does not appeal.

We continue our descent along the dank corridor leaving behind the harrowing cries of the tortured thieves. We approach the eighth pouch yet cannot access it without scrabbling on our hands and knees, for we are crawling downwards on rocks and gravel which form a makeshift staircase. I notice the corridor suddenly drops at a steep gradient, with makeshift steps formed of wooden platforms and enormous boulders which coil downwards. With each tread I know we move deeper into the cavernous depths of Hell, closer to its mighty demonic core, for I am profoundly aware that, here, all light has left us. It is black, dismal, sinister; frightening and I understand that at each point it has become more dangerous for we barely leave each pouch with our lives. These rampant demons show violence with much ease but, too, there are snakes and hounds and serpents and dragons and fire most terrifying. It is perilous and I am lucky to be alive in this realm of the cursed dead.

I am unsure how we are to safely navigate these steps for we will need to jump or scramble, such is their depth. After much exertion and, I confess, fear, for I am mortal man who might easily plummet to my death, we reach a platform that seems relatively secure. We sit upon it and gather ourselves for a few minutes then look down into the pocket. It is a dark ravine, deeper than the thunderous waterfall wherein appeared the grotesque monster Geryon, with only dancing flames to illuminate it, as giant fireflies on a fetid swamp. The flames flicker and, aghast, I soon realise why. For swathed within each resides a sinner, burning, squirming and writhing and each time the wretched soul moves in protest at the agonising scorching it receives, so does the flame, as if labouring in the wind.

I cannot imagine what sin has been committed for a soul to endure a torture thus and I ask Virgil, but not before a screaming double flame dances its way towards us for, within this blazing tongue of fire appear to be two naked bodies, flailing and floundering, roasting and burning. Virgil tells me these shades are the Greek warriors Ulysses and Diomedes, the pair responsible for the removal of the sacred statue of the goddess Pallas, that which Zeus threw down from Mount Olympus to protect Troy from attack. Thus when they stole it from the Temple of Athena, it rendered the city conquerable, as was proved when the Grecian troops invaded. So, I now know the eighth pouch to be reserved for the Evil Counsellors, for these committed wicked deeds with the most severe consequences and this atrocious pair are punished thus, united for eternity, burning within a scorching flame such that I, too, feel I roast alive.

Virgil vehemently rejects my idea to discourse with them for, he says, my accent will do me no favours. Instead, he introduces himself and asks them to relay the tale of their deaths. Between shrieks of agony, Ulysses obliges. Bored with life and seeking exciting new challenges, he sailed to the western-most point of the Mediterranean where, legend said, no man had voyaged for, to do so, would be to sail off the earth's rim to certain death. After a few weeks, an enormous mountain came into view and, with the edge of the western point now in sight, this plucky mariner braced himself to either plunder or succeed. However, in the moments before he reached the rock, a violent tempest whirled about him and carried the sailing vessel into the abyss. It intrigues me that in life as in death, Ulysses was punished for his sins, for God was not going to permit him to enjoy eternal glory as a celebrated mariner following the desecration of 15,000 innocent souls at Troy.

We bid farewell to the miscreant pair and continue carefully around the pouch whereupon there are more flames and, as before, we can just make out the naked bodies within, writhing, howling, flailing. From one corner a violent scream is heard, its owner pierced with pain, such as a dying animal. I turn to Virgil and he can tell from the horrified look upon my face that I expect to find within a brass bull, the hollow medieval torture chamber. This barbaric torment, whereupon lowlifes were forced inside; interred, encased, entombed, metes a punishment most grave, for it is set on fire and the ensnared prey is burned alive. Writhing, snorting, dribbling, kicking, screaming, moaning, dying in the claustrophobic sweltering grave, the imprisoned souls within emit the harrowing sounds of a bull surrendering as the burning metal takes hold. Virgil looks into the pouch but there is no brass chamber. I am relieved, yet not consoled, for I still do not know what I can expect to find here and from where the violent scream came. Virgil points yonder for he realises it is a shade experiencing inordinate pain within the flame in which he is swathed. He is trying to speak but I cannot decipher the words over the unremitting howls until, somehow, he manages to dance over to the ledge.

Eventually he approaches close enough for conversation and his words reach the tip of the flame. He addresses

Virgil, for he wishes for news of his hometown, Romagna. Virgil pushes me forward, for I am the man's compatriot and I confirm that although not at war, there is tyranny and violence within. I am eager to know this soul's name and he whimpers between tormented howls that it is Guido da Montefeltro. He admits he readily reveals his identity, for although he recognises I am of the living, he does not believe me to be leaving this brutal place and is thus confident his secret, of which he is most ashamed, shall not become knowledge on Earth, for I shall not be returning there. In fairness the man does not yet know I am on a mission set by God Himself, prayed for by the blessed Beatrice and watched over by the Virgin Mary in Heaven, that, too, I am ably assisted by the maestro who is Virgil. I shall be returning to the living Earth. I have faith in God's capacity to arrange this, but I shall not reveal Guido's secret when I am back there, however much he chastises me today.

Guido tells us that he was a soldier and a scoundrel, for he lied, cheated, snitched and backstabbed. He found the light, for he found God and thus repented, becoming a Franciscan monk in the ardent hope he might absolve his sins. He served the new pope, the unpopular Boniface who, in return for his allegiance against the Christians planning revolt and uprising, promised Guido absolution upon his death. In a moment of weakness or fear, or both, Guido acquiesced. Upon his death, as Guido ascended and approached the gates of Heaven, for Pope Boniface had assured him absolution and a direct path, he was intercepted by a demon of death who swooped down, plucked him up and delivered him unto Minos in the second circle. For, as the demon logically stated, absolution cannot be granted in anticipation of redemption such that redemption cannot precede repentance and repentance cannot precede sin. Minos and his tail declared Guido a fraudulent counsellor and cast him to the eighth pouch of the eighth circle, wherein he shall eternally writhe in a scorching flame, for his path to Hell was guaranteed upon his self-serving promises to Boniface. Upon re-living his death and the circumstances leading up to it, poor Guido is overcome with grief and thus disappears within his flame to the other edge of the pouch. We make our way down to the next, descending ever deeper into darkness. If only we had not.

I cannot speak. I am mute and wish I was blind, for the sight I behold herein is tantamount to massacre. For, walking in perpetual circles are thousands of naked souls butchered in such a manner that another human soul alive or dead could not possibly have performed the barbaric deed. These shades are slashed and maimed, dismembered and mutilated in a wanton display of brutal carnage. For, as they pass along the battlefield that is the ninth pouch, crazed fiends whip and hack away with their swords; piercing, slicing, dissecting, decapitating. All howl, scream, moan and cry out in a crescendo of despair, for they suffer in such severity they are grief-stung to madness. Some, with entrails drawn and hanging from their midriff, others, holding dismembered limbs, yet more, pierced in the throat, with noses, ears and tongues sliced off rendering them quite impotent for they are mute. Thus, they may never beg forgiveness, they may never atone and, all know, without contrition there is no absolution and without absolution there is no salvation. And here, salvation is denied. For here there is no mercy.

A soul passes me, his slaughtered windpipe stained crimson with blood. Another, maimed, with bleeding stumps where his hands should sit. One more grabs at his chest and pulls it apart, screaming, such that I can see his shattered ribcage and organs within, yet another passes and has no arms. It is a horrifying and sickening scene. As they complete the circle, the body heals and reforms and they are re-made whole, ready for the crazed fiends with their swords to begin hacking and slicing at them again. This woeful suffering plays out for eternity, as does the soundtrack of howls of anguish and misery, for these are the primal screams of abject agony and horror. Of torture.

Such a punishment surely defies all sins known to man? For, to my mind, to unify all sins as one is to still not sin enough to be punished thus and the carnage is as one thousand battles. This is grave indeed. And we are still only in the eighth circle. Please God, I can take no more. I cannot endure further distress for I cannot stop the suffering of these beleaguered souls who are mangled, mutilated; maimed. Indeed, did not the Gods show mercy upon Prometheus, dispatching Hercules to destroy the eagle who so pecked at his regenerating liver each day, for even they knew barbaric punishment could not be eternal; that no man, immortal or otherwise, could endure such brutality. I wish for my cherished angel, Beatrice, to show herself, to pluck me from this scene most disturbing and hold me to her bosom such that I may smell her sweet scent, feel her heart beating in her breast, be comforted by her warm embrace, for I fear that I shall never know purity of thought again, such has my mind been so viciously molested.

I ask Virgil what sin can possibly warrant such a violent, disturbing and rabid punishment and he informs me the ninth pouch is reserved for sowers of discord; the schismatics, for those who caused divide amongst men in life shall so be divided themselves in death. He points to the man who spread open his chest and identifies him as Curio, he who persuaded Caesar to betray Pompey thus starting the civil war in Rome. So too, Ali, cousin of Prophet Muhammad, whose failed succession to the caliphate divided Muslims into Shi'a and Sunni.

As Virgil and I discourse, the Italians in the pouch call for me for, again, my accent causes excitement amongst my compatriots here. They know me to be of the living and thus beseech me to impart messages and words of love to their friends and kin on Earth. I confess, such is their suffering, I do not believe anything I may say or do shall alleviate their misery but I tell them I will do their bidding upon my return and, in this moment, have every intention of doing so.

A soul moves towards us from within the depths of the

pit carrying something heavy in his hands. I know not what it is until he stands opposite whereupon, in horror, I see it is his head! He lifts this up, as a lantern, for his disembodied voice is released from his mouth and tells me he is Bertran de Born, the man who notoriously convinced Prince Henry to rebel against his father King Henry II and in doing so, caused rift and divide within the monarchy. Naturally, his eternal punishment is to suffer his own divide. Thus, separated from his head, he crowns himself the most pitiful soul in Hell and I am minded to concur.

I can look at his lantern no more and search the pit instead. There is crimson everywhere I look, for it is a blood bath. Blood on the floor, splattering the pouch walls, bloodied stumps and bloody wounds, even blood-curdling screams as the demons' swords slice into bodies, maiming, wounding, disfiguring, mutilating. I cannot look yet I cannot remove my eyes from this scene, such that it is so abhorrent. I am transfixed yet traumatised. I am incredulous that a mind can invent a punishment so wicked, for that mind cannot be sane, rational, healthy. I am mesmerised, utterly gripped, yet broken-hearted and appalled.

Virgil rebukes me for, again, he has caught me staring. He says this is not the time to tarry, for the eighth circle is a vast landscape and the hours are precious, for he has calculated that tomorrow must be Easter Sunday. He knows that despite there is no sleep in this realm, for the wicked enjoy no respite or peace, I arrived in The Dark Wood at the dawn of Good Friday and a second moon is due shortly. I continue to glimpse into the pit, for I cannot ignore the anguished screams within and I weep tears of despair as I watch these afflicted souls being sliced so viciously by raging demons with not one ounce of humanity in their empty hearts. Suddenly I am distracted, for in the distance, I swear upon God's name I can see the face of my ancestor, my relative Geri del Bello, and tears again come to mine eyes such as the waterfall wherein lived Geryon, the winged monster.

Virgil admonishes me, for despite having the romantic soul of a poet, he is not one for emotive displays and thus gestures for me to heed him, for he observes del Bello is jumping and pointing, screaming at me and clearly not seeking a gentle reunion. He was killed in a bloody battle with an ending most violent and is furious his death has remained unavenged. Virgil firmly tells me revenge is not my obligation, for del Bello existed many lifetimes ago, thus takes my arm and leads me away. We proceed cautiously along the bridge that takes us from the penultimate to the final bolga, for we are now at the tenth, the pocket of the Falsifiers.

It is dark and bleak and already my ears are contaminated by screams and wails and cries, for these are the howls of pain, of torture. My nostrils, too, sense the suffering within, for here the stench is rank, fetid; grim. It appears there are four pockets within this final pouch and we come to the first whereupon naked shades are huddled in heaps or sprawled out on the ground, writhing in agony, for they are sick and ailing. Infected scabs crust their entire beings which they rub and scratch incessantly, frantic and feverish, for they are plagued, diseased; leprous. Two afflicted souls lean upon each other, for they are weak and fragile yet are fighting, scratching and clawing with as much violence and ferocity as they can muster such that I believe they wish to soothe the infernal itching they endure.

Virgil interrupts in an attempt to offer them respite and asks if they know of any Italians within this pocket. Indeed, they say *they* are Italians and pause momentarily to ask Virgil what his purpose is here. He gestures towards me on the ledge and tells them about the course that has been plotted within the nine circles for me. They are intrigued, as are others, for they see I am of the living and interest is piqued such that a myriad of souls begins to gather and necks are craned to catch a glimpse of me. Virgil thrusts me forward so the innumerable yet contaminated sinners herein can view me with greater ease. It is an opportunity for me to learn of their names and stories so I venture that in return for sharing their tales, I will ensure that upon re-entering the living world, I shall spread news of them to their bereaved kin.

The first, Grifolino of Arezzo steps forward boldly. He had told an acquaintance of the Bishop of Siena he could teach him to fly. The Bishop, much angered at this heresy then discovered that he practiced the dark art of alchemy and he was immediately burned upon the stake for it. Thus, his path to Hell was ordained and Minos directed him here with eight coils of his tail. Another scabby shade squeezes himself forward declaring to be Capocchio of Siena, also an alchemist of the highest order. He, too, was burned alive at the stake. So, the first pocket is reserved for the falsifiers of metals and their punishment is to rot violently upon the fetid earth, scabrous wounds causing incessant itching and ceaseless aggravation, for they eternally writhe and squirm, their thrashing and wriggling a futile attempt to remove the leprous scabs, as steel blades descaling a fish. It is a pitiful sight yet, in truth I am glad for it, for I am relieved I do not find them on blazing stakes herein, eternally burning alive in death, flesh melting and dripping in a punishment most cruel and barbaric such that I have already witnessed.

We move forward to the second pocket whereupon my ears are again set aflame by screams of hideous pain and cries of agony. For the naked sinners within are biting each other, tearing at each other with their teeth, gnawing and chomping huge chunks of flesh. I am reminded of the stories of antiquity whereby through extreme suffering, and engulfed by madness, starving men turned upon each other as wild animals. I witness the same turmoil here, brutal and ferocious, for the fighting is fierce, and compassion is there none. It is as cruel a sight as I have seen within the eight circles. I meet Gianni Schicchi, he who impersonated another to benefit from his friend's will. I see the princess Myrrha, she who disguised herself as another to enter into carnal relations with her own father in order to gratify her severe lust. For these are the souls who falsified other persons and, in death, they are barbarians indeed.

We walk on in the darkness and eventually reach the third pocket whereupon the most bizarre vision appears before my eyes, for a man has a body contorted and moulded into the shape of a lute! He has no face to speak of, for the flesh is rotting away and he is bloated, horribly distended by the dropsy disease, which gives him the distinctive swell to his belly. He is Master Adamo and has a raging, perennial thirst, that which only the river Arno of his home town could quench and one he thinks of often. But he will see no water here, for his punishment is to crave the refreshing waters of the Arno in all perpetuity. For this is where he counterfeited coins and thus performed his own sin of falsifying. He shows no remorse, no self-pity even, just anger at the soul he accuses of convincing him to counterfeit, and he seeks revenge. Perhaps he should meet with my ancestor Geri, for revenge is a game on his mind also…

Always descending and clambering, finally and after a long haul, we are at the fourth pocket reserved for liars, the falsifiers of words. Accusations fly around, for the wife of Potiphar continues to insist Joseph tried to seduce her, Sinon of the Greeks who deceived the Trojans into pushing the horse unto their precious city still promotes his innocence. Each pore upon the skin of these souls smokes, such that they are afflicted by fever so high it causes their flesh to burn from within. The sight is macabre indeed and the stench most repugnant. Their cries are haunting such that the pain of roasting from the inside out is too much to endure, but endure it they must for they have sinned against God and now they suffer for eternity.

A row breaks out between Master Adamo and Sinon, for the former insults the latter such that angry words turn to violence, for Master Lute has leapt into the fourth ring! I confess that, despite the misery, I am riveted. Sinon makes to attack Master Adamo then flicks his bloated belly which sounds as a gong, an amusing diversion for all who hear it.

But Virgil is affronted and admonishes me severely, for he decrees it shameful that I stoop to watch this pointless argument between afflicted and accursed souls so desperate for respite. I am straight back in the Forest of Suicides, embarrassed into contrition, utterly mortified, for I seek Virgil's respect and hang my head. I am ashamed that he thinks me a voyeur, observing the downfall of man at his lowest. He senses he has upset me, for he wraps his arm around my shoulder in gentle embrace and, unfathomably, we immediately fall asleep where we stand.

We awake to find ourselves in motion, already walking, the screaming souls of the feverish falsifiers of words now far behind us. We continue along the dark spiralling path, for we make our way unto the core, the final circle of nine, the absolute nadir of the nefarious Underworld. Indeed, we approach the central wall of Malebolge. As we descend deeper into the heart of the funnel we find ourselves blinded once more, for it is void of light and all is black. Instead, we let our ears guide us for we are drawn towards a thunderous bugle's blast which crashes through the atmosphere. We advance to a sorrowful chorus of lament, a roaring symphony of haunting, harrowing wails and groans of woe. With each step forward the volume rises, reaching a deafening crescendo whereupon scores of rocketing towers can be seen to rise out of the mist ahead. As we approach I realise these are not towers but, rather, naked giants, colossus titans; the Custodians. So enormous are these goliaths, of both height and girth, that their navels are level with us at the rim of the eighth circle yet their feet are to be found fathoms below, standing within the very depths of Hell, for they are trapped, entombed, embedded within the ninth circle, at the very base, the heart and core of Hell itself. In truth it is a fantastical sight and I am quite mesmerised.

One speaks but he is unintelligible and I cannot understand a word of his booming voice for he speaks utter gibberish. Virgil tells me this is Nimrod, the Babylonian king who, by building the soaring Tower of Babel such that man could reach the Heavens without spiritual effort, brought upon the wrath of God whose response was to splinter Earth's single language into a thousand incoherent ones - nonsense, prattle, foreign tongues. He then condemned Nimrod to the inferno whereupon Minos banished him to the very depths and deprived him the use of his own language as punishment.

Virgil names some of the other giants, for there are a great many here such that the pit of Hell is a vast landscape and has the capacity for hundreds of these defiant rebels, despite their gargantuan forms. We come across a raging ogre bound in chains, arms restrained behind his huge body, stomping and flailing, spitting and screaming, trying to escape the bonds. Virgil explains that this is Ephialtes, son of Neptune who, in scaling Mount Olympus and taking up arms to dethrone the gods, so angered them that his punishment was to be deprived the use of his own. We talk of other giants and, upon hearing the name of one, Ephialtes is so enraged, he lashes out, stomping and tramping his feet thus causing an earthquake!

We make haste and, unharmed by falling rocks and debris, continue along the spiralling corridor. We stop alongside the navel of Antaeus, lion-eating son of Poseidon, who Virgil intends to persuade to help us down into the pit. I am shocked, for was not this invincible a murderer? Did he not construct an entire temple of human skulls to honour his father? Indeed, he challenged his helpless victims to wrestling matches knowing that he was always to be victorious, never to be conquered. For his powers, given by his mother the Earth goddess Gaea, ensured that whilst his feet touched the ground he would remain eternally triumphant. And the bones lining the temple demonstrate the immeasurable casualties of his violence. In truth, I fear I may be the next.

I am alarmed, for I did not expect that we would venture so close to the heart of Hell in all its gore and horror, but Virgil seems unconcerned. The giant Antaeus listens intently, nods and agrees. I am unsure quite how he intends to execute this task, for there is little room in which to manoeuvre, so tightly packed are the giant bodies, and the base of Hell, whereupon his feet are embedded, is a long way down for I have looked into the dizzying depths of the crater and only see darkness. However, within a moment, we are there amongst enormous feet and ankles as thick as the oak tree! For he has simply picked us both up in one hand, bent over and deposited us on the floor whereupon we find ourselves in the inhospitable, barren, desolate vestibule of the ninth and final circle of Hell. For this is the domain of the unforgivables. The traitors.

9TH CIRCLE OF HELL -TREACHERY

Have I not said that to attain salvation is to bask in the glow of God's love, to feel the comfort of His tender embrace? For not to do so, to deny the Divine, shall cause you to be cast adrift to a wilderness furthest from the warmth of His love where there will be ice and all the coldness, muteness and numbness of a life without redemption? And it is here. For the ninth and last circle is a hostile tundra of ice. A frozen surface furthest away from the warmth and bliss of Divine love, in which we all wish to wallow. For here, mercury plummets.

I have witnessed fire in Hell. The burning furnaces, the scorching, torturous flames; the inferno. I have beheld the damage and pain inflicted by intense heat and all the suffering and misery that charring, roasting hotness does to a soul. The torment, anguish and agony of fire that causes a shade to screech as a piglet and snort as a bull. The pain of red rain, flaming tombs, scorching sands and melted flesh. But what I see today is beyond compare and, indeed, beyond description. For we are at Cocytus, the fourth river of Hell.

It is a lake of ice, frozen as a glass sheet so dense it would not shatter even were two score mountains to collapse upon it. I am flummoxed to find ice in Hell; to know that the toxic bosom of the nefarious Underworld is a frozen terrain. I confess this is most unexpected despite my initial prediction, for this was metaphorical speak only and I am dumbfounded, for the inferno has been a raging fire with all the pain and torment, suffering and misery that fiery flagellation inflicts. But this is ice. And there is cold and frost like no mortal man has ever sensed and my blood freezes.

I know us to be far from God here, for when you bask in the glow of God's love, enveloped by His warmth, you shall have attained salvation. And there is no warmth here, no glow of love, no ember of faith, no comforting embrace. For we are within Caina, the first ring of the ninth circle wherein lie traitors to their kin, so named after Cain who, envious that God failed to acknowledge his paltry sacrificial offering of grass and seeds, preferring instead the fat sheep presented by his impoverished brother, so wickedly slayed that man Abel in a jealous rage. Thus, treachery and frigidity of hearts is what unites sinners herein.

As we walk gingerly upon the frozen river of pain I look down and check for cracks but am met with an horrific sight for, at my feet, are the heads of men otherwise totally submerged in the frozen water below. Their faces snowy, lips blue, hair frosted, teeth chattering, for the pain of intense cold burns as that of intense heat, and I pity these poor wretches their eternal suffering in this freezing sea of death. We encounter a pair of twins, locks entwined such that not even the gap of one hair's breadth separates them. They are mute, for their tears have frozen to their faces, icing their mouths firmly shut. To communicate they butt heads most violently so another soul identifies them as the Bisenzio brothers, here for they murdered each other over political disagreement and, clearly, they remain incandescent because of it. It is a pitiful sight, I will not lie.

We continue across the frozen lake of woe and witness human form turned to beast by the freezing temperatures, for souls howl, wail and bleat, crying out for warmth yet still denying their sins. I am horrified for, not taking care where I place my feet, I accidentally kick a man full in his face! Naturally he is furious, incandescent, for my clumsiness has caused severe pain. He curses me, of course, so I bend down to offer profuse apology and immediately I recognise the cur as Bocca degli Abati, an Italian traitor! I tell him I shall kick him again and this time in the teeth, that I shall rip out his hair and punch him in the cheek, such that he showed such treachery to my beloved Italy. Indeed, for he is frozen I can, and do, tear out a tuft of his hair and leave him to suffer in the ice, happily so, as Virgil and I progress along the solid carpet of frost to the second ring, Antenora. For this is the realm of betrayers against homeland, so named after Antenor, the treacherous Trojan warrior who enabled the Greeks to overthrow the city of Troy.

I am appalled to see two sinners immersed in the ice yet in combat, one devouring the other's head, which he has clamped firmly in his jaw. It is a shocking sight, for he bites most violently in a manner quite barbaric. Naturally curious to understand what has led to this bizarre yet brutal occurrence, I stop and ask, adding that if he so wishes, I may spread word of him back on Earth when I return there. He pauses from his feast (for truly, it is as if he eats the face in front of him) and the sinner thus begins his sorry tale, but not before he has wiped his mouth upon the hair of his dinner's head.

He introduces himself as Count Ugolino and his meal as Archbishop Ruggieri, both of Pisa. He continues that the Archbishop had condemned him and his four young sons to prison as traitors yet the Archbishop, Ugolino declared, was himself the traitor. Denied food and destined to die of starvation in a freezing tower, he listened in abject hopelessness to the weakening cries of his hungry children as they huddled and cuddled in their prison cell, frantic, despairing and inconsolable. Out of the darkness they heard the welcome sound of footsteps approach the door, relieved that at last they would attain respite and sustenance, for their bodies were weakening and their hearts fading. Alas, their joy turned to despair when, instead of the food they desperately hoped to receive, realised instead they were condemned to certain death when the door was violently nailed shut. Witnessing their beloved father's utter woe as he bit his own hand and mistaking this as a sign of severe hunger, his sons offered up their own flesh to him. He refused, naturally, but they died regardless in a pitiful display of starvation and deprivation. He turned blind with grief and, having resisted the temptation to feed upon their flesh, through desperation and in the darkness, finally succumbed.

Having recounted the tale, and wild with grief once more, baying and weeping copious tears for his lost boys, Ugolino bites down on the Archbishop's skull again, this time harder, forcing a howl of pain. I am utterly distraught to hear this pitiful tale for, even if the Count was guilty of treason, his sons were most certainly not. There is an injustice that I do not understand but as we continue along the frozen lake of despair to the third ring, I am moved again to tears as I recall the love the young children demonstrated to their father, such that they gave themselves unto him in his hour of need. Also, for the suffering he has had to endure, for the memory of that tragedy will remain with him for eternity and it affects him greatly.

In this moment and as I wipe the freezing tears from my cheeks, I question what I am prepared to sacrifice. Would I, as mortal man, tear off my flesh, eat and devour it if He so commanded that I would be spared an afterlife in this dark hole? It is unlikely I confess. And that of my child, my son? That I should be required to eat the flesh of my own kin, nay my children, of my blood, of my heart? I simply cannot contemplate such a wicked thing. Who is God that He asks such a grotesqueness of anyone? If I concede, am I to gain salvation? For this is a trickery surely? A game one cannot win. For in committing the sin of violence against kin, one would be cast into the bubbling river of blood, submerged in the scorching liquid of the Phlegethon wherein burn the murderers and plunderers, the lowest of the miscreants in this cesspit of doom. It is a conundrum, I will not lie.

We continue onwards, mindful not to slip on the frozen river of pain and find thousands more souls, this time lying prone in the thick ice with just their faces positioned upwards to the skies, protruding out. We are in Ptolomea, the third ring reserved for traitors to their guests, so named after Ptolemy who generously hosted a magnificent banquet only to murder those he invited. Always I am reminded that violent death has affected so many. Always I am shocked at humankind's capacity to sin. These reprobates concentrate hard, for they know to cry is to condemn themselves to eternal pain for the tears will become ice, hardening over their eyes, a frozen canopy of crystal thus rendering them blind. On my neck I feel a blast of chill wind stirring from the front. I ask Virgil if he feels it too and what it is. He tells me to be patient for we are about to enter the final ring of the ninth circle, the intense climax of my journey and when we do, I shall discover the root of this icy blast for myself.

Just then, a soul cries out from the surface of the ice. He pleads with us to remove the shroud of frost from his eyes for he seeks a moment's respite as he wishes to cry more tears, which frozen eyes deny him. I say I am not a sinner, for he has mistaken me to be one, but that I will gladly do as he bids if he furnishes me with his name and tale of woe. He announces himself as Alberigo and begins thus; that he was a grower of fruit and a poisonous crop caused the death of his beloved family. He was punished as an assassin and now resides in Ptolomea, a penalty he deems excessively harsh for this unintended transgression. I am confused at the dates he has cited and ask him if he is of the dead or, as I, of the living. At this moment, another shade voices his tale and I believe him, Branco, to be the same. And it transpires that what I suspect is true for, Virgil tells me, the ring at Ptolomea can remove a soul to Hell without the sinner first dying. For if a sin is considered so grave and a soul is obliged to enter Hell, a demon possesses the shade's body on Earth and hurls his spirit to the depths of the inferno.

Having relayed his name and story, Alberigo asks me to honour my promise to remove the frosty veil from his eyes such that he may release more tears. I confess I am compelled to refuse, for I did not know then what I know now; that he is a traitor of the worst kind, an assassin who committed treachery against his own family, for he is considered wicked beyond evil such that his soul already resides in Hell while he still lives on Earth. Indeed, upon reflection I am disgusted with this pair, so without offering assistance, Virgil and I make our way out towards the fourth and final ring, heading for a great figure hiding within a misty fog.

Yet before we reach it, for it is far into the distance, I am startled to see bodies lying underfoot, beneath the ice, completely submerged. They are contorted, twisted, as a foetus yet they do not move for they are totally immersed, frozen into the icy river of despair, entombed in this glacier of the Underworld for eternity. For these are the most evil sinners of all - those who committed treason against their benefactors. I cannot assist nor converse, for although not yet eternally dead, they are unmoving, silent, mute, deaf. They were traitors, so I am not stirred to help them although I confess the sight of them is haunting, quite pitiful even, and I am strangely moved.

HELL'S CORE

Virgil nudges me forward and we advance into the misty, freezing fog for we are now at Judecca, the last ring of the ninth circle; the final, the absolute. I know this to be the utter nadir of Hell's pit but, inevitably, we cannot complete our journey without passing through it. I know not what or whom dwells here. I believe I have now witnessed the punishment of sin in all its evil and inhumane guises yet there remains one final act, one more horrific unavoidable scene and, in truth, I am not sure I will endure this apocalyptic climax. For Virgil tells me I am to meet the Black King of Hell, the worst traitor of them all; a supreme evil. The banners of Hell's monarch draw closer. For he is Lucifer. And he is come.

Words fail me. Strength fails me. Hope fails me but I pray God is resolute for what stands before me is an abomination indeed and in this moment I cannot tell if I am of the living or the dead, for I have lost life's breath such is my confusion at what I witness. He is Satan, Dis, Emperor of the Universe of Pain and he is the origin of all that is evil. He stands taller and wider than Nimrod and Ephialtes combined, nay than the scores of giant custodians conjoined. He emerges from the icy lake, furious, ferocious, rising up entrapped in the frozen pit, sharing fetid air with his crew, his vile acolytes, the most ignoble of the Damned. Torso, arms and head appear proud of the icy surface; genitals, legs and feet immersed below. He is seething, rabid, consumed with bitterness, hatred and rage. And, in my terror, I am utterly mesmerised.

I retch, for the stench is foul. A grim, decomposing, fetid mixture of rotting flesh, burning skin, excrement, brimstone and sulphur. All that is rancid decay. All that is disease. It sticks in my craw such that this squalid air is a musty solid yet I hold my vomit, for I shall do nothing to attract the attention of this nefarious being, he who is Satan. He has ice in his heart for he is devoid of love, of compassion, of feeling. And my body feels this ice as violent shivering overtakes, for my muscles contract but they do not generate the heat my body requires to survive. Is this how I am to die? Is he the last my eyes shall see before death takes me?

I fall to my knees, cowering behind Virgil, weeping tears of despair. My brain cannot endure Diablo's screaming for it pierces this putrid miasma and enters my ears as shards of glass, as frozen debris impaling my fragile eardrums. Do they bleed? I fear so. I gasp. My heart cannot embrace such ugliness, for it is repulsed by this foul, repellent and vicious being, he who is defiled by violence, obscenity and wickedness. He who is defiled by sin. In this moment I know I look upon evil in its most vile, disgusting and immoral guises and I am aghast.

Appalled but transfixed by the grotesque that stands before me, I know not where to look first for this creature that is Dis has three heads, yet it is clear I do not witness the Divine Trinity. He has three faces; of red, yellow and black (for the Devil), each with eyes weeping profusely, wings flapping furiously behind, in perpetual motion. But these are not of gentle white feathers, soft velvety plumes as the beautiful angel he once was, the most magnificent in

Heaven; God's favourite. They are black, hairy and veiny as a bat and the cause of the unforgiving frosty blasts and icy winds that froze the Cocytus.

Of his faces, one looks forward and the two that flank, backwards. All are contorted into hideous snarls, bawling perpetual tears, howling eternal screams and all are eating at flesh, three mouths gushing blood. The central, chewing at Judas Iscariot, he who betrayed Christ, disappearing head first into the abyss that is Satan's mouth, back skinless, enduring a punishment of endless torture but never death, for the Devil is ceaselessly tearing, biting, maiming. The others, Brutas and Cassius, those who murdered Caesar, suffer the same fate but their legs are being chewed and torn, chomped and mutilated as their faces, locked in terror, display the agony and eternal suffering they endure.

Enraged, engorged by anger, Diablo's fists smash at the shackles that is the frozen river of torture, yet he shall never be free. I pray he does not see me in these shadows, for should he do so and pluck me from the darkness, flesh and soul of this mortal man would certainly be separated if forced into the raging mouth of Hell. For this beast is The Black Emperor and he would surely crush my bones as a petal under a rabbit's foot.

The cacophony of sound is breath-taking. For the voices of the Damned rise in a furious crescendo as Satan's rabid crew endlessly howl their dissent, wail in anger, shriek in rage and screech in triumphant exultation at their sovereign. For this is the bosom of the Underworld whereto the faithless demons and Supreme Devil feed at the teat of denial. For they have denied God. They have disobeyed God and His Divine Law and they face eternal punishment in this cankerous, leprous land because of it. My heart thumps yet it is quite shattered such that it cries out in sorrow for the suffering my eyes witness, for this is torture unequalled.

Is that a whimper I hear amongst the baying and howling? I believe it to be so, for Satan is indeed a tormented animal, burdened with the weight of the entire universe that bears down upon him. Yet who may provide that final denouement and release this suffering beast from his eternal pain? None. For he has forsaken God, so absolution has vanished upon these icy winds. My heart weeps, for it aches; it is broken. Mankind is broken and so, too, is my spirit. For I have seen millions of souls in this desolate place that is the funnel of Hell. Inferno. This is the sewer of the universe, a realm of agony, suffering and despair. For here there is no joy. No love. No light. No mercy. No salvation. For here there is no God.

Virgil motions to me. For now I have witnessed the damage that sin can do, seen the cesspit that is Hell in all its gore, violence and evil, we need to make a hasty retreat. Satan was a sight to behold but I wonder that Virgil does not leave me linger a while longer for, God willing, I shall never see this again in my lifetime. There was not sufficient time to examine what I was witness to and should I aim to deter, to prevent and avert the living on Earth from meeting this beast, I must describe him with an intricacy Virgil's haste does not allow. For this is Lucifer, God's preferred. The most beautiful of angels reduced to a grotesque; a shrieking, bestial and reptilian distortion. For he screams in anger for eternity and, albeit the size of ten thousand temples, he is shrunken to proportions of a tragic parody of the trinity, of the lack of Godliness he represents, a mockery of everything that is pure in sound and vision. He is pitiful. Yet undeserving of pity.

Cast from Heaven for the ultimate betrayal; for disobeying the Lord, for denying the Divine. For is this not the greatest sin of all? Indeed, his exalted ego served only to heighten his desire for glory and honour, that possessed by God alone, such that to overthrow the blessed Father and secure the golden throne for himself triggered the War in Heaven. The might of God triumphed. Lucifer and his demonic crew were defeated and violently hurled, banished to the icy sewer for eternity. Yes; his pride cometh before his fall.

Yet are we to perceive him as fearsome and dangerous, for indeed he is a writhing, thrashing, growling deformation and he is terrifying to behold. Or is his bestiality, for he has no human traits that I may see, evidence that he is no more than a beast, a creature, a fiendish swine? For one such as this is not bestowed with intelligence, nor mind, nor acumen, nor aptitude. He cannot educate, nor connect, nor evangelise or convert. He cannot communicate, not even his rage other than with perpetual agonised and tormented screaming and, therefore, he may not repent, so will never attain salvation. He is, simply, unable to save himself.

Is it to me therefore, to save others? To save mankind? To bear witness to this grotesque travesty of love and warn the living of the dangers they face should they deny God, should He cast them here to this place that is rank and fetid, bleak and unforgiving? For God has scorned him, forsaken his beloved Lucifer, now Satan, and we are all to view him with contempt. Yet, we must look to him as an example of the might of God, for He can forsake us as easily as He did his favourite angel and banish us to this place, the base of Hell, the circle of Judecca.

I wish to discuss man's spiritual fragility with Virgil, for a moment's weakness will have him exiled to this sewer of terror for eternity, but he reaches out for my hand, impatience etched upon his face. I know not how he manages it but from nowhere and with much force he pulls me onto his back and then, to my horror, leaps upon Satan's scabrous body! The stench is intense for my face touches his flesh, his dishevelled hair, inhaling foul odours of sweat and filth and all that is rank and decaying. I retch, yet somehow, I do not vomit. Using tufts of his frozen devil pelt to grip as we traverse across his matted and leprous torso - as wide as the Nile it seems - we reach his navel whereupon Virgil changes course and heads down to the midpoint. When we reach the surface of the icy lake, Virgil takes us beneath the Cocytus to Lucifer's hips. I fear I am to drown for we are about to submerge in the river Cocytus proper, yet we do not. I cannot comprehend what he does next for he reverses taking us back up the hole we have just clambered through and begins to ascend back up Satan's torso, from whence we came. Is he taking me back into Hell? Do we return to the core of the ninth circle? I cannot bear it! Only it is not his torso that appears above. It is his waist then his genitals then his legs. His head is now below the surface line of the frozen river, for it seems that Satan has completely inverted!

I am at an utter loss to explain what has just occurred and look at Virgil, puzzled and bewildered, as we hang on to Satan's hairy thigh waiting for the right moment to swing off back onto the icy tundra, which is ice no more, for even though we have reversed and retraced our steps, this place is different to where we met Diablo. It seems that we hang for an eternity, violently swaying as he kicks and flails. Virgil ignores me for he concentrates to calculate the precise moment we may dismount without harming ourselves. I am mystified and as I cling to Virgil while we swing in the air, gather my thoughts enough to observe the terrain. We are in darkness, yet I can see at least we are upon dry ground, a vast landscape with a flat topography which pans out for miles. In the distance is a passageway, a cave perhaps. Virgil releases his grip, we drop and, praise be, land safely, ready to begin our long trek in the direction of that opening.

I am not compelled to speak to Virgil of Satan, the Black Emperor of the Underworld, the monarch of misery and pain, for I believe I understand the complexities and tragedy of what I have witnessed. It is transparent, for it is merely a message, a representation of what man risks if he strays from the earthly path of truth and righteousness. For if he seeks the light and bliss of God he shall not find it here. Thus, to bask in the radiant warmth and glow of salvation, to spend eternal life in the glory and majesty that is the celestial heavens, man must use the greatest gift God bestowed upon him, that of free will, to remain steadfast in his faith, to not succumb to distraction or temptation; to remain firmly on the path of light. To remain free of sin.

As we begin our hike away from what was the frozen Cocytus, I turn to Virgil, for my mind is bamboozled at what has just occurred. For, one moment we clambered about the wiry pelt surrounding the Devil's navel, diving below the surface of the frozen lake towards his legs and, the next, we retraced our steps through the void whereupon we came not back to his torso and the icy tundra but to a new terrain, a new landscape, a new but familiar territory. For it was Earth. Virgil smiles and explains thus: that in the moment we descended through the opening, we passed through the centre of the earth. For, when Lucifer dishonoured himself and was cast from Heaven as an exiled rebel, plunging headfirst into our planet during his fall from grace, his body became trapped at this central point. Much like the earthquake that occurred when the enraged giant Ephialtes tried to escape his chains, the impact of Lucifer becoming wedged at the earth's core was to cause the moon and sun to spin in different directions and all the lands of the southern hemisphere to migrate north, leaving only sea and one mountain in the south.

It is in this southern hemisphere we now find ourselves as we make our exit from this grim place, Virgil upright and calm, me stumbling and flagging. Yet I have triumphed. For I have met the Devil and I have survived thus I know I have faith in my heart. I am glad and relieved to leave this place behind us, yet until I see light or the sun or the stars I shall not know I am rid of it. After many footsteps covering many miles we reach the entrance to the cave where there is nothing but darkness, though I care not, for with every stride we take forward, we are one further from the pain and suffering of the inferno, that vile, miserable cankerous place, the pit of eternal woe and suffering. We walk silently within the narrow passageway and, eventually, come upon a bubbling stream. This is the beginning of the Lethe, Virgil tells me. The fifth river of Hell, leading to and running through Purgatory; the river of forgetfulness. We follow the water, for what is a babbling brook if not life, and we emerge, hours later, to find ourselves at the surface of the earth upon a vast open plain.

Here, I look up to the dawn sky, for there are stars within and if these are not shining examples of God's hope and virtue, I know not what is. Two worlds collide in this moment; those of destruction and genesis and I have experienced both. For I am reborn unto Earth. Unto life. Unto God. No longer am I left in the realms of the abandoned, the forsaken, the Damned. For I have met the Devil, the fallen angel Lucifer. I have looked into Satan's eyes and felt the putrid heat of his breath on my face and I have survived. I may now safely meet God, look into His eyes and know I am loved. I am absolved. Salvation is mine. I am the resurrection. For God did not abandon me such was my fear, rather He has saved me. He did not desert or forsake me and for this I declare my loyalty unto Him and proclaim that He alone is my master, my saviour.

I shall pray that my faith remains steadfast, that my trust in and love for Him is unerring, for in this place I have been driven to the very depths of despair, witnessed the punishment of sin in its nefarious forms and I do not wish to be cast away from God again, to suffer infinite separation from Him in such a vile, iniquitous and torturous wilderness. I seek eternal life, not eternal death, for this is a retribution I cannot endure. Thus, resolved to pursue an earthly life of virtue and serene faith, in His name, I renounce temptation and sin.

The light of a new day is upon us and it is glorious. For what is light if not God? I bask in this heavenly glow, heart bursting with gratitude and relief, enveloped in Divine love, confident and reassured that, beneath a celestial umbrella which holds the sun and the moon, the planets and the stars, I may savour the warm embrace of our most gracious benefactor for eternity. We pause to breathe in the air; fresh, dewy and crisp. I inhale slowly and allow it to replenish my lungs, for I need to remove all that is cankerous from within my own flesh such that the dark place of despair we have left behind was steeped in depravity and stripped of all humanity. I fear it taints me. We are at a new dawn and my fervent desire is that it instigates rejuvenation, renaissance; a life transformed, invigorated by faith, joy and light, for we have stepped off the perpetually rolling wheels that are the wicked and vicious circles of Hell, and the eternal suffering is no more. Please God, this new dawn brings new beginnings for me.

PURGATORY

As we climb we cleanse the moral grime that is sin.
For only through purification of the soul may a spirit
ascend to the celestial Paradise.

THE SHORE

Under a sky of sapphire blue, we make our way in silent contemplation across the vast plain, upon sands untouched by the feet of mortal man. Virgil speaks, but only to tell me we are of Easter Sunday, three mornings since we began our harrowing quest through the eternal prison of the inferno. In my heart I know I could not have completed the gruesome mission without him; endured such torture and depravity, and prevailed, despite the insufferable inhumanity I bore witness to, so thank him in all sincerity for his advocacy, for he is nothing if not wisdom and fortitude. I know that in him I have had a champion most dependable so we embrace as brothers, for I entrusted my life unto his hands, he has delivered me safely out of the darkness into the light of salvation and we are now kin. But he is a shade, so embrace is not possible.

For many miles we venture on, reflecting quietly thus, pausing momentarily, for being deep in thought and not noticing the changing landscape, we see ahead an enormous elevation. This mountain rises calm, proud, erect, out of a windswept sea, bathed in a pure and beautiful sunlight, for a new dawn begins and now we are out of the dungeons of Hell the radiance of God shines upon it. This is a day of resurrection indeed. We pause to search for the invisible peak, mouths agape, for we are quite in awe of this magnificent mount such that as surely as Hell descends ten thousand leagues, this rock must rise the same. Virgil informs me this is the Mountain of Purgatory, the only piece of land in the southern hemisphere, thus left when the seas displaced, as Lucifer plunged into the frozen Cocytus during The Fall, that same island to which Ulysses attempted to sail seeking triumph and glory. And, indeed, it is an extraordinary sight. One I suspect no mortal eyes but mine shall witness.

We stand at the shoreline surveying the breath-taking scene when I am distracted by a robed ancient hobbling across the sandbank, furiously waving his staff. The bearded elder draws near and breathlessly introduces himself as Cato. He is not known to me or Virgil but announces his role is to secure the approach to the mount, for he is the guardian of the rock. He is curious, sceptical even and begins an interrogation, for he is distrustful of our presence here suspecting one, if not both, to be lacking in faith. Have the rules of the inferno been broken, plunging it into chaos, he demands to know. Has the vile will of Satan shattered the gates of the eternal prison? Is he to expect an avalanche of corrupt sinners in this place where all strive to repent? Shall the quiet sands herein be deluged with errant souls, those tarnished with immorality, blemished with vice and failure? For the nature of our arrival suggests we are direct from Hell and Cato is unnerved. But, by my breathing, he knows me to be of the living and, after explanation, Virgil persuades he is but a virtuous pagan of Limbo. Still, he retains a wariness.

Virgil informs him I have been sent by God, for I am to purge my sins. I am intrigued. Is it thus, that my mission is not yet over and there is one final task to complete before I may meet my heart's desire in the flesh? I know that to purge is to cleanse, to purify, to exonerate. But am I to ascend the Mountain of Purgatory? I cannot believe so, for it is huge; a colossus, as tall as all the giants guarding the ninth circle placed head to toe, for its summit disappears sky bound, unseen into the clouds. I am earthly man, of the living and, as such, have no chance of successfully navigating this beast. Indeed, it cannot be possible for mortal man to scale this dazzling height such that it peaks in the mists of Heaven itself, where the air is pure and the light is as a stunning effulgence, up yonder in a celestial place that earthly eyes cannot see.

Do I find myself at the start of another unavoidable journey? And if it is thus, as I rise skyward, reaching closer to Heaven and God's embrace, shall my soul be purged, purified of sin? As I emerge at the summit will I be rid of all imperfection; cleansed, sanitized and sanctified? If I struggle and exert, will I become worthy of attaining salvation that I shall find God, celestial joy and eternal life? I pray this is true, for I seek Him and the Kingdom of Heaven that is the golden light upon the hilltop and, if reconciliation is assured, I will continue on this journey most gladly. But, Virgil says nothing.

Cato capitulates and we fall into a comfortable, more genial conversation. Virgil relays the story of our difficult and perilous journey through the wickedly torturous underworld and our brief but terrifying encounter with the Devil. Cato listens attentively and, after our discourse, instructs Virgil to wash my face in the grassy dew and gird my body with reeds. It sounds as if I am to be baptised. Is this a ritual purification that Virgil is to perform upon me? For what is water if not cleansing? Has Hell tainted me that I need to be washed of its infernal filth before I am purged? It appears so. The reed, Virgil tells me (to my astonishment it regrows immediately he breaks it from its root) is to remind me that humility should direct my mindset here and that I must be prepared to bend and flow, as indeed the reed does in God's breeze. As he ties them to my waist, I notice inexplicably that, as Cato, we wear the long, hooded robes of a monk.

Just as Virgil secures the last stem, we hear the sound of water lapping and turn to the sea, whereupon a boat approaches steered by a magnificent angel bathed in a red glow. This, Cato informs us, is the Ship of Souls carrying within one hundred spirits of the Redeemed, penitent shades seeking ascension of the mountain. In truth, my eyes are blind to any passengers, for my gaze is locked upon the heavenly messenger, a feathered titan basking in scarlet (the sacrificial blood of Jesus) and he is glorious, for his enormous wings act as sails as he guides the boat to shore.

Cato explains that to cross the seas is the only way to reach the rock for, upon Judgement Day, souls are delivered here by the Divine to spiritually prepare for eternal life in the celestial heavens. He sends His winged messengers to transport them from Tiber's mouth, for it is His will they ascend the mountain to glory. For as they climb the rock and cleanse the moral grime that is sin, so shall they undergo a transformation, for their souls, full of the misery and woe of turpitude, shall regenerate to a state of grace and blessedness. Indeed, only by honestly searching the nadirs and complexities of our personal humanity through reflection and contemplation, he says, may man truly reach the pinnacle of human spirit. For to know oneself is to know God. Thus, through purification upon the mountain, souls may present themselves spiritually cleansed ready to meet their Creator in the perfection and splendour that is Paradise.

It is clear then, that no residents of the inferno will travel here as we. Those nefariously corrupt and poisonous souls deemed too wicked to embrace the light of the celestial spheres, who remain eternally separated from God in the darkness, shall never know the dawn sun nor these sparkling waters of lapis, nor shall they rejoice in the radiance of truth nor achieve a state of grace through redemption. For He has judged they shall never attain salvation and, as such, will never enjoy the bliss of eternal life in the golden heavens.

It is true they endure inordinate violence and torture, suffering and torment, but they are not to be released to offer repentance and atonement. For without these, a soul may not redeem himself and, without redemption, salvation is not possible. In His wisdom God has deemed such sinners unworthy and, through His providence, has willed those wretched spirits carried across the River Acheron no prospect of redressing their sins, denying them passage upon the Ship of Souls. Thus, they shall only know eternal pain and eternal death.

I revert my eyes back to the vessel which is nearly upon the shore as another approaches in the distance. The souls aboard, clothed in hooded robes as we, are heartily singing the psalm *In exitu Isräel de Aegypto: When Israel went out of Egypt,* an apt tale of exodus, and I confess I am glad, for this angelic scene is far removed from the rivers of Hell, those fetid cesspits of anguish and woe where the brutal sadists Charon and Phlegyas ferried the desolate miscreants to the Underworld. Virgil bids me to kneel, for the angel alights and I am to show reverence to this impressive celestial messenger whom I can barely see, such is the glare of light that engulfs him, now a dazzling white effulgence. I willingly lower myself to the sand and watch in awe as this enormous seraph signs a cross with his open wing upon each head that leaves the boat.

As they disembark, it is clear these unfamiliars know not where they are, for confusion reigns and they look to us, bewildered, as they search this alien terrain. Virgil explains we are just as much strangers as they, also here for the first time, albeit our journey was significantly more treacherous than theirs. He gestures to Cato who gathers a group about him such that he may offer instruction. A soul makes towards me and it is with great joy I see he is my friend Casella, a musician! I attempt an impossible embrace, for he is a shade where I am not and thus we hug air. Despite this he is in high spirits and we sing and chatter, enjoying a reunion most hearty, joined by other penitent souls who notice my breathing and find themselves quite distracted.

Cato decides we have lingered too long and haughtily sends us on our way, rebuking me for making light of this solemn occasion, for souls are here on a ritual journey of transition, he says, seeking spiritual change and are not to be diverted. But he is mistaken. For Casella was fascinated that he finds me here in this place of the dead when my breathing tells him I am very much alive. I was merely explaining that God had set me an onerous mission, a harrowing quest through the circles of Hell that I may better understand the punishment of sin, a task which I had only completed this very morning. And now, as he, I am here to purge my own.

THE MOUNTAIN

Virgil and I break from the group and move towards the enormous volcanic elevation, the splendorous mount. It is as the conical sewer of the inferno but inverted, a towering mirror image standing proud, strong, rigid. In truth it is a magnificent structure, a triumph of His creation. It is of rock and clay, as the Old Man of Crete, yet without the gold and silver threads. Without the tears. There is a series of ledges, terraces, openings and stairwells which coil upwards around the outer perimeter. Indeed, all a soul requires to ascend and all of which I have navigated before, albeit descending.

I am concerned, for the mountain is vast yet the passageways are narrow and steep, crumbling and collapsing. There is no protection from a drop most sheer and if a pilgrim was to slip and tumble, he would plummet to a violent, bone-shattering death. Indeed, to the flank, waves crash forcefully against the lower cliff face such that any soul would certainly, should he not snap his neck on a protruding ledge first, be destined for a meeting with Poseidon in his underwater palace. I confess I am unnerved, for I am mortal man, of the living, and am anxious that death awaits me here. Yet, Virgil still does not tell me we are to climb.

But were we to navigate the rock I would be certain to meet God for, unlike the descent into the toxic funnel of Hell, we would rise upward, ascending, where there are hues and colour and scent and life. We would climb to where He is in Heaven to a summit so high it is not within my earthly vision so my spirit would be challenged to rocket, to soar like an eagle, rise as pure as a dove, as an angel with wings of glory to reach the crest, the zenith; to greet Him who is the Almighty.

I am inspired! I feel great joy, a bliss in my heart and am overcome with emotion, again close to tears, but Virgil cautions me, for this is not quite Heaven or Paradise, nor Bliss or His kingdom, he says. It is Purgatory; a place where souls are cleansed of misdemeanours, for ascension of the mountain frees man of the filth and wounds of sin. For to sin is to stain, to err is to tarnish and a soul needs to cleanse before it may be forgiven. For whilst it remains imperfect, blighted by the blemish of sin, it may not ascend to the heavenly realms. Thus, to purify is to exonerate. To sanctify is to unshackle. To cleanse is to liberate. For once a soul has decontaminated through penance and purgation, it may achieve redemption and thereby attain salvation. For one may not repent without purifying the memory, leaving the past behind in a place one may never access again.

Virgil tells me an ascent on this scale will be an ordeal most gruelling, for the mountain is steep and dangerous. It will require significant endeavour and endurance, for the rock is titanic. Yet, he says, what is penance if not struggle? What is repentance if not to demonstrate contrition through diligent exertion? And what is atonement if not to evidence sorrow through dedication, commitment and effort? His words are wise, for he wishes me to understand that purification of sin will not be attained easily. For where earthly man strayed from the path of Truth, he shall purge that sin in death upon the mountain through suffering, whereupon his soul shall undergo purification that he may attain salvation in the heavens above.

And now I understand the reason for God's displeasure with the giant, Nimrod. For in constructing his soaring tower at Babel, that which rose to celestial heights, he removed the need for man to journey to Heaven through spiritual endeavour and suffering. For indeed, should he choose the rebellious giant's route, man would forego the need to cleanse himself of sin, to purge himself of vice, to purify his soul. Yet in his heart, man knew he would not be invited to Heaven without first demonstrating his faith and was therefore not surprised when God's thunderbolt struck and the tower was razed; crumbling, tumbling to the ground.

As we stand near the base and study this vast elevation, Virgil informs me that unlike the inferno which was focused on punishment, Purgatory is concerned only with purification of the soul for, here, suffering is endured merely to attain spiritual growth. For upon the mount sins are absolved through penance, and penance brings only peace and serenity, not pain. As such, I shall be witness to the capital vices through examples first of the opposing virtue, thereafter of the punished sin for, here, sins are deemed conceptual; more of the mind. It may thus be deduced, he says, their roots were in motive rather than action and, as such, I shall not be witness to cruelty and brutality. He assures me that upon the rock souls are already saved, for this process of purification is intended to restore innocence to enable mankind to return to a state of existential origins. I confess I am relieved to hear this for, truly, I do not believe I am capable of re-living the terrifying punishments and woeful misery of the Devil's bowl ever again. Yet, more importantly, he confirms at last that we are to climb.

As I crane my neck to search for the hidden summit, Virgil tells me of the topography and what I may expect to find here such that the rock of nine terraces is divided into three components; the lower slopes of Ante-Purgatory, the main cliff itself and, at the summit, the gardens of Paradise. It is upon these terraces, he advises, we will witness the saved souls enduring their penance in order that they may attain purification, for God's will is that they achieve spiritual growth through suffering. Finally, he teases, we shall meet a glorious angel standing guard at each Pass of Pardon, for God bids him to direct us to a secret crack in the rockface wherein spirals a sacred stairwell from which we shall emerge to locate the next terrace as we rise in ascension.

We look to the mountain once more and, indeed, I see again the terraces coiling the perimeter, taking the form of a colourful maze of paths and passageways, though they rise to unfathomable heights. I am shocked to hear I am expected to scale this rock, for I have not the earthly words even to adequately describe its size. It is immense, vast, enormous but this does not accurately record its stature, its girth, its sheer volume. I am unnerved, I confess. But, it is thus. I am to climb, to ascend to the summit where lie the terrestrial gardens of Paradise and, on my journey, as I renounce my sins, I shall meet our Father's heavenly creatures, His messengers; the angels. I know these shall not be as the Damned, the ignoble crew of demons, terrifying and gruesome, vicious and tormenting for, here, angels shall be kind, virtuous and benevolent. For God exists on this mountain. I am certain of it.

Virgil talks more of the terrain and stresses this ascent shall be gruelling for the ledges and passageways are narrow and steep. There will be danger and turmoil, for I am mortal man and just as the terrifying depths of the cavernous abyss that was the inferno would take my life should I have stumbled and fallen into the cankerous pit, here I shall scale heights that, too, should I slip, will have me plummeting, dramatically cascading to a painful death. Yet, he promises most enticingly, should I succeed and reach the summit, I am to find something and someone quite beautiful. He knows then, that I am likely to triumph, for already he tells me that I am to experience beauty in all its forms. My emotions soar at the thought of a meeting with my beloved muse Beatrice, for she alone is beauty and owns my heart. Or, does he refer to the guiding force of the Virgin Mary, the blessed Mother herself, who I know watches over me? The reeds of humility remind me this honour is unlikely.

We stand at the base of the mountain but there is no way up, for this section of the rock face is sheer and flat. It stands at a height of two score men or more and I have no idea how we may navigate it, for we have no ropes or ladders so must rely on cunning and brute strength. Virgil concedes the lower cusp will be troublesome and arduous, for the straightforward path is blocked by crashing waves, but effort and endurance will ensure success and that, as we rise, ascension will become less demanding for the gravitational pull from the satanic core of the inferno shall weaken considerably.

The Maestro remains steadfast and constant by my side, yet I am aware that although he is a supreme teacher and I could have none wiser to lead me towards the light of salvation, he is not of this place and is therefore as unfamiliar with it as the Redeemed upon the Ship of Souls. Yet, he is masterful and quick-witted so I am satisfied he will direct me as God intended despite his lack of knowledge of this new terrain. We study the stone for nooks and crannies whereupon we may slot our toes and grab with our fingers, for our destination is a ledge, way up yonder. We begin our ascent and, after many hours of significant toil and struggle, we approach the ridge.

It has been gruelling, for I have been encumbered by my robes and the reeds and have no expertise in climbing, but I understand that struggle is needed to cleanse the soul, to sanctify the spirit in order to attain the purity required to enter the kingdom of Heaven and already I feel closer to God. I have been appraised and I gladly accept His judgement if it will gain me salvation. We pause for breath whereupon I spy an armada, for the Ship of Souls, guided by the magnificent wings of the glorious angels, is as a fleet approaching the shoreline. This itself forms as a vast expanse of desert plain, untouched by any mortal man but me, that which we traversed as we left that black and dismal hole, where all is darkness, misery and woe, when we walked out towards the light.

ANTE-PURGATORY
THE EXCOMMUNICATES

I look back to Virgil who tells me we are about to
encounter the Excommunicates, a collective of indolent,
unshriven and preoccupied souls banished to Ante-
Purgatory, for it was only death's door that prompted an
utterance of repentance and for this delay they pay a heavy
penalty. Indeed, immediately we spot a bunch of
Purgatorios reclining in the shade of some large boulders.
They have made themselves as comfortable as they can,
given the limits of the stony cornice, and lounging against
the rocks, they somehow manage to sleep. Virgil scoffs, for
he says these souls embody all that is typical of a late
repentant; sloth. Yet, he confirms, all shall be permitted
entry to the mountain proper for, indeed, all have genuinely
repented. Until that moment, each will languish; delayed
here for a length of time commensurate with the moment
of atonement. For, just as these souls delayed their
repentance in life, so shall the opportunity to purge their
sins be delayed in death. It is clear then, these penitents bide

their time, for exertion is pointless if ascension is not due for years to come.

Just beyond is the primary ledge which reveals itself as a crumbling shelf wrapped around the impossibly wide rockface. A huge tribe of robed souls appears from behind the curve and Virgil explains these are the Indolent; deathbed penitents who waited until their dying breath to repent. Thus, for being contumacious and stubbornly refusing to obey God's law until their last moments, each soul serves an additional sentence, wandering aimlessly herein for a period of time that is thirty times longer than that they exhibited such wilful spiritual disobedience in their earthly lives.

Upon spotting us, the horde casually approaches. I look to their faces for I fear they must be impatient to ascend, frustrated that their opportunity to atone is impeded so, yet all I see is incredulity. I follow their confused gazes, which one minute are at my face then the ground, for they see my shadow and nervously realise I am of the living. Virgil gently tells them not to be afraid, that although I am indeed mortal man amongst the dead, I am sent here by God and all we seek is a way up the mountain that I may purge my sins for, as they, I find myself on a journey of purification such that I may ascend to the glory that is Heaven.

They are astonished and suddenly burst into life, for excitement fills them to giddiness such that with much noise and jostling they clamber to make my acquaintance. Virgil tries to calm the swarm but is interrupted by a soul who introduces himself as King Manfred. History teaches us that Manfred sustained two fatal wounds during the battle of Benevento whereupon he pleaded for Divine mercy, beseeching the Lord God upon his deathbed, repenting for his sins with his last breath. He apologises for their zealous enthusiasm and states the commotion is solely because a prayer from a living Christian in good grace with God may lessen sentences upon the rock. Thus, any opportunity to expedite their entry to the mountain proper that they may begin their journey of redemption is greeted with great joy and howls of anticipation as we now witness.

Yet how does he expect me to respond to this entreaty? By praying for their souls? This inordinate number who I do not know, whose specific sins I may not recount? And with their clambering and jostling do they not see they may send me plummeting over the edge, for already I have gazed down and see we are at a perilous height! Virgil senses my distress and reminds Manfred we need to make haste. He begs directions that we may continue our ascent but is interrupted by an excited cry coming from a group of Indolents yonder, for they have espied a crack in the rockface and discovered a path inside the mountain.

We make to approach when a shade introducing himself as Buonconte accosts us! For he is eager to relay that despite his own violent death, having suffered a fatal laceration to the throat, he managed to offer a late repentance as he lay dying upon the banks of the River Archiano. A man of violence himself, a demon raced to snatch him up and deposit him in Hell, condemned to suffer eternal damnation in the boiling river of blood. Instead, thwarted by an angel from Heaven who, having heard his dying words of atonement, plucked him from the demon and delivered him unto the banks of the Tiber whereupon he took passage aboard the Ship of Souls. I am much fascinated by his tale of victims and perpetrators, of angels and demons, but Virgil has already moved on, for he wishes to inspect the slither in the rockface.

Surrounded by the Indolents, he does so and declares that despite the restrictions and danger therein, for the opening is miniscule and the stairwell is uncomfortably narrow and dangerously steep, it will suffice, for it will be safer than navigating the open cliff where the waves crash violently upon the mountainside. I confess I was not expecting beauty within. For although it is cramped there is light enough that I may see the mountain interior is of rhyolite, the pink volcanic rock. An amber hue sparkles, for between the cavities of this igneous stone, fire opals glisten, so too red beryl, topaz, jasper and agate as jewels in a trinket box. Indeed, it is a cave of treasures and I am much distracted. Yet as we ascend my mind turns to the onerous trek.

Oh! That we had wings, an eagle to pluck us from the depths of the mountain, for the struggle is too much for a mortal man as I, such that I am expected to climb these perilous steps to infinity or so it seems, when my shoulders brush both walls and I cannot even see where this rocky staircase ends. Yet, I am on a quest, thus I diligently follow Virgil despite the ascent is gruelling. My muscles ache, for there are many thousands of steps and I am hindered by the long robes and ridiculous reeds that he girded tightly around my waist. It is already late morning yet I fear that despite traversing two hours, we have not made good progress, for the Indolents clamber about me blocking my view, stumbling across my path, crying out for my prayers, jostling and pushing in their bid to reach closer to Purgatory proper, although I know not why for their ascension will not occur for many years to come and they put my mortal soul in danger with their recklessness.

I beg Virgil to pause, for breath no longer comes easily and I fear that in my weakened state I shall stumble and plunge to a brutal death within this rocky interior. I am much heartened that he takes pity upon me and gestures to a ledge where we can attain much needed respite. I ask how much longer I am expected to climb but he does not respond other than to reassure me that as we ascend my journey will become easier. We continue upwards without the Indolents for, thankfully, Virgil has dismissed them. The hike remains gruelling, for some steps are perilously tall, others miniscule in depth such that my heels overhang, the cliff walls touch me on both sides in a manner most claustrophobic and I need all my focus to stay upright to meet the inexorable demands of this physical challenge. But, eventually, and after another hour, maybe more, I have cause to be uplifted, for we approach the second spur of Ante-Purgatory. Despite the inordinate danger, for we have already scaled unfathomable heights, I have prevailed, thanks be.

As we emerge from the stairwell the sun tells us it is nearly noon and, in the welcome fresh air, we make our way along the shelf, that which coils steeply around the mountain as a maiden's golden ringlet. With relief, I note we have outclimbed the dangerous waves that crash the flank wall yet the wind blows as a tempest and, naturally, I am unnerved, for we have scaled a great distance such that I feel as a bird in flight. Virgil distracts me and gestures to the Unshriven, those spiritually idle souls who failed to gain absolution, for in meeting violent deaths they died without their sins being forgiven. As such, they must delay their ascent of the mount for the same period of time they lived upon Earth.

Noticing the shadow cast by my body, they too see I am of the living and greet me with much excitement, for they wish me to convey entreaties to their loved ones, should I return to Earth, in the avid hope family prayers assist in speeding their ascension. Amongst them, an intriguing beauty named Pia de Tolomei catches my eye. This unfortunate married was murdered that her husband could elope with his mistress and, unprepared for her sudden execution, in the absence of repentance and absolution, thus finds herself delayed upon this spur for a period of twenty-two years, the entirety of her short lifetime. It is a sad tale but I cannot help, despite her fervent plea.

Virgil encourages me to listen to the petitions of the Unshriven but reminds me not to delay my own rise to grace. He gently pulls me away and draws me into conversation about the power of prayer, for he says that pagan prayers will never reach God, only those of the faithful. Indeed, until the sacrifice of Christ upon the cross, all prayers were ineffective and therefore wasted. I wish to discuss this concept further but he remarks that my cherished Beatrice will explain it soon enough and, indeed, far better than he. So, I am certain to be reunited with my love, my heart, for this is not the first time he has mentioned that such a union will occur.

THE VALLEY

Leaving the Unshriven behind, we climb the shelf, pushing forwards unsuccessfully, for everywhere we look is a labyrinth of twists and turns and we are tricked into paths that lead nowhere, for the light is fading and Virgil cannot look to the sun to guide us. We have again traversed the sea wall without drama for, praise be, the waves lack force as we ascend the winding path. Eventually, we stumble upon a lone soul who sits upon a ledge and beg him for directions. He introduces himself as the poet Sordello and demands to know where we are from, for he suspects it is Hell.

Virgil states that he is originally of Mantua but concedes his afterlife is of Hell where he resides in Limbo, a painless border reserved for contemplation and reflection, for he is keen to assert he is a virtuous pagan and not a conscious sinner. He confirms I am of Earth, a living man, here on a pilgrimage of purification such that my cleansed soul may be free to ascend to the celestial heavens. Sordello is not much interested in me but upon hearing Virgil is of his own homeland, leaps up and embraces him most heartily. It will be his pleasure and privilege, he says, to personally guide us up the rockface, but explains the rules of the mount strictly forbid any ascent without sunlight thus, we shall need to camp out as night already approaches.

It does not surprise me that we have been scaling the mount for one whole day and still have not reached the first terrace, for this rock is a colossus, taller than five thousand temples and the climb has been gruelling. Despite Virgil's frustration, for he is keen to continue with haste, we are compelled to heed Sordello's words. He indicates a group of souls in whose company he feels we would be comfortable and we make our way over, for we are to spend the night in the Valley of Negligent Rulers. Herein reside the Preoccupied; those too busy taking care of earthly business to focus on heavenly matters. Thus, as they neglected to take care of their spiritual souls leaving them unprepared for the gates of Heaven, so God neglects to aid their ascension, for they must linger in the anteroom of Purgatory a while longer.

Just as we are unable to climb until sunrise (does God wish us to ascend bathed in His Divine light?) so are we unable to clamber down into the valley until after sunset. But Sordello tells us that from the ledge, even in the dimming light, we can see into the valley and study the souls therein and we thus move across while he points out some of the residents. There is Emperor Rudolph who failed to restore glory to Italy, along with Ottokar II. Hereto Philip the Bold who lost a major battle thereby disgracing France, along with Peter III. Also, Charles II of Anjou together with Pedro of Aragon, all three pairings bitter enemies of the throne such that discord and disharmony overtook their earthly lives, leaving insufficient time to devote to spiritual endeavours. Thus, for their earthly life of dissonance and unrest, they are joined in accord and harmony in death until they begin their spiritual purification.

Once night has fallen, Sordello leads us along the spur, which disappears inside a hollow of the mountain itself, into the Valley of Negligent Rulers, a place, as we have seen, brimming with the souls of distinguished nobles, resplendent in their robes and finery. They begin an evening hymn *Te lucis ante terminum, rerum Creator, poscimus: To thee before the close of day, Creator of the world, we pray* and their voices rise in chorus as two enormous angels descend from above to join us. Sordello explains the angels are of Mary's bosom in Heaven and are here to guard the valley against a vicious serpent. They are clothed in green, their faces illuminated white from the heavenly glow in which they bask and their swords are aflame, burning red. All know these colours represent the theological virtues of faith, hope and love but I confess I am panicked at the thought of the serpent, for I witnessed these in Hell in all their nefarious forms and they were most savage.

I am approached by a noble shade who beckons me so I walk towards him. In the dim light I see it is Judge Nino, a man known unto me, for indeed he is a friend I hold most dear! He concedes his earthly preoccupation with his public duties precluded him from considering the spiritual welfare of his soul such that God has denied him ascension and, albeit disappointed, accepts it is His will, for he knows he shall meet the holy angels soon enough. He is intrigued that I am alive upon the mountain where all are dead, more so when I explain that having witnessed the punishment of sin in the inferno, I now climb the mountain on a second quest, such that I may purify my spirit, reach the celestial heavens and, as he, meet the blessed souls of the holy angels.

Suddenly, Sordello grabs the Judge and clutches him close. He points at the ground for the slick streak of evil, the hissing serpent is arrived and slides between the grass and flowers, licking his own back in a manner most narcissistic. One can imagine it did thus as it tempted Eve with the succulent, ripe fruit for it is a vainglorious creature indeed. Out of nowhere, the green-winged angels swoop down and there is a furious stand-off before the serpent slopes off into the grass from whence it came. I am shocked at what I witness yet all around me seem unphased at this incident. Sordello explains it is an event occurring each evening, with the angels always victorious. Is it that they are watched by the celestial stars that have appeared in the night's sky, shielding and guiding them with heavenly light? Maybe. For there was no light in the inferno, in the realms of the phantasmagorical whence the pit of serpents triumphed so mercilessly over the souls of the thieves.

Our small group converses a little longer but I confess the gruelling climb of the lower mountain has depleted me. I cannot endure without rest so, utterly exhausted such that sleep was denied us in the inferno where the wicked shall never know peace, I curl under a blanket of cobalt sky. Although the hour is not late I fall asleep immediately, for today we have traversed Ante-Purgatory in its entirety and I am weary beyond words. Yet slumber is not relaxed or replenishing, for my dreams are tumultuous. In one, a huge eagle snatches me up and takes me hostage, carrying me away from Virgil, from my darling Beatrice and from the heavenly light towards the silvery planet of Jupiter, whereupon we burst into flame, setting the night sky ablaze.

When I awake I am shocked to find myself laying upon a rocky ledge before a large gate, yet I know not how I arrived here. It is as when I was cast to the heights of the precipice at Limbo from Charon's boat during the tempest. Virgil informs me it was St Lucia who plucked me from my torrid dreams and brought me here, to the Gates of Purgatory, leaving Sordello with the noblemen in the valley. This great lady was honoured by Rome for her courage in defending the faith, he reminds me, having lost her life during the persecution of the Christians in the fourth century. Such that I could gain her strength, bravery and constancy in this moment, for now a new day has dawned, it appears we are to enter Purgatory proper.

THE GATES

An angel, enormous and regal, sits upon an alabaster throne at the Purgatory Gates, but before we can reach him, we must first navigate three steps; one of white marble, one of black rock and the final, of the red stone porphyry. Virgil tells me these colours have significant relevance, for they represent, specifically, the purity of a penitent's soul, mourning (the black step is cracked as a crucifix) and, finally, the blood of Christ, for this reminds us of the sacrifice man must make to achieve ascension to the heavens. Each of these demonstrate one of the three steps of repentance; recognition of sin, contrition and atonement. He says the entrance is named Peter's Gate and the angel standing guard is the custodian of it, having been handed the gold and silver keys by St Peter himself.

We move to approach God's glorious messenger but he holds out his hand, within which is a sword, for he refuses us entry! It is as if I am cast back to the raging demons guarding the gates to the flaming citadel of Dis, to the black crumbling tower whereupon hung the Furies where I was denied the right to pass. Virgil steps forward and informs him that I am delivered by St Lucia for I am instructed by the Divine to ascend the mount in order to purge my sins that I may enter the celestial Paradise. The magnificent herald of the heavens beckons for us to climb the stairs and, again, I am grateful that the wisdom and rectitude of Virgil's intercedence has protected and guided me. As we reach the angel, he raises his sword, glistening in the reflection of the dawn sun and, before I can protest or stop him, uses the tip to carve the letter P seven times into my forehead!

He has drawn blood which drips upon my face. I am appalled, astonished, for this is an act most heinous but Virgil is unconcerned. He looks into my eyes and calmly explains the letter P represents the Roman word *peccatum*, meaning sin, and the angel has carved seven into my brow, for they represent the documented number of cardinal sins that I will witness here upon the mount. He continues that as I ascend and move through the terraces of Purgatory, so shall my soul be cleansed and purged of sin. He further assures me that an angelic porter will stand guard at each terrace and remove a letter as I progress up the mountain. With the deletion of each letter so shall I notice my passage upwards becoming easier, for each has the weight of vice and shall initially drag me down. Finally, he warns me to journey looking only forward and upward, for should I glimpse behind as Orpheus, I will be returned to the place whereupon I now stand, with not a second chance to ascend. Indeed, he cautions, a backward glance may be deemed evidence of my reluctance to expunge the urge to sin or demonstrate an averseness to repent.

I suddenly feel an inordinate heaviness about me as the encumbering invisible burden of sin takes hold. Satisfied I am prepared for my ascension this Easter Monday morning, the angel produces Peter's keys, one silver and one gold, for spiritual and temporal authority, and unlocks the gate. As he does this, Virgil whispers that the keys represent atonement and redemption for, armed with these, a soul may achieve reconciliation with God and attain salvation. Thus, with salvation, he may enjoy eternal life with Him in the kingdom of Heaven. As we ascend the three steps and pass through the gate, a rousing angelic chorus of *Te Deum laudamus: Thee, O God, we praise,* greets us. The gate clangs shut, although I am mindful I have no cause to turn and view it. Immediately, we are in Purgatory Proper.

I eye my surroundings. There is a little vegetation, some plants and bushes, a tree here and there but, naturally, mainly rock. Rocks and boulders, stones and pebbles of irregular shapes and sizes; some protruding, some smooth, others rough, some coloured, some dull. Virgil tells me there are seven terraces and we shall visit them all, for each pertains to a cardinal sin. For clarity he reminds me the root of these sins are gluttony, sloth, greed, lust, wrath, envy and pride. He begins to talk of love, which confuses me, so I interrupt and ask him why, for surely love does not correspond to sin other than the overbearing lust experienced by the eternal lovers Paolo and Francesca and their ilk. But Virgil says that the link between love and sin is undeniable, for just as love flows through God in its purest form, in humanity love flows too, albeit contaminated. I must look perplexed for he expands thus: that too little love can be evidenced by sloth; too much by gluttony, greed and lust and improper love by wrath, envy and pride. I am intrigued, for truthfully, I had never considered any correlation between the two but can see now that, indeed, there is a connection.

Paths and passageways twist and weave in a chaotic maze, taking every direction of the compass and confusion abounds, for I know not which route we are to take. Virgil says we are not immediately at the terrace, for we need to climb another rockface to reach it. Having made innumerable wrong turns previously, I am relieved to see ahead a set of large stones, vaguely resembling a stairway, to aid our ascent. I feel the heaviness of the carved letters upon my brow weighing me down and already I am fatigued despite having climbed but a few stairs this side of the main gate. With significant struggle we clamber up the crude but effective stairwell and stagger to a ledge which Virgil says should direct us to the next terrace.

The cliff face is tall, having a height of five men or more. He warns me I shall need to take heed and hug the wall, for the corridor twists and turns most dramatically, and one slip could send me plummeting to my death. I wish for more comforting words from my companion but he has none to offer, for I remain a mortal man and thus caution is to inform my every movement, for this quest is to be perilous indeed. Already my thighs ache such that the muscles within are aflame, for I carry seven invisible weights and they impede all progress.

My breath is laboured and sweat drips from my brow across my open wounds and into my eyes. The reeds girding my robes flick back into my face in a manner I find most annoying but I have little option than to leave them in place, for Cato instructed Virgil to perform this ritual in order that I may ascend. This climb is an ordeal and I am permanently reminded of the extensive efforts of the Avaricious and the Prodigals as they relentlessly pushed their heavy stones but I reassure myself that my endeavours have a purpose, whereas theirs did not. For, as I purge my sins upon the mountain through penance and suffering, my spirit undergoes purification that I may be rewarded with eternal bliss in the celestial Paradise.

I fear we are lost, for after many hours gruelling ascent we have not found the terrace and are weary. From the corner of my eye I spot a shelf opposite, less steep than the one we stand upon and it invites us, for it is constructed of polished white marble and there is greenery so it has a prettiness which, other than the Valley of the Negligent Rulers, is mysteriously lacking in this place. Upon the resplendent cliff face appear to be a number of intricate carvings so, carefully, we make our way from the ledge upon which we stand, to the shelf opposite. It encircles the great mount and Virgil announces we have, at last, found the first terrace of Purgatory. He reminds me that I am to observe capital vices, first through examples of the opposing virtue and then of the punished sin itself. It is surprising to find no souls here but it gives us an opportunity to draw breath and examine the friezes and sculptures which adorn the pure white marble walls herein the corridor. Virgil explains that the first three terraces relate to sins caused by perverted love; those that caused harm upon others.

TERRACE 1
THE PENITENT PROUD

Upon this first terrace we shall meet the Proud penitents and thus, he says, the friezes on the wall ornately illustrate the redeeming virtue of Humility, some with tales of the Bible and others, the Classics. Indeed, I gaze upon a carving beautifully depicting the Annunciation, the conversation between the Angel Gabriel and the Virgin Mary, for it is here he announces she shall birth the baby Jesus, son of God; that she shall be his mother. In all humility, she replies unto him *Ecce ancilla Dei: Behold, the servant of the Lord.* Another shows a poor widow begging Emperor Trajan to avenge the murder of her beloved son. He cautions delay, for he is due to leave for battle (indeed, he is already mounted upon his favourite steed) but she beseeches him, for if he does not return she is unconvinced another will help. She declares he neglects his duty thus he acquiesces, for he humbly understands that obligation and mercy dictate it shall be so.

I become aware of sounds as a crowd of one thousand or

more approaches slowly along the shelf, yet if they are man or beast I cannot quite determine until they are upon us, for they are squat, crouched down, chest almost upon the marble floor as giant turtles, such that they have no pace and all movement is an effort. Their moans and groans are quite audible, for indeed, they are souls of human form and now I can see that each carries an enormous boulder upon his bare back rendering him almost immobile, for he is bent double beneath its weight, almost prone to the floor.

Virgil explains these souls are the Arrogant Proud whose penance is to lug crushing weights along the terrace, the intention of which is to flatten their pride. Indeed, as they failed to bend upon Earth as the reed of humility, they do so now to cleanse themselves of the blemish of sin. As they stagger up the terrace shouldering the burdens they did not in their earthly lives, struggling under the hampering weight of the stone, so they endeavour to look upon the artistic examples of the virtue Humility on the cliff face and thus benefit from the wisdom within. It is an ordeal indeed for, ascending many miles with such a boulder upon their backs, it takes every effort to stand to view them and, in truth, not many manage it.

I am confused, for Virgil told me I was not to witness pain and torture upon the mount but to my mind what I see here is exactly that. For I am reminded of the gilded procession of the Hypocrites in the Inferno, those sinners clothed in capes lined with lead, such that their stance is the same for they are both encumbered; heads bowed, shoulders hunched, knees caving. Virgil explains that it is merely discomfort they endure, not pain or torture, and as these penitents understand it is necessary to suffer in order to undergo purification, they welcome the solace it brings. For, in being invited to repent upon the mount, they know they are destined for the heavens above and this brings them much comfort.

As they advance closer, I realise they recite the Lord's Prayer albeit it is punctuated with the sighs and moans of exertion and struggle, for they cover an inordinate distance. They pray not only for themselves but also man on Earth, that he is delivered from temptation and vice. Virgil asks for directions, for the quickest route to the second terrace, for he tells them that I, too, suffer under the weight of Adam's sin and we have already taken significant time to reach this place. A soul breaks from the procession and introduces himself as Omberto Aldobrandesco, a Grand Tuscan. He endeavours to straighten up such that he wishes to witness the sight of a living soul amongst his fellow penitents, but his face remains bent to the track since the burden is too heavy to stand erect. I crouch down that he may see me better and he asks for my earthly prayers such that they may expedite his progress unto Paradise.

We enter into discourse such that I am curious for news of his downfall and, sighing, he reports it was conceit and self-importance that brought him to this place. His family were so wealthy, with land and property holdings so vast, they could reside in a different castle at each sunrise and this they did in a display of wanton superiority and haughtiness. Thus, with years to reflect upon his wilful pride and, embarrassed into contrition, he laments the shameful arrogance of his kin. He welcomes that God has shown mercy in his invitation to atone upon the rock and he vows not to be discouraged by the pains of penance, for he seeks eternal life that redemption brings, thus endures his suffering, without which he will be denied absolution and the salvation he seeks.

From the back my name is called, so I move towards the shade, for he must know me having recognised my voice. He remains squat and uncomfortable and I sense his distress so again I crouch and, with much pleasure, see from his face he is my old friend Oderisi, a most talented artist and illuminator! I wish he was not suffering thus but he is happy to see me and we enter into a hearty discourse. We converse in earnest and he tells me of his art and successful career, for he was engaged by Pope Boniface to decorate manuscripts in the papal library. Indeed, he confesses, it was his vanity and arrogance at being thus commissioned that secured his place on this terrace of the Arrogant Proud. But, he feels blessed that God has judged him worthy of salvation and considers his penance a gift from the Divine, for he knows he is destined for Heaven.

There is a pause in our conversation at which moment Virgil takes my elbow. We move forward and he gestures to the ground for upon the shelf beneath our feet are more illustrations and ecclesiastical sculptures albeit, from the violent and ugly depictions, I know these not to be of the virtue Humility, rather punished Pride. They include Lucifer himself, falling from Heaven, Nimrod and the tower at Babel and, finally, Niobe, gloating at her pro-genitive prowess given her fourteen children, all of whom were later murdered by Apollo and Artemis. Thus, Virgil explains, as the penitent souls herein endlessly scale the terrace of the Proud, they reject the sin of pride underfoot and embrace the virtue of humility above.

As we continue along the shelf of white marble, upon which exquisite sculptures illustrating humility and punished pride stand proud, Virgil checks the sun and tells me it is already noon, that we have been ascending for three hours. I follow his gaze upwards and my eyes meet those of a majestic angel, a resplendent celestial being who smiles and bids me approach for he stands guardian at the sacred Pass of Pardon. This is God's messenger, the Angel of Humility who, in raising his wings and gently brushing my forehead, erases the first P, for he confirms I have purged the sin of Pride.

He whispers the words *Beati pauperes spiritu, quoniam ipsorum est regnum caelorum* to mine ear: *Blessed are the poor in spirit, for theirs is the kingdom of Heaven*. I am much reassured by this benediction and confess I am overcome and again brought close to tears, for now I know the mountain to be a place of purification not punishment, where penitent souls may release the burdens of sin, despite the ascent is gruelling, for the terraces are steep and eternally winding. Indeed, I know, too, that God wills them to succeed in their penance such that He wishes them to triumph and rejoice in the glory of Heaven. Momentarily, the lion of The Dark Wood appears in my mind, for he represented the sin of Pride, that vice I have now purged. So, he is gone and I may release my fear, for I am certain there are no beasts or behemoths in this realm of purification.

TERRACE 2
THE PENITENT ENVIOUS

The angel points to a secret opening in the rock wall and guides us up this Pass of Pardon. It is here we must begin the next phase of our ascent, but I believe this will be slightly easier, for a glimpse in reveals it is not as confined, nor steep as at the base. However, we are already at a significant height and I cannot throw caution to the wind just yet, for the sacred stairwell is long and spirals upwards to infinity, thus a stumble would send me plummeting to my death. Again, the amber beauty of the fire opal glistens through the pink volcanic rock within, so too red beryl, topaz and jasper. It is as a cave of jewels and I am much heartened. The shade of the inner mountain is a welcome relief, for we have been climbing in the midday sun and although we are of Easter and therefore April, it is warm and I remain clothed in cumbersome robes and girded in restrictive reeds. Yet, as the angel at the Gate of Purgatory promised, it is less arduous than the previous climb, for a significant weight is lifted with the removal of the letter from my brow and thus our pace quickens slightly.

Finally, and after a lengthy climb with Virgil taking the lead, we emerge from the stairwell into a maze of passages and corridors, paths and gates and we know not which to take. There is no one to ask for directions and Sordello remains in the Valley of Negligent Rulers so Virgil looks to the sun for guidance and states confidently that we shall follow its beams, for sunlight is sent by God and we are directed by Him. He moves forward, clockwise and we ascend. The path is steep and it takes effort to climb, for it is long, wrapping around the mountain circumference twice, maybe three times. Frustrated and hot, after two hours, possibly more, we finally reach the second terrace, that place where the sin of Envy is purged, which, as the first, is empty of souls.

I suggest to Virgil we rest and wait for signs of life but he wishes to push ahead, for once the sun sets, ascent is forbidden and we are already of mid-afternoon. We continue on for a mile or so and I am disappointed to see there is no vegetation: no flowering bushes, no spring crocus nor a violet; not a blossoming tree, even. The rock has a blue-black hue, for it is of slate, metamorphosed from shale and is stratified thus the cliff face is empty of friezes and sculptures. Indeed, this is a barren and unappealing landscape with no beauty for eyes to rest upon. In the distance we hear disembodied voices crying in the air, although we do not yet encounter any souls. The sounds are as an ethereal murmur until we reach closer, whereupon I realise they relay tales of love and kindness such that Mercy is the correlating virtue to Envy. Indeed, I can hear *Love those who have shown you hatred* then, *Mary, pray for us!* How different this is to the screams, groans and cries of misery that greeted me in Hell.

Presently, we arrive where the penitent Envious hoard, those souls from whom the voices emanate, a long row of repentant shades sitting as blind beggars upon the inside ledge, leaning one against the other or reclining upon the rockface, all touching his neighbour. A hand rests upon a shoulder, a robe is clutched, an arm is linked. I say they are as blind beggars for they are dressed in old cloths, woven from dark hair which mimics the hue of the cliff face yet, most disturbingly, their eyes are sewn closed with iron stitches! Virgil tells me these penitents derived earthly pleasure from witnessing the downfall and misfortune of others, blind as they were to the moral merits of their neighbours. Thus, upon the mount, as penance, they shall be deprived of sight, denied even a glimpse of the light of Heaven. Such suffering is macabre indeed and I am distressed for their torment, although they do not appear as in pain.

They are many in number; three thousand, maybe four and, as a giant python, they follow the cornice all the way round until they coil out of sight, beyond the bend. I confess I am nervous, for the terrace is narrow with no barrier to stop me from tumbling off so I must hope they do not make a sudden move and send me hurtling over the ledge, plummeting downwards. Upon realising visitors are amongst them, for they have heard us talk, they begin to weep, rust coloured tears emanating from between the iron threads dropping upon their cheeks. Indeed, I cry as they, for in this instant I am filled with much compassion for their suffering. I wish to comfort and encourage these wretched souls so assure them that the heavenly light of God will shine upon them one day as surely as it does today and that once purged of their sins, they will witness such glory with their own eyes.

In the background I can hear murmured and melodious tales of love and generosity, such as the story of a mother and son at a wedding celebration, much lacking in wine. The mother, she is Mary, says unto Jesus: *Vinum non habent; there is no wine* and he performs his first miracle thus. Another voice calls out: *Love those who have done harm to you* and in the distance: *Pray for them that persecute and calumniate you!* I realise sadly that, without sight, examples of the punished vice of

Envy and corresponding virtue of Mercy are announced orally, for those without eyes may not see the messages conveyed within the illustrations and sculptures that adorn the rock face as at the previous terrace.

I wish to discourse with a shade here to better understand their journey so ask if there is one from my land who will converse with me. From the distance I hear the voice of a young woman who introduces herself as Sapia of Siena. She explains her earthly downfall was an overwhelming jealousy for those enjoying good fortune or blessing, such that it quite outshone any personal prosperity. Indeed, whilst witnessing a savage battle whereupon were killed her countrymen including her own nephew, a great rejoicing arose in her heart purely for she so envied the power held by the military leader, her uncle. On the brink of death, she spoke unto God to make her peace and, but for the intercession of the scrupulously honest hermit, Pietro Pettignagno, she would be found enduring a life-long sentence with the other Late Repentants upon the spurs of Ante-Purgatory. After much deliberation and reflection upon the mount, she still cannot account for it. Sapia bows her head and praises her merciful God, for in allowing her to atone upon the mount He has ensured she will achieve spiritual purification and, through His forgiveness, the glory of salvation.

We meet with more souls of the penitent Envious, among them two noblemen who understand I am of the living yet, as themselves, journeying to Heaven. They are most anxious to talk, for they seek comfort from an earthly soul graced by God and recognise from my accent that I am from near the River Arno. One, Guido del Dua, tells me so forceful was the envy he felt for those happy with a good life, his spite was as a furnace burning in his heart. Yet, it was God's will that he should purge that sin and he was thus awarded the privilege of a voyage upon the Ship of Souls such that, through penance, he may purify his spirit to secure eternal bliss in the kingdom of Heaven.

As we continue along, stories continue to be shouted in the air, one signalling Mercy, another punished Envy and these play on a continuous loop of echoes as we pace upwards along the terrace. An unexpected thunderous boom of *I am Aglauros!* which has me clasping at Virgil's arm, is countered with a gentle and melodious *Love your enemies.* I recall that Aglauros was Cecrops' daughter, jealous of Mercury's love for her older, more beautiful sibling, and she was turned to a mute statue as a result of her envious actions.

I am transported back to the ninth circle when I hear the tale of Cain through the prophetic cry of the penitents: *Whoever captures me will kill me*, he guilty of the sin of jealousy of his younger brother, for Caina is that icy prison wherein lie traitors to their kin. I confess I find this terrace plays havoc with my mind for there is an element of chaos here. Blind beggars, screams of envy, tales of woe and death, the Gospels and the Greeks and confession, yet no real sense of remorse, thus many years of repentance will delay these souls their ascension. I am not an overly jealous man, thanks be, so to know when my time is come I shall unlikely spend time here comforts me somewhat.

We finally reach the end of the second terrace and I am glad to see the back of it. A glare of bright light blinds me such that I am as the beggars we have just left behind, and I wonder if this is lightening to accompany the thunderclap of words roared by Aglauros. But it is not, for a magnificent angel bathed in white appears before me, he who is the Angel of Mercy. He gently wields his wing across my face and the second P is erased from my brow. So, the ritual cleansing of the terrace is performed by the shining celestial body and I am now purged of the sin of Envy, but not before Virgil mysteriously tells me I shall have need to become accustomed to this shining light.

The angel gently whispers a benediction unto my ears *Beati misericordes quia, ipsi misericordiam consequentur: Blessed are the merciful, for they shall obtain mercy* and, again, I understand that purification of the soul is occurring in this place and I am emotionally moved because of it. But what is this shining light to which Virgil refers? Am I to reason it is the light of God, the glow of the Divine and that I shall bask within it and achieve salvation, that I shall meet Him in the glory that is Paradise? I turn to ask him but the angel has spread his wings and gestures to the sacred Pass of Pardon uttering the words *Lift yourselves here to travel to Paradise* whereupon I see that Virgil already moves towards the secret crack in the cliff, for he wishes to make haste to the third terrace.

TERRACE 3
THE PENITENT WRATHFUL

We leave the shining angel behind and as we venture onwards through the narrow crack in the rockface can hear him singing *Tu es praevalusiti, iam laetus eris: Thou that hast prevailed, be jubilant!* Virgil and I ease into a slow but rhythmic pace up the winding, but wider, stairwell and he reflects upon our time on the second terrace, for he wishes to discuss, specifically, the poverty of mankind and the infinite benevolence of God. He tells me that human envy is born of a misconception that if one man has more, another has less. In the celestial heavens however, one soul's happiness is a cause for all therein to rejoice and God looks to invite as many as possible to share in the joy.

He wishes to prepare me for the third terrace by explaining the differences between earthly and heavenly possessions, which he does thus: earthly possessions are physical, temporary, unreliable and, ultimately, worthless, for they may be stolen, lost or broken, they may choke the desire for God and cannot be exchanged for redemption of the soul. In contrast, heavenly treasures remain in the heart as a mark of one's moral character and spiritual servitude, for these are invaluable and, pertinently, attainable. As such, they are everlasting, eternal. It is not lost on me that during this discourse we gaze upon the twinkling gemstones of jasper and fire opals which sit invitingly as gilded treasure amongst the pink volcanic rock of the mountain stairwell.

As we climb, he discusses the virtue of Meekness and its partner vice of Wrath, for next is the terrace where that sin is cleansed. He tells me in order that I may examine this set of pairings more fully I am to be shown visions in my mind, a notion I find peculiar, for meditation does not come easily to me. But, until we arrive there and as we continue our ascent up the unending sacred stairwell, Virgil delivers another discourse on Love. He wishes me to understand, particularly in relation to earthly and heavenly possessions, that upon Earth man may inspire envy if he possesses a thing which may be divided and shared but keeps it whole. So too, once a thing is split into pieces, man is dissatisfied with small portions. However, if his desires are for heavenly treasures, there is no envy, rather love and happiness, for as more people seek, cherish and share celestial riches, the more love and joy radiates in that place.

We emerge from the stairwell and begin our search for the terrace. We continue along a maze of paths and passageways, climbing and scaling boulders and ramps with surprising abandon given the dizzying heights we have reached. After two hours, maybe three, we arrive at a shelf of scoria, the burgundy rock that solidifies airborne as it is majestically ejected from an erupting volcano. Already it is mid-afternoon so the sun glares brightly and I have cause to close my eyes to shield them from its brilliance. Immediately I am sent three visions to my mind, such that they are hallucinations, each of which exemplify the virtue of Meekness for, Virgil tells me, I am to understand how it triumphs over Wrath.

In the first, the Virgin Mary gently questions her child,

Jesus, who stayed three days at Temple without informing her but she does not scold him, for she knows his intention was pure. In the second, Pisistratus forgives the man who embraced his young daughter despite his wife seeking a punishment of execution and, in the third, I am shown Stephen with the stones, the young man killed by an angry mob who, with his dying breath, prays to God in Heaven to forgive his tormenters.

We walk on in silence along the upwardly spiralling terrace for an hour, possibly two, and the afternoon's light begins to fade, for it is nearly evening. We watch as the sun begins its slow descent on my second day upon the mount and I am minded it is about time for Vespers. Suddenly, a fog of thick shadowy smoke approaches, rolling across the terrace and we are shrouded, enveloped by a blanket of black. To my mind I am plunged into The Dark Wood where everything was darkness and hung heavy in my lungs. Virgil tells me this thick smog represents the blinding effects of anger, for we approach the souls of the Wrathful.

I confess I am fearful, for in the bowels of Hell they fought and bit and tore and punched such that their punishment was to suffer eternal violence. Yet here it is different and gentler, he reassures, as they stumble around hooded and blinkered by the black cloud, for their punishment is to be denied sight such that they were blinded by rage upon Earth. I, too, am quite unable to see in the thick mist so cling to Virgil for I am worried that a misstep could send me hurtling off the rockface. My fingers pass through him so he grabs at me, and orders me to be vigilant and hold on, for he is determined we shall not be parted in this fog. He has no need to tell me twice. We hear voices in the distance and it is there we direct ourselves, for these emanate from the shades who seek penance upon this terrace.

As we approach I realise they recite Agnus Dei, the prayer of the penitent wrathful and the words *Lamb of God, who takes away the sins of the world, have mercy upon us* echo around the shelf. Despite the black fog, there is a harmony here for the wrathful work together to find their way around the terrace, in contrast to their earthly lives where they fought directly against each other. Bathed in the dense acrid cloud and unable to see clearly, they too experience hallucinatory visions. Within these they witness the same scenes as I, exemplifying the virtue of Meekness that they may better purge their sin and, indeed, curb their desire of succumbing to it.

A man addresses us, for although he is blinded by the mist he believes me to be of the living and is fascinated to meet a mortal man who, having successfully navigated the sewer of inhumanity that is Hell, now rises in ascension of the mount to triumph in Heaven. He introduces himself as Marco Lombardo, a Venetian nobleman, an interlocutor renowned for his wit and conversational skills albeit, too, he was choleric and famed for his violent temper. Today he feels a righteous anger and sadness that the world is full of sin and corruption, that morals have strayed and I wonder if he thinks man's depravity is Heaven sent or due to earthly influences? He states he believes that Heaven impacts mankind in every endeavour, for life is preordained from above.

I ask him for his thoughts on free will, for his ideas on Heaven suggests that it does not exist. Indeed, he agrees most heartily that it does for, without it, there would be no Hell. For, just as man may then not be commended for his virtues it follows that, too, he may then not be castigated for his sins. To his mind, Heaven merely whets the appetite and it is for man to choose how to respond to this hunger, which he may do by asserting free will. In conclusion, therefore, he believes that mankind, in all his corrupt and arrogant guises, is responsible for the demise of virtue, setting the world onto a path of depravity and immorality for he, ultimately, is responsible for exerting his own choices.

Lombardo is most learned and I believe Virgil feels so too, for he has not interrupted the discourse. I ask him to accompany us to the end of the terrace, for like the blind man upon Earth, he is aware of his environs and can guide us safely through the black fog to the angel guarding the Pass of Pardon. He graciously agrees, within the limits of the rules of the terrace and, while we walk, I ask him to disclose the events of his arrival at this cornice, which he relays thus: that being a benevolent character he was excessively generous with his riches. However, his temper, which he concedes was most vile, landed him in prison and, by then, penniless and impoverished through his charitable philanthropy, and with the means to gain his freedom only through financial contributions from his countrymen, resolved to die a jailed pauper rather than accept fiscal aid from his neighbours. As such, God granted him passage to the mountain on the Ship of Souls where he willingly serves his penance, for he eagerly awaits reunion of spirit and flesh that he may enjoy eternal life in the beauty of the celestial spheres.

As he finishes his tale he stops and gestures right, for we are to part here before the angel appears and espies him. He entreaties me to pray for him once I am arrived back on Earth such that I, a mortal man in good grace with God, may expedite his journey to Heaven. With this, he turns to venture back into the fog. Before us, the black cloud dissipates, for God's light shines upon the angel who draws near and the dark mist is no more. I see the sun begins to set in earnest and know that once I am deemed purged on this terrace, the final of perverted love, we shall bed for the night for the rule of the mount is that ascent is strictly forbidden without daylight.

Despite the dispersal of the black cloud and therefore the restoration of my sight, I am sent further visions. These relate to examples of wrath and the first tells of Procne who, upon learning her husband raped her sister, cut out her sibling's tongue to prevent her from revealing his terrible crime. Incredulously, she then killed her own son and fed his cooked flesh unto her despised spouse. She is thus punished for her cruel vengeance in murdering her innocent child in order to wreak revenge. The second vision tells of Amata who, in instigating a deathly battle between her daughter's two admirers, hangs herself in a rage when the wrong suitor triumphs, thus denying her daughter a mother and a husband. The third, of the biblical figure Haman of Persia, so enraged when a servant failed to bow down to him that he declared all servants be executed that very day. The intervention of Queen Esther ensured it was he who was sent to his death and Haman was promptly hung at the gallows. It is clear to me then, that the black clouds blinding the penitent wrathful also warn that anger clouds judgement and obscures the mind.

The visions over, my eyes open to behold the Angel of Meekness who stands before me waving his soft wings across my face. The third P is thus erased from my brow as into my ear he whispers the benediction *Beati pacifici, quoniam filii Dei vocabuntur: Blessed are the peacemakers for they will be called children of God*. As with each blessing I am moved to tears, quite overcome with emotion, for this time I know I am half way up the mountain thus already I am purged of the vices of pride, envy and wrath. In one more day I shall be so close to God I may feel the warmth of His embrace upon my flesh. We are directed by the angel guarding the sacred stairs at the Pass of Pardon yet fear we will not make it up before the sun has completely set. Virgil grabs my arm and drags me with much exertion, ascending through the funnel of pink rhyolite, sparkling and glistening with fire opals and agate towards the fourth terrace, that of the Slothful. The angel's voice carries in the air behind us up the endlessly winding stairwell with the words *Pacifici, who know not evil wrath*.

For the pace and steepness, we are suddenly overcome with exhaustion and weakness such that I cannot lift even a limb, and collapse on the top step where we lay half emerged from the stairwell, which is timely, for night has arrived. Virgil bids me to get comfortable for he wishes to discourse a while longer on the nature of love. He reminds me we have already discussed that the sins purged upon the mountain relate to love in its varying degrees. But he now wishes to expand on this and examine love in the context of natural and rational thought, for he is of the firm belief that deeds are influenced by one or the other. For he reasons, is not love the root, the seed of all action, both virtuous and corrupt, such that love flows through God in its purest form and through man in its weakest?

But if, as Virgil says, love is thus and that nothing but love drives a man to action, then how is free will applied? For, I say, if indeed it *is* God who controls and directs all actions through love, how is man responsible for those actions? And why does He not direct all action to be virtuous and pure, thus removing the need for punishment and suffering in the inferno? For surely, by directing all actions to be honourable, He could ensure all of mankind triumphs to bask in the eternal bliss of the glorious celestial heavens?

Virgil ponders, for he gives my question much consideration. He talks of the differences between natural thought; a preordained love that flows from God influencing or motivating man on a subconscious level. This he juxtaposes with rational thought; that which influences or motivates man to reason and thus distinguish between good and bad, right and wrong, virtue and sin. For it is *this* action which God may hold man accountable because he uses free will, His greatest gift to mankind, to make that decision in relation to his action.

I confess I am much impressed with Virgil's ability to use reasoning and language most suitable to enable discourse on any topic and, indeed, facilitate me with answers through compelling argument. In truth, I find these more persuasive than Marco Lombardo's. I have spoken of this man many times and at almost each have declared he has the wisdom of five thousand scholars for his sagacity, acumen and judgement is truly second to none. I am surprised then, to hear him tell me that Beatrice will explain it far better than he for, he says, it is her belief that free will is best demonstrated by the ability to control one's desires.

He continues his discourse on the theme of love and reminds me that the three vices we have witnessed to this point on the mount demonstrate love in its perverted form: Pride, for through the denigration of another, one hopes for glory; Envy, for when one is outshone he fears his own loss of power and, finally, Wrath, for through grievance one seeks vengeance. Next, he wishes to draw my attention to love in its deficient and misdirected forms and it is apt that the fourth terrace, whereupon we rest now until sunrise, will demonstrate flawed, inadequate love for, in the morning, we are set to meet the penitent Slothful.

TERRACE 4
THE PENITENT SLOTHFUL

The sun is almost, but not quite, set. My eyes are heavy
and, despite Virgil's voice in my ears, I begin to doze. I
awaken suddenly, startled by a throng of loud, semi-clothed
Purgatorios who dash past excitedly yelling examples of the
vice, Sloth and its corresponding virtue, Zeal. For these are
the penitent Slothful, those spiritually lazy and negligent
souls who, upon Earth, failed to act in pursuit of love and
all things good and virtuous. Thus, as penance here upon
the mountain, they are engaged in ceaseless activity. Some
yell out in condemnation of the uncommitted and
undetermined, others countering with cries of: *Mary ran to
the hills in haste!*

As they tirelessly speed around the ledge of chalk, I hear
an account of the Visitation: a newly pregnant Mary rushing
to the hills to visit her elderly cousin Elizabeth, who, upon
their greeting and embrace, finds herself newly pregnant as
her son, John the Baptist, dives into her womb. The story is
told of Aeneas the Greek, son of Aphrodite, hero of Troy,

zealously fulfilling his destiny to complete a quest to discover Italy, allowing his descendants Romulus and Remus to become founders of Rome. Finally, the impressive thunderbolt who is Julius Caesar, the great emperor and warrior who, with feverish ardour and courage, marched onwards from battle to battle in his eagerness to successfully complete his military campaign.

To correspond, some tales of indolence and apathy including the story of the Trojans who, for their lack of determination and courage, refusing to endure hardship and suffering, failed to commit to follow Aeneas further into Italy by remaining in Sicily. Another, the lamentable tale of Moses' followers who, despite Divine intervention upon the lands and seas of Egypt during the great exodus, transgressed and resisted, failing to commit to this enormous quest and thus God denied them entrance to the Promised Land.

Virgil tries to hamper the group for he wishes to ask directions now so that we may be prepared for our journey at first light, declaring that I will say an earthly prayer for whoever obliges, but no one does, for sloth is nothing if not the sin of distraction. A few moments pass and on noting us seated and resting on the stairwell, a spirit stops briefly to converse. He bids us not to take offence with the unobliging group for these penitents wish to make haste and use their time productively, for they declined to do thus upon Earth. As such, they exuberantly repent for their laziness upon the terrace such that, with God's mercy, they will triumph in the glorious heavens. He is eager to demonstrate vigour and fervour himself thus begs his leave that he may continue with his energetic penance and, in doing so, atone for his sins that he may find his way back to the path of light.

The penitent slothful continue to run around the shelf shouting their words exemplifying sloth and zeal so, regrettably, I am unable to quiz one to better understand what actions brought them here. Once they have disappeared into the distance and we can hear them no more, the moon rises and the stars disappear in the lunar glow. Much as they wish to continue their zealous activity, the rules of the mountain forbid it and thus they must cease with their endless exuberance which, in truth, I find exhausting. When my eyelids can take no more they close and I settle down to my second night of slumber on the mount, for tomorrow is Tuesday and already we have purged the three collective sins of perverted love and now, the fourth, of deficient love. We stand at the threshold of the final category, that of excessive love and it is these penitent souls we shall meet tomorrow when I wake from my slumber.

My sleeping eyes rest upon a woman, withered, squinting, sallow of complexion, with maimed hands and crippled feet. I gaze upon her for, in truth, she appears most ugly and yet, the more I search in her face, the more beautiful and desirous she becomes. She begins to sing and I confess I am spellbound such that her voice is pure of tone, dulcet and melodious. She looks upon me and announces she is a Siren, a temptress seducing the likes of Ulysses himself amongst many mariners of the sea. A holy woman approaches, Virgil too, and he commandeers my dream, seizing the Siren and thrusting her forward unto me for he wishes me to understand she represents the greed, gluttony and lust of disordered love, of allure and aversion. The stench from her stomach is fetid, polluting my nostrils with a smell most putrid that immediately I am awake!

Virgil admonishes me, for he has called me three times already, so keen is he to make haste with our ascent. The dawn sun has risen, although from its low setting I can tell it is only recent, so we have not delayed by many minutes such that we may only climb in the daylight. For an hour, perhaps more, we make our way upwards along the winding terrace whereupon, bizarrely, discarded robes carpet the floor but, if they have slipped from the ceaselessly writhing bodies of the penitent slothful herein or, in haste, been neglected in dressing, I cannot tell. We dodge the repentant shades who continue to charge and rush around crying out examples of zeal and punished sloth. I confess I find their persistent fervour draining and I am terrified that in the mêlée they shall crash into me, sending me hurtling off the ledge.

A most welcome diversion stills us, for a tender voice calls out thus: *Veni, huc iter est: Come, here's the path*. I turn to see who utters these words and before me stands God's messenger, the magnificent Angel of Zeal. He points to a secret crack in the wall whereupon I see steps leading up to the fifth terrace. On retracting his fluttering wing, for he too demonstrates the opposite of sloth, he gently wipes it across my brow and the fourth letter P is erased. I have thus purged the sin of Sloth and am free to enter the Pass of Pardon, which we do to the benediction spoken by the Angel: *Blessed are they that mourn, for they shall be comforted.*

TERRACE 5
THE PENITENT COVETOUS

The stairwell is wide, less steep yet still winding but more inviting, for my shoulders no longer brush against the walls, yet Virgil can tell I am distracted and it is not the gentle pink hue of the glistening mountain interior which diverts my attention. I relay the tale of the ancient witch in my dream and he tells me she merely symbolises the ugliness of vice, transforming to beauty once the soul has undergone purification upon the mount. I am to have faith, he reminds me, to keep trusting and look towards the King. Yet another sign from him that I am to meet my maker and this cheers me considerably. While we climb, Virgil tells me we are shortly to arrive at the first of the final three terraces, all of which right the wrongs of misdirected, excessive love. Upon the first of these, the fifth of Purgatory, we shall encounter the avaricious Covetous. Indeed, we are met by a band of penitent souls the moment we emerge from the sacred steps onto the shelf of pumice, an abrasive rock formed during explosive volcanic eruptions.

They lie naked on the shelf, stretched out, face down, weeping and sobbing, reciting the prayer: *Adhaesit pavimento anima mea; my soul clings to the ground*. In truth it does, for their penance is to lie prostrate, for a soul helpfully cries out that in Purgatory, they must look to the earth such that they spent life searching for earthly goods rather than seeking the comforts of Heaven. These penitent shades are considerable in number, many thousands and I confess I am filled with anxiety for, to avoid treading upon them, I must travel at the very edge of the cornice leaving me much exposed and vulnerable, for I have looked down though I now barely see the sands from such a height.

Gratefully I kneel as, between sobs, a cleric engages me in discourse, for it is he who has cautioned the nature of the punishment here, himself atoning for his wanton worldly ambition. He does this with good grace despite that he is shackled with the chains of justice, for he feels blessed that God has not denied him eternal life in the celestial spheres and gladly endures the suffering today, for tomorrow he will rejoice in the radiance and bliss of the glorious heavens. On realising he is a pope, indeed he was Peter's successor, I bow my head whereupon he stops me, embarrassed, for in the afterlife he tells me, the very honours the avaricious coveted on Earth do not exist. Indeed, they are meaningless such that all are equal in the eyes of God. We bid him farewell, for he wishes to continue with his purification but it is no great matter that he disappears with the other beetles, for upon this terrace are thousands of souls such is the prevalence of the she-wolf of greed and it will be no hardship for me to engage with another.

Indeed, immediately I find myself with a man calling out examples of Liberality and Generosity including *Dulce Maria! Sweet Mary!* for her poverty decreed she birthed the baby Jesus in a barn. I crouch down as he tells me he is Hugh Capet, the founder of the dynastic Capetian Kings of France whereupon he recounts the tale of the Consul Fabricus, he who chose to impoverish himself and thus died penniless such that the state had to bury him. This story he tells with cries of: *Possess virtue in poverty rather than great riches with vice!* Also, the tale of St Nicholas, generously providing dowries to enable young girls to avoid succumbing to brothel life. He extols thus, willingly, for he is honoured that God has blessed him enough to allow him to cleanse, to purify, to purge himself of sin on the mount that he may journey with the righteous to the lights of Heaven.

At night, penitents are required to continuously voice their denunciation of hoarding and spending, which he himself does by reproaching his own descendants for their greed and covetousness, for they accumulated substantial wealth within minimal time such that their avarice became all encompassing. Indeed, their rapacious desire for power grew as fervently as their riches such that they turned to poisoning, pimping and emotional warfare to attain it.

Condemning avarice and prodigality, we hear the tales of Pygmalion, Queen Dido's murderous husband, so keen to secure her considerable inheritance he resorted to assassination. Also, King Midas of the golden touch, so desperate for wealth he greedily requested as a gift from Dionysus the ability to turn anything he touched to gold and, finally, the tale of Heliodorus, sent by King Seleucus to the temple in Jerusalem to pilfer charitable monies pledged to the Apostles, those primary disciples of Jesus Christ and pioneers of the New Testament.

From nowhere, the great mountain shakes and trembles in its entirety, jolting like an earthquake, such did the island of Delos when the goddess Latona birthed her twin son and daughter, Apollo and Diana, the sun and the moon. I am aghast, for if the rock crumbles or I should fall from this dizzying height, my death is most assured, for I am a mortal being and would not survive. I wonder that these penitents do not know this, for in truth not one has remarked on it upon this terrace and neither do they check after my welfare. Virgil reminds me it is only laying prone with eyes trained at the rock floor rather than to me they are unaware, not that they lack interest. He assures me all will be well for he is here to protect me; that in this moment I have nothing to fear.

It seems the penitent souls prostrate on the ground have no fear either, for they jubilantly cry out the song of praise *Gloria in excelsis Deo: Glory to God on highest!* The mountain stills itself and, in that moment, faces down, the souls begin to weep once more, calling out examples of generosity, tears collecting in the cavities of the porous pumice. I confess to confusion for, in the moment of danger as the mountain shook violently, they burst forth into joyous song and now that it stops and we are safe, they resume their sobbing. I am bemused by their actions. Indeed, my need for answers is as a thirst, one that cannot be quenched but for the water that gives grace, yet even the wise Virgil cannot offer me an explanation and is as curious as I.

We continue along the winding path, dodging the thousands of weeping souls laying prostrate upon the terrace and from behind, quite unbeknown to us and most unexpected is a shade, although for his stealth he could have been Jesus himself reborn and emerging from his rocky tomb! Startled, we jump as this upright penitent greets us, kindly and warmly with a: *God give His peace unto you* and asks how we come to be here on the fifth terrace, for he has seen that we have ascended through the secret pass of the sacred stairwell. Virgil tells him to look upon my brow at the letters etched therein by the Angel of the Gate and know that God has sent me, a living man, here. He adds that he himself stands beside me as my guide, that having strayed from my true path need shepherding back to the bosom of my honourable flock, for it is my destiny to reign with the righteous.

Having answered the shade's question, Virgil poses one to him, for he asks about the earthquake that caused the trembling of the mountain. The penitent soul is much animated for he reminds us that the mountain of Purgatory is unaffected by weather be it tempest, hail or snowflake, as any such natural forces may only reach to the three steps at the main gates whereupon the angel porter stands guard holding Peter's keys of gold and silver. The quake therefore, he continues, was not of nature, rather of Heaven. For in that moment, a soul judged he had been completely cleansed, purged entirely of his sins and was released, ready for his triumphal journey to the glory of Paradise. The mountain thus shakes with a proclamation of joy, for this soul has achieved spiritual purification and may now delight in true ascension to the palace of God. And while this happens, the souls hereupon the rock rejoice. In celebration, they sing in chorus the prayer *Gloria in excelsis Deo*, which indeed we have just heard the prostrate Avaricious calling upon this very ledge for, he says, no one shows envy to that soul as each knows at some point his own ascension will occur. Once the trembling stops and the mount retains its stillness, they return to their weeping and sobbing, face down to the ground reminding them to reject their avaricious desire for earthly goods.

When Virgil seeks clarification that it is the penitent and not God that judges sins have been suitably purged, the man nods in confirmation and confesses that he himself was the reason for the trembling of the mountain just this moment past. For he has been upon this rock for nine hundred years and only now feels the time is right to rise up from Purgatory to the kingdom of Heaven and thus tentatively makes his way to the celestial steps. We are much shocked, for an entire millennium, or almost, is more than a lifetime, indeed it is ten! We ask his name, for we have conversed for some time without introduction. He tells us he is the poet Statius, author of the poems Achilles and Thebes and that his time upon the mount has been split between the fourth and fifth terraces for he needed to purge both the sin of sloth and prodigality, the sister vice of avarice.

I exclaim that he must be much disappointed to have remained here for so long and he says he has a deeper regret than even this. I cannot imagine what it may be for, indeed, nine hundred years in continual penance without imminent purgation would play most heavy upon anyone's mind. He turns to me and, in earnest, for genuinely I do not believe he knows who stands beside me, says that to have lived at the same time as the great and lauded poet Virgil, to have met and learned from him direct was his greatest desire and if it were possible to do so, he would gladly delay his ascension to Paradise by another year, ten even, to have enabled it. He shows much sadness at this moment, one I feel is quite equal to the degree of his desire. It transpires that the poems of Virgil encouraged him to purge his sin of prodigality, for in reading them, particularly Aeneid, he was directed towards God and this was his salvation, for his path to the inferno was thus diverted.

Immediately Virgil looks to me, for he does not wish Statius to know him but a misfortune has occurred. For, upon his confession, a mischievous smile crossed my face which he spotted. Indeed, he demands to know why I grin so and now I am caught, for if I stay silent to oblige my friend I risk offending this kindly and wise gentleman who stands before me. Virgil can see my predicament and reluctantly gestures that I may reveal his name, which I do by gently teasing both poets. Overjoyed at this wondrous revelation, Statius throws himself at Virgil's feet to offer an abundance of kisses upon them but, embarrassed, Virgil gently rebukes him.

In the moment Statius is lost, for he quite forgets Virgil is as he, just a shade in this place but one whom he loves in such quantity, he is lost in his desire to treat him as a mortal man. Indeed, close to tears and quite overcome with emotion, the words *ardet intus quanto vos: how much love within me burns for you* are whispered from his lips and we know they are formed within his heart. Regaining composure, Statius readies himself to leave and begin his ascension to the Divine realm of Paradise, thus he attends with us as we progress on, much invigorated to be in Virgil's company.

We three encounter the Angel of Liberality who raises his

wings as if to embrace us, but instead erases another letter from my brow for I have successfully purged the vice of Avarice. As he does so, he whispers the benediction *Beati qui esuriunt justitiam; Blessed are they who hunger and thirst...* but stops short of the final words albeit I understand his message; that the avaricious should hunger for salvation not earthly treasures. Again, I am overcome with emotion, for this guardian angel is God's messenger and he speaks direct to me and through him, does God. I am aware too, that only two terraces remain on this mount, that my ascent is almost over and, as Statius, I shall shortly make my way unto Paradise. The angel points us to the Pass of Pardon with the words: *Come, ye that have faith that you may rise to grace*, for it is here we shall begin our ascent to the penultimate cornice.

TERRACE 6
THE PENITENT GLUTTONOUS

We disappear into the secret crack in the rock face and begin our climb up the sacred stairwell, for as we ascend we head towards the sixth, enveloped by the pinks and ambers of volcanic rock and fire opals sparkling as a million comets in a moonlit sky. Virgil tells me we are still of Tuesday, about midday, which means we have spent five hours, maybe six, on the terrace with the Avaricious. He and Statius continue in intense, earnest discourse but they seem happy enough and question each other back and forth. I am quite content to eavesdrop, for they are celebrated poets and I shall unlikely be in the company of such esteemed linguists again in my lifetime.

As we climb, Virgil asks Statius to impart details of his own sins of greed, for we found him on the terrace of the Avaricious and this does not sit comfortably with him for, indeed, he finds his fellow creative a most pleasant and learned man. Statius explains that he was a spendthrift thus his penance was not in relation to avarice, rather prodigality and reminds us that both sins are purged on the same cornice. Thankfully, he realised and changed his ways with sufficient time to save himself from the inferno where he would find himself heaving a stone boulder across the deep ditch for eternity. However, before his time on the fifth terrace, he resided upon the fourth for he, too, had to purge the sin of Sloth.

We continue our dizzying ascent of the secret stairwell, for the spiral tapers noticeably and within a short time we cover a significant height. He tells how, having studied Virgil's writings and being drawn closer to Christ, had a moment of clarity and became a Christian. However, for fear of persecution by the troops of the pagan Emperor Domitian he kept the news of his conversion hidden, thus it was for cowardice he was cast to the terrace of the Slothful. Virgil nods and smiles knowingly. He speaks of reciprocation of love that is kindled by virtue, for he explains that Statius' love and respect for him was demonstrated by the prayers he sent down to Limbo. In turn, knowing who directed those prayers, Virgil reciprocated with thoughts of love and respect, for he is a pagan thus God does not hear his entreaties. At this, Statius asks for news of Limbo, for he is keen to know of the Romans and Greeks now residing there. Virgil obliges and they fall into yet another conversation, this one on the various resident poets including Terence, Plautus and Homer.

Finally, we emerge from the sacred stairwell and the sun tells us it is early afternoon. We alight onto a ledge of obsidian, black volcanic glass which is eerily beautiful as the sun reflects upon it. Statius indicates to turn right, for we search for the sixth terrace. I notice with some relief the journey no longer seems an ordeal, for five of the seven invisible weights have been erased and I move all the faster for the loss of the burden, plus the pull of the inferno is no more. Indeed, I am much invigorated until I look over the edge to an undulating carpet of lapis many fathoms below, such that I realise how far we have climbed, the heights we have reached and the dangers we face thereupon, for Poseidon and his palace still invite.

We continue along the smooth, black ridge which wraps around the conical mount whereupon appears a tall tree, branches hanging down, laden with ripe, succulent, sweet smelling fruits; figs, I think, from this distance. It takes its nourishment from a shimmering waterfall adjacent, which rains down upon the leaves and gives sustenance to the fertile soil, for these fruits are bursting. I confess I am much excited by the thought of these plump delights and, as we approach, I reach out to pluck one from the bough that I may get a taste of Heaven. An anonymous voice from within the tree, as those of the Forest of Suicides, forbids me, crying out: *This food shall be denied to you!* I am most confused, until Statius tells me of the sin purged herein. For we are at the terrace of the Gluttonous, those who indulged in food, drink and bodily comforts upon Earth, where so they are now starved in the presence of mouth-watering nourishment, taunted; for the temptingly succulent fruit is forever denied.

The voice from the tree continues, but now cries out examples of Temperance and Moderation, for these are the corresponding virtues for the vice of excess. We hear it relay a tale of John the Baptist; he, who while wandering alone in the wilderness wearing a shirt of camel hair, survived eating only honey and locusts and I hear again the story of Mary sharing Jesus' gift of wine at the wedding at Cana. Also, the women of Rome for drinking no wine, such that abstinence protected them from shameful behaviour and, finally, of Daniel who, in a bid to gain wisdom, rejected the nourishment of food and wine.

We continue along the terrace whereupon, echoing in the air, we hear the words of the hymn *Labia mea, Domine aperies et os meum adnuntiabit laudem tua: Oh Lord, open thou my lips and my mouth shall proclaim your praise.* Virgil tells me we are shortly to meet the gluttonous repentants, for they are desperate to purge their sin of excess thus sing these words in order to atone. Indeed, within a minute or two, emerging from a bend in the terrace appears a band of these pitiful Purgatorios. I am much shocked at the look of these shades who stand before us; emaciated, skeletal and gaunt, for they are the souls of the penitent Gluttonous and I thus expect gargantuan silhouettes as the elephant and the giant hog. Instead, we are greeted by bodies swamped in their robes; withered, malnourished, pinched and shrunken. I am reminded of the prince Erysichthon, he who felled the favourite oak in the sacred grove of Demeter, Goddess of Plenty. His punishment was eternal hunger and, thus, he ate at himself although here, as there, there is no flesh on any bones to comfort a starving man.

A feeble soul approaches, eyes as hollow as gem-less rings, cheeks sunken, clutching his stomach, for the hunger pangs yield cramps, yet he bids me a hearty welcome for he recognises me! I confess but for his voice I would not have known him for his face is much altered by starvation but, yes, I can see it is my good friend Forese Donati and I am much relieved to meet him, albeit he begs me not to reproach him for his thinness. We enter into robust discourse, for we spent many years on Earth ribbing and chiding each other such that we were known for our verbal sparring and we are happy to return to a version of it now. I am compelled to ask about his emaciated state and, indeed, that of his cohorts here and he tells me that as gluttony was their companion in life, so has hunger become their attendant here on the rock. For, as they failed to achieve a holy and healthy use of food and wine in their earthly ventures, so they are deprived of sustenance upon the mountain that is Purgatory.

He asks if I have seen the tree abundant with plump fruit for, he says, the waterfall adjacent sprays the leaves purposely, for in doing so it releases a scent, a sweet perfume, stoking a further desire to devour the delicious bounties from the branches, an act these penitents are denied. He has no fear he will succumb, for despite the temptation of the aromatic and fleshy fruits, they are always unattainable. Instead he has faith; that their suffering and torment, such that they do starve in all actuality, is no real hardship, for he sees it as a gift; solace. For they follow in the footsteps of Christ which draws them closer to God. He tells me he does not suffer and I believe him for it.

We exchange news and he talks fondly of Nella, his own woman, for it is she he credits with his incredible advance through Purgatory, such that he has only been here five years (when Statius was nearly one thousand!). He recognises that through her fervent prayers and tears he has been shown mercy for, he asks, what is love and forgiveness if not mercy? I ask after his sister Piccarda and also for the names of the shades here who stare at me, for they have seen my shadow and know I am of the living. He is most excited to relate that Piccarda already resides in Heaven for her temperance and virtue were recognised by God. That he may join her there at some time is of great comfort to him.

At this moment he declares his disapproval for Florentine women, their characters and their fashion, for he says they exhibit no such meekness and is lucky Nella is not of that place. Indeed, if she were, he says, he would be here for eternity such could he not rely on a Florentina's good grace. I am affronted at this unwarranted attack on my compatriots, but he begins to get heated so, to distract him, I introduce Virgil and Statius. Indeed, I gesture towards Statius and proclaim he is the cause of the tremor of the mountain but a few hours before. I discourse further on poetry and then Forese interrupts for he is interested to know why I am here on the mountain amongst the dead, for he can tell I am no shade for he, too, has seen my shadow.

I describe my ecclesiastical quest, detailing my journey through the Underworld such that I met sinners and demons and beasts and giants, that my own eyes were witness to punishments most depraved and wicked. In truth, but for my sage guide Virgil, who accompanied me

172

there as he does here, I might not have entered unto Purgatory to be cleansed of my sins. Without him I would not be properly groomed for a meeting with my beloved Beatrice before I ascend to Paradise, if indeed, this is where I am headed. I am of the view that Virgil has expedited my ascension, I am sure of it, for without him my progress would have been much hindered, perhaps as Statius although in truth I have committed no serious sin as he. Yet, as we have learned, to climb the mount is to make straight those men whom sin made crooked and, for some, repentance takes more time.

At the sound of the name Beatrice, another skeletal soul approaches and to my great delight I see it is my poetic predecessor, Bonagiunta of Lucca! Indeed, he remembers that it is she to whom I refer in my poem La Vita Nuova when I wrote: *Ladies who understand the truth of love*, a poem to which he gave considerable praise for, at the time, he declared it of a new sweet style. Despite we are almost strangers we engage in conversation but, before we do, Forese departs with some gentle chiding such that when I ask when I may expect to meet him again, his riposte is that it is entirely dependent on when I expect to die! With no further distraction from Forese, I turn back to Bonagiunta and we discuss the differences in our poetry, such that he honours me by declaring me the superior bard.

Virgil is keen to make haste, for it is mid-afternoon, time for Evensong, thus we three bid a speedy farewell to my poetic champion and continue our ascent along the sloping terrace of the Gluttonous. A second tree is spotted ahead, greater in stature than the first but boughs, too, weighed heavy with ripe, succulent treasures. Ravenous, desirous and tormented souls jump and reach up, grasping, crying out in desperation, for the bounties within are tempting, tantalising and these shades are famished, for they are frighteningly malnourished. Yet, for the branches are too high, there is no low hanging fruit for them here, for God will not ease the path to trespass against Divine law.

The tree remains impassive to their pleas and tears, and as we approach they give up their efforts and move on, chewing upon air, suffering for their gluttony, reluctantly accepting that through hunger and thirst they shall attain purification. As they pass, they are startled to see my shadow upon the floor, yet they do not linger, for they are desperate for sustenance and despatch to locate some. Sighing, disappointed and shaking his head, Virgil tells me that those illuminated by bliss and grace hunger only for salvation, thus these penitent souls will spend many years upon the mountain before they enjoy a taste of Heaven.

A voice from within the branches speaks a warning to stay away, for it cautions the tree is an offshoot of another, the Tree of Knowledge, that which tempted Eve with its juicy apple, that to whose enticement she succumbed. We make haste, for I do not intend to fall as Eve but can hear the tree citing examples of indulgence being punished as we continue on. One, relating to the cursed centaurs, well known for their bouts of debauchery who, upon feasting and drinking at a wedding abducted the bride which led to the Battle of the Centaurs and Lapiths and, another, of the reckless troops who heavily indulged in wine giving cause for Gideon, the great military mind, to abandon them prior to the battle at Midian, which he fought with only 300 soldiers.

Our trio continues to climb and Virgil tells us it is late afternoon or thereabouts, time for Vespers, so we have spent more than three hours amongst these starved souls. The terrace is narrow but long and winding and I cling to the verge, for in hugging it I am less likely to fall albeit everywhere I look there are emaciated souls, bones evident despite their garments which hang loose and I am much distracted. We continue to ascend along the path in thoughtful silence for I need to concentrate in this difficult and dangerous task. It occurs to me that as I climb this magnificent mountain of Purgatory, I meet sins in the reverse order that I did when I descended into the funnel of

Hell, possibly for the souls of the virtuous here may taste the eternal joy that is Heaven whilst those sinning souls in the inferno are in the reverse situation but, I must focus, for I am at a perilous point.

We walk upwards for ten thousand paces or so it seems, for we are as ships with the wind caught favourably in our sails, when a voice rings out startling us all. It is the majestic Angel of Temperance who glows as red as the apple that tempted Eve. Into my ear he gently whispers the benediction *Beati qui esuriunt et sitiunt iustitiam quoniam ipsi saturabuntu: Blessed are those who so hunger and thirst after righteousness, for they shall be filled.* I have heard these words before, indeed when we entered this terrace the last angel spoke them but at the time did not finish the blessing. The Angel of Temperance accompanies us to the Pass of Pardon with the words: *Ascend here to the heavens, servants of God,* warning us to turn right when we emerge from the sacred stairwell, else we shall lose our way to the final terrace. As he gestures with his wing, he brushes it across my face and the sixth P is removed from my brow, for, praise be, the sin of Gluttony has been purged. We are shown a secret crack in the rockface whereupon we spot the wide stairwell and the angel bids us climb to glory.

TERRACE 7
THE PENITENT LUSTFUL

We three poets climb high and steep within the glowing
amber stairwell, for now we approach the seventh and final
cornice, we near the summit. It is no hardship, for the
invisible weights of vice are nearly no more so we ascend
with considerable ease and emerge onto a terrace of
soapstone. This metamorphic rock, Virgil tells us, is heat
resistant. Why he imparts this knowledge I know not, unless
we are so close to the sun we shall see Apollo himself!

Statius tells us we are at the most western point of the
mount but I am appalled to see the ledge is minuscule, as
narrow as a bale of corn and, indeed, we rise so high, we
surely must reach the heavens, for wispy clouds are close
enough to touch! For safety, we course along it in single file
and again, I hug the cliff face but even with this precaution
I feel my heels must extend beyond the ledge and at any
moment I may plummet to my death. We are almost at the
summit and to fall from this height, ten thousand leagues or
so it seems, does not bear consideration so I close my eyes

tight as if Medusa approaches, gather my thoughts and sidle to my right, inch by inch, praying that nothing will distract me. However, I cannot rid my mind of a thought which perplexes me and, noticing, Virgil bids me to speak.

We continue upwards along the terrace which coils around the tip of the mount as Minos' tail and I declare that I wish to understand how so the gluttonous shades appeared so gaunt and bony. For, without doubt, emaciation occurs and I know not why the bodies of these penitent souls take on the opposite earthly form in this place where a soul has no physical body. I look to Virgil, who unexpectedly invites Statius to respond. I am surprised, for Virgil is nothing if not wisdom but Statius concedes that an understanding of spirituality is required and begins to answer, for Virgil is his hero and I suspect he will not deny or embarrass him.

We listen attentively as Statius offers an explanation thus: that after death a bodiless soul is dispatched to Hell or the shores of Purgatory. The flesh is no more until the Final Judgement when, upon resurrection of the dead, blessed souls are reconnected with body. Until that day, Divine and human powers radiate blissfully around a soul such that the surrounding air constructs a form much like a shadow, whereupon it takes on the mantle 'shade'. At such a time it takes the imprint of the penitent's desires. Thus, in seeking purification through hunger it takes the form of an emaciated, malnourished hollow, only for it desires the pains of starvation in order to attain solace.

Satisfied with this effective elucidation, we continue along the narrow ledge of the crag, me hugging the rockface, cautiously following every protrusion, twist and slope. As we approach the terrace bend and make a final turn on to a wider trail I have cause to cry out, for I see that from an opening in the cliff face, a raging fire spews across the very track we intend to follow! Indeed, a wall of flames blocks our path, churning out flares and fire, intense heat as a furnace and, to add to the danger, a strong wind blows from somewhere (it must be Heaven) which I fear may carry me with it! Virgil explains the raging blaze represents the searing heat of desire, for here reside the sexual sinners, the penitent Lustful.

He has spotted a strip of path free of flames, for it appears the purpose of the wind is to hold the wall of scorching fire back that we may pass safely and, indeed, it seems we are able to make our way there without coming to harm. He advises me to take precautions. He does not need to tell me twice for I confess that with fire to one side and a perilous drop to the other, indeed hazards to every direction I look, I fear that caught between this rock and a hard place, I may not survive the challenge. We shuffle past the roaring fire in single file and it comes to me that when I am in greatest need of help and assistance, I must look to God, not my fellow man.

We walk on and the path widens. I am aware of voices, nay a song and am horrified to realise it comes from within the fire ahead, for moving inside the scorching flames are penitent souls! Virgil orders me to look away but I cannot, for I am transfixed such that despite the heat of this raging mountainside inferno, the shades are walking in a nonchalant manner, singing a hymn of praise; *Summae deus clementiae: God of supreme clemency*. In truth, they do not appear unduly tormented albeit I am shocked, for I am reminded of those burning, charred souls in the sixth circle, at Dis, those trapped in the burning tombs, those dancing within flickering flames, those with melting faces as candle wax, all of whom displayed upmost pain and suffering, for the torturous fire meted out severe punishment. Yet, these do not appear to suffer as they. Indeed, it seems they willingly accept their punishment and Virgil says it is because they know this is the last wound that must be healed, for once treated, they are close to meeting God, for they are destined to ascend to Heaven, such that they are of the final terrace.

On completion of the hymn they begin to call out examples of chastity and marital fidelity for these souls are purging the vice of Lust, repenting for their misdirected earthly sexual desires and they wish to hasten their purification. I hear them talk of the virtues of marriage, of the Virgin Mary, she who is the paragon of chastity and purity for they cry out her words to the angel Gabriel at the annunciation *Virum non cognosco: I know not man!* There is a tale of the virgin goddess Diana, she who expelled her nymph upon hearing of her pregnancy, thus upholding the virtue of chastity. They resume their singing and then recite cautionary tales of excessive love including the story of Pasiphaë, she so overwhelmed with desire for a handsome white bull, positioned herself within a fake cow and tricked the beast into mating with her. Indeed, she was successful and thus was born the minotaur. It is a bizarre opera, I cannot lie.

The sun's arc lowers for it begins its slow descent, yet its light is robust enough to form a shadow of my silhouette in the flames, creating much excitement from the Lustful souls within that very furnace. Virgil tells me this is because the penitent souls here thirst for life, as a desert nomad thirsts for an oasis. Indeed, a lustful penitent steps forward but, mindful to remain within the raging fire itself, for he must continue to burn, does not venture onto the path.

He asks who I am and why I am alive, for my shadow says I am not of the dead. I make to begin my response but in that moment the wind dies down and, alarmingly, the flames roar across the path for there is no breeze to hold them back. Virgil tells me we need to pass through the wall of fire in order to reach the other side, for without doing so we shall not be able to continue along the trail. I refuse to indulge this ridiculous notion, for it will lead to certain death such that I am mortal man and cannot possibly withstand such a firestorm.

A welcome distraction comes in the form of a second group of souls thundering along the terrace who dive into the searing flames, whereupon with a touching caress, they swiftly embrace the first group within. When they have done this, remaining within the fire, both groups continue in opposite directions along the terrace whereupon the second calls out examples of punished lust, of indecent, lascivious love as they pass us by. These include the words *Sodom!* and *Gomorrah!* for these biblical cities and their inhabitants were decimated by fire and brimstone so sinful were their sexual transgressions and peccadillos considered.

The first group make their way back to us, for they wish to hear the answer to their question: why do I share their terrace on the mount if I am alive? Dodging flames, I relay details concerning my quest; that I am set to reunite with my beloved, most gracious Beatrice and that God has endorsed my climb of this magnificent rock, for in witnessing the purgation of sin that souls may be spiritually purified in preparation for ascension to the celestial Heavens, I shall be compelled to embrace the virtues of righteousness and truth upon my return to the earthly, mortal world.

They murmur amongst themselves but appear satisfied, so I ask of them and the other group, for my journey feeds my need for knowledge. One steps forward from the fire, yet I dare not move closer, for as a mortal man I find this heat unbearable and am quite petrified of burning alive in the flames of lust. He informs me that the two groups are lustful penitents but one purges natural lust whilst the other, misdirected. He gestures to his own group of sexual sinners and announces they performed acts of natural lust in that they were desirous of and enjoyed excessive carnal activity whilst the other, now gone having dispersed into the fire behind me, practiced misapplied lust in that their chosen erotica included wanton depravity, sensation and salaciousness.

With this neat explanation he introduces himself as Guido Guinizzelli whom I know to be a poet! Indeed, he was one of the first proponents of the *dolce stil novo*, that description which Bonagiunta of Lucca flattered me with upon the terrace of Gluttony. In truth, I see this gentleman before me as much as a father to my creative children as I do Virgil. He is much embarrassed by my praise, citing himself quite unworthy and gestures towards another soul whom he tells me is Arnaut Daniel, a poet recognised as a true maestro, for he is famed for his poetry and love songs and now, for his incapacity to control his lustful desires. Guido invites me to a say a prayer for both himself and Arnaut and upon this request, leaps back into the core of the furnace!

Again, Virgil urges me to pass through the wall of fire but, naturally, I refuse. I cannot comprehend how he expects me to plunge into such flames of death and I will not be convinced. We remain thus, in discord, Virgil persuading, me denying, for a significant time, perhaps an hour, maybe two for we are nearly at dusk and the sun continues its slow descent.

The sky takes a pink hue as the light fades, yet I can see the Angel of Chastity approaching from the other side of the raging fire, beckoning, for he stands at the base of a staircase, a ladder carved of rose quartz, a celestial stairway winding around the uppermost section of the elevation. Statius whispers this pink stone represents the unconditional love that is Mother Mary, she who is tenderness, compassion, healing and comfort; she who is love and grace. For these are the Holy Steps, those which lead to the mountain summit and, thus, to eternal joy.

The angel opens his wings in welcome embrace and calls out, for he instructs me to step through the fire of the Lustful in order that I may access the sacred path and conclude my quest. I implore him to have mercy, but my entreaty is ignored. Instead, he smiles and whispers softly that God is near, that He watches over me, for His desire is that I succeed and ascend to the celestial realms. If I need strength, he says, I am to heed the benediction within the song of the flames. He looks into my eyes, and in an instant I am overcome with a wave of peaceful serenity, a calmness as my panic and fear dissipates.

Virgil speaks. He tells me that Beatrice is waiting for me beyond the flames and if I pass through, I can find her in the Earthly Paradise. I need no more persuasion than this and wonder that he did not mention it before and so, despite the intense heat, the scorching furnace and searing wall of fire, I follow Virgil who has plunged headfirst into the flames, with Statius immediately behind me, at the rear. In this moment I am unharmed. I am unaffected. I am certain I am embraced by God, for what is His love if not shield and protection? For I have put my trust in the angel and through him, God and He has delivered me once more. Indeed, as I pass through the fire I hear a dulcet melody and the words *Venite, benedicti Patris mei: Come, ye blessed of my Father* so I am hopeful He watches over me. Indeed, I know He does.

We three are safely through the wall of fire, praise be! The Angel of Chastity, whose wings are still outspread, performs the ritual cleansing of the letter P from my brow and whispers the beatitude *Beati mundo corde quoniam ipsi Deum videbunt: Blessed are the pure of heart for they shall see God.* Tears abound and I confess that again I am quite overcome, for I do believe this to be true. In this moment, the leopard of The Dark Wood comes to my mind, for he represented the sin of lust and now that I am purged, purified, cleansed of that vice, the beast can affect me no more. As the final letter P is removed, I am reminded, too, of the eternal lover Paolo for, God willing, I am to be reunited in perpetuity with my own Francesca, the blessed Beatrice.

The angel gently ushers me towards the sacred stairwell of Holy Steps and urges me to climb the giant treads of rose quartz, for there is still daylight, even if only for a few minutes and thus we make haste to press forwards and upwards along the magnificent Pass, enveloped in the night sky and guided by the soft glow of the pearl moon. As the rule of the mount forbids ascent without sunlight, we each take a step on this sacred ladder, for the sun has set and slumber calls. We try to make comfort and my eyes close, for I am exhausted from the strains of the day and I drift off to sleep, as a goat between his two shepherds. I notice the glistening stars in the night's sky, as big as planets, for these are the last my eyes lay upon this third day, for tomorrow I shall enter unto Paradise.

Just before Wednesday's dawn, within my mind, a dream forms. Not of the eagle who carried me away from my beloved Beatrice, nor the seductress siren enticing innocent mariners with her beauty and song, although there is a woman at the heart of it and indeed she is most welcome, for I am presented with a scene most pleasant. Upon a riverbank, Leah, she once married to Jacob, gathers flowers, for she is young and beautiful and despite having seven children to look after, plans to create a floral garland, for she is always labouring with one task or another.

She sings a tale of her sister, Rachel, Jacob's second wife who spends her time studying her reflection in a looking glass, yet devoid of vanity. I immediately understand that Rachel's actions reveal her more contemplative nature. The dream tells me that although those with active lives may achieve more and enjoy happiness and a good life, it could reasonably be argued those who follow a more serene and contemplative lifestyle may actually achieve the best happiness, for they may attain a better state of spiritual bliss.

Rousing from my dream, we awaken, for it is dawn and the Wednesday sun is just risen, its glow lighting up the sacred stairwell of the Holy Steps, for its beams reflect against the rose quartz. I am refreshed, for the dream was not as a nightmare and I feel I understood the message within; that with contemplation one may achieve Heaven. Virgil breaks my thoughts, for he tells me that today all my desires shall be fulfilled, as a sweet fruit quelling an insatiable craving and we begin our concluding ascent to the summit. His words excite me indeed and my pace quickens because of it. We continue our climb, for the final step is in view and from there, Virgil tells me, we will have sight of the Earthly Paradise.

And what a sight indeed! For ahead, upon a flattened landscape, is an immense meadow, abundant with flowers and blossom, surrounding the form of a shimmering orb, a golden, celestial sphere upon which a bloated sun sits in a sapphire sky. As we stand and take in the beauty of the view, for this is the Garden of Eden in all its glory, I spot Virgil looking at me. I am in awe of the scene, of the gleaming sphere set within such colourful and fertile pastures and cannot comprehend why he does not focus his sights upon it. Indeed, he looks to me with sadness etched upon his face. Before I may ask what ails him, he speaks.

He is as my father, for his emotions overwhelm him as he confesses his pride, praising my displays of endurance upon the mount. Indeed, within the funnel of the abysmal inferno too. He announces gently that he resigns his office as mentor, for his art and intellect can take me no further on my journey. Desolate, despairing, I voice my anguish, nay my objection, but he tells me that, as intended, my mental love has been perfected and, as the reeds of humility, bent to God. So understanding as I now do the temptations of sin and living within their limitations, for the truth of virtue is shown unto me, it is safe for me to follow my desires and pleasures. Indeed, he continues, for I am at the pinnacle of the mountain, it is now spiritual guidance I seek, that which, as a pagan, he is unable to provide. He states that he has uttered his last words and that I may expect no further sign from him. Statius thus urges me to continue through the Earthly Paradise for there I shall find Beatrice.

What do I hear? That Virgil deserts me? He denies me his presence before I travel into the afterlife that is Heaven? Why does he not wish to share in this glory with me? To experience Divine love in all its forms? For this is a moment I have desired since my journey began nearly six days hence in the Dark Wood and who, if not Virgil, deserves a glimpse of the celestial kingdom that is Heaven? I am distraught, for in crowning me master of myself he thus confirms his presence redundant, just for he is without the means to provide what is necessary to progress to Paradise. But it was not just guidance he provided. We were friends, as brothers; kin. I heard him tell I am to meet Beatrice, but I am distraught. For in gaining her, I must lose him and I am bereft.

MATILDA

I expect to find myself alone once more, for the first time in six days, but my two guides Virgil and Statius walk behind me, observing diligently as I continue my journey, yet saying nothing. This time I am unafraid, for I am purged of my sins, cleansed and purified, ready to meet God. I feel blessed for I am about to enter the heavenly forest I observed from the terrace, that which sits at the mountain peak. In an instant I am surrounded by breath-taking beauty, exquisite floral scents and loveliness in abundance. For this must be Paradise. There are trees and birds aplenty and the air, although breezy, is fresh and fragrant and blows just enough to bend the boughs without disturbing the birds therein, or their song, and golden blossom falls bountiful, as summer snowflakes. I wish to explore, for I am free and the exquisiteness is utterly absorbing such that I am eager to relish in it.

I walk for some time basking in the abundant beauty herein and come upon a brook of shadows for, untouched by sun or moonlight, it is a stream of darkness, yet I confess a water more pure I have never seen. Upon the floral bank a lady sings and gathers flowers but it is not Leah from my dream nor, sadly, my true love Beatrice. She is most graceful and I confess I am beguiled by her innocent beauty, for her eyes sparkle, her smile dazzles and her hair glistens in the golden sun which shines upon it as rays of pure love. She lifts her head, yet remains modest, and greets me with a face more beautiful than the nymph Daphne, she who tempted Cupid's arrow. She tells me she is Matilda and that I am arrived in the terrestrial heavens for this is The Divine Wood, the Garden of Eden, the birthplace of Adam and Eve, the place where they were created by God. She advises that I see it in its most beautiful state, for it is as it was conceived by Him, a place of bliss in which mankind could bask for all eternity, before that devious pair committed the original sin and plucked the ripe fruit from the Tree of Knowledge.

There are two streams here, she continues, sourced not from a spring but a fountain of unchanging purity; the Lethe, which washes away memories of sin, and the Eunoë, which restores memories of good conducts and actions. In order to benefit from their powers, one must first savour the Lethe then, immediately after, the Eunoë, for as we cast away our sins, forgiven by the mercy of God, so we remember the goodness in our hearts and are compelled to act with good grace in the future. I am reminded of the sacraments and reconciliations of baptism, for do we not bathe specifically to purify and regenerate our souls, to cleanse flawed doctrine such that we may be admitted, sanitised, to the Church of our Father?

I ask after the breeze, for weather did not affect the mountain such that it stopped rising beyond the gates at the third terrace. She tells me the celestial orbs above revolve and their constant rotation is responsible for the soft wind which carries not only seeds from the flowers and trees, but also the Music of the Spheres of Heaven, created by the stars, which may be heard echoing within the Earthly Paradise, a celestial soundtrack for this precious wonderland. Indeed, this place is sublime and one where I feel I could remain for all time, for surely there is nowhere more beautiful and joyous than this? But Matilda speaks, for what I witness here is not intended to be enjoyed permanently, rather it is just a promise of the glory and delights offered in Heaven which, she assures me, I shall soon discover. For here is not a destination, rather a signpost to an even more beautiful, more glorious and magnificent place. Souls are not permitted to enjoy longevity here for, as Adam and Eve were quickly cast out upon committing the first sin, man's sojourn in The Divine Wood is short, and merely serves to remind us to keep our gaze towards the heights of Heaven, for the gates are now open unto mankind as He welcomes us back through the life, death and resurrection of His son, Jesus Christ.

Espying Virgil and Statius behind me, she talks of a golden age of man's innocence and happiness, now but an enduring memory though once found in this place and one which ancient poets dreamed of and used as subjects for their prose. I turn to my guides and, smiling, they imbibe this information as bees to nectar, as beguiled by this innocent beauty as I. We are all perfectly content and so I return my gaze to Matilda who begins to sing *Beati quorum tecta sunt peccata: Blessed is he whose transgressions are forgiven* as she walks along the bank. She sings direct to me, I am certain of it.

THE PAGEANT OF THE SACRAMENT

I mirror her steps on the opposite bank and together we follow the twists and curves of the Lethe upstream, heading east. She is coy, as a nymph of the woods and I am mesmerised, so to follow is no hardship. From nowhere, lightning flashes as a bright glare and I am blinded. But this is not lightning, for it lasts much longer than a momentary snap. She calls out for me to be watchful and listen and in no less than one hundred steps I realise why. For emerging from the forest within the bright light is a celestial procession. In truth, I know not what else to call it.

A charming melody drifts through the air, echoing in the meadow and in this moment I am lost, intoxicated by all the beauty I behold. I find I am furious with Eve and her weakness, for through her wanton desires and fall from innocence in performing the original sin, man is denied these wondrous pleasures and, in turn, me a lifetime in this place. The voices are roused to the crescendo of a choir; dulcet, passionate, joyous. The sight and the sound are more than my eyes and ears can behold, more than my brain may record so I summon the Muses to help me make order from this ecclesiastical vision, for I wish to remember it in detail such that I intend it to form my poetic works.

Approaching us from within the light are seven golden trees, glowing and glistening. It is only when they advance closer I realise they are not trees, but a candelabra formed of seven single candles, each shining more brightly than a full moon in the midnight sky! I turn to Virgil, for truly this exquisite vision is symbolic of something and I wish him to enlighten me. But, for once, he cannot speak, for in truth, this spectacle is of the Divine, and thus Virgil's pagan wisdom may not help unravel my confusion. I am transfixed.

Matilda calls from across the bank. She rebukes me! For, in passing my eye over only the candles, which she says represent the gifts of the Sevenfold, I have ignored the individuals robed in white behind them. I had not even noticed these men, such that their clothes glared so bright and had cause to be reflected in the candle flames but now that I do, I see a rainbow trail, for each releases a banner of colour behind him, a wondrous prism floating through the air. Next, no more than ten paces behind, a procession of 12 pairs of elders, the writers of the Book of Revelations, each swathed in white, a wreath of fresh lilies upon their heads, singing, albeit they move slowly yet with much grace and serenity.

Four creatures pass by, evangelists of the Book of Ezekiel, each with six wings, plumage of angelic proportions, feathers of seeing eyes and crowned with a coronet of leaves such that mortal words may not do justice to describe their magnificence. For they are Matthew, Mark, Luke and John, hereto immortalised as the winged ox, lion, eagle and man. Between them, within the centre, for this cavalcade acts as a guard of honour I am certain, is a chariot so grand, so ornate, that even the majestic griffin that pulls it, wings so tall I cannot see the tips, is reduced to no more than a spear carrier. His plumes and everything of him that is the eagle is golden and that of the lion is white and red.

Yet who is transported within this triumphal celestial carriage? Is it Jesus? The Virgin Mary? Or God himself, for only a deity would ride this two-wheeled throne towards Paradise, for it is more magnificent than those of the emperors of Rome or Apollo of the Sun, even!

To the left of this magnificent chariot, a trio of graceful dancers pirouette and twirl and again I am reminded of the holy virtues of faith, hope and love for one has skin green as an emerald, another red of the blood of Christ and the third white, as virgin snow; purity. Four maidens follow to the right robed in violet for, undeniably, they are a reference to the cardinal virtues of temperance, fortitude, justice and prudence. Finally, a further seven elders, at the procession rear, and in white as the first (of Revelations) but crowned with red roses which, from a distance, suggest their heads are aflame. The Pageant of the Sacrament has reached us, and in this moment a mighty thunderclap bursts as a roaring volcano, splitting the very sky in two! The ground shakes as a hundred giants dancing and the procession is dragged to a halt. For the chariot has stopped, triumphal, resplendent, magnificent. And it is level with me. And my heart pulsates with a thousand beats, for the passenger steps forward to reveal himself.

A choir of one hundred angels begins to sing: *Blessed art thou that comest* and as they do, they scatter a curtain of flowers from the sky thus the passenger remains hidden, as the sun behind a morning mist, as a virgin's face behind her floral veil scented with the fragrance of ten thousand rosebuds. Finally, she is revealed unto me. A woman. A blessed woman, for she wears a crown of olives, that which represents the highest of all seven gifts of the Sevenfold. For she is wisdom. Her veil is white and she covers her red dress with green robes for, again, these colours are those of the sacred virtues of faith, hope and love and in her they are brought to life. For who, more than any other, symbolises these better than God's best creation? For she is my woman, resurrected. She is Beatrice. We are reconciled. As one. For she has come back unto me.

I cannot muster breath. My body trembles as the mountain releasing a purged soul, for I am overcome by the mighty power of ancient love. I am astonished and must tell Virgil, for he has prepared me for this moment yet still I seek reassurance that it is she. I spin around for he stands behind me but, he is gone! My eyes dart east and west, north and south but he is not here. He is vanished with no final word and, but for Statius, I am alone, orphaned. Tears cascade down my cheeks, as Niobe mourning the loss of her 14 children for I, too, am bereaved!

Before I may digest this dismal and bleak news, for I confess my emotions are in turmoil at this realisation, Beatrice approaches. I await gentle words of comfort, a soft touch of hand maybe, a small gesture of love perchance but she beseeches me to stop weeping, for she says that the Earthly Paradise is a place of sublime beauty and joy where all men should be happy. Mysteriously, she adds that I will need to save my tears for a more worthy cause, then immediately she rebukes me! I am admonished, for she challenges my attendance here and says I do not belong of this place! My face must show a confusion, for she asserts that I have committed sin by straying from the earthly path of Truth that she herself had placed me on.

I confess that in this moment I hang my head in shame for, observed by this celestial audience of angels and nymphs, elders and griffins, she reproaches my earthly misdemeanours most heartily. I am disgraced. As I glance down, my face is reflected in the brook and it is so sorrowful that indeed I am engulfed in pity for myself. The angelic choir immediately bursts forth into song and I am much comforted by the psalm within *In te, domine, speravi, non confudar in aeternum: In you, Lord, I have trusted, let me now be confounded in eternity*. I suspect they appeal to Beatrice to show mercy, to take pity for they too, may feel she has put me to shame.

At this entreaty I am quite overcome with emotion and

the tears flow again. She gently chides the angels, for she says she merely conveys a message and attempts to explain it to them thus: that when I was a youth, all the spheres, all God's graces, the heavens and the skies showed favour by bestowing poetic talents and artistic gifts upon me. With virtuous Beatrice at my side, and led by my love for her, I followed her along the path of Truth, a straight and just path towards the light of Heaven. Upon her death and without her righteous guidance, I abandoned her to follow another whose virtues were lacking and strayed to a crooked path, one which led me towards counterfeits of goodness; wandering, squandering.

Despite her attempts to intrude upon my dreams and lead me back, I failed to heed until, finally, having sunken to such depths and in danger of finding my soul beyond all redemption, she had no recourse but to intercede and cast me to the circles of Hell to journey among the souls of the Damned, to experience all the horrors within such that I may be set back upon the road to salvation. For this purpose she sent Virgil to guide me safely through the inferno to the Mountain of Purgatory, and I now find myself purged of sin, just steps away from Paradise proper, although she owns she cannot let me pass just yet.

To say I am affronted is too strong, I admit. Yet, am I now not compelled to question her love for me? I confess I am incredulous, for I understood it was God who sent me unto the inferno, that it was He who cast me into The Dark Wood to encounter the terrifying she-wolf. That it was He who insisted I should witness woeful punishment and suffering to better understand that to avoid a harrowing afterlife in the rancid cesspit of the Devil's basin, one of eternal separation from all that I love, I should redirect myself away from sin to the path of righteousness. To know it was my beloved, my heart, my muse, who cast me there to that place of danger and depravity, cruelty and brutality is devastating for, in truth, I would not wish man nor beast to suffer the torture, indignities and evil therein. She took a risk, did she not, in assuming that I would succeed? For if I failed in my quest, it would not be at her side in the celestial Paradise where I would spend eternity, for that was her intention I am sure of it. Indeed, I would be cast to the inferno upon my Judgement Day, with no recourse, no respite, no chance at redemption and thus we would not enjoy and savour eternal bliss, rather endure eternal separation.

I know it is me to whom she directs the tale though she articulates it to the angels. It is the truth she speaks for, indeed, I did squander my talents such that when she left me, abandoned unto death, I sought the easy path which was one of misdirection. Her harsh rebuke leaves me quite incapacitated such that I am humiliated before this celestial jury. She presses me for an explanation, for she insists I address my audience and list those obstructions and temptations that impeded my path, for they must have been many in number and strength that I could stray from the Truth so easily and quickly. Head bowed, I concede they were but she is not ready to release me. Indeed, she commands I announce my tribulations, for I have not yet passed through the Lethe and thus my memories remain intact. So, I tell them in earnest that I am without honour, void of integrity; I am but a husk yet in this moment know I am full of remorse.

I explain thus: that as I felt abandoned by her in death, so I abandoned the Divine path and, with no guiding light, for I felt I had been forsaken, I fell astray, deviated and betrayed her honour. I release this tirade of words as a bow pulled so slack the arrow barely flies and falls far short of its intended target. It is thus as my words spew forth but what with my sobbing and breathlessness, she cannot hear me. But had she, my confession would have resonated in her ears. I am ashamed. I cannot speak but she says the shame will stop me from sinning again, from succumbing to temptation and with that, she gently informs me of a more proper action. That despite her absence in physical form, knowing her to be virtuous and true, I should have continued to follow her, to lift my wings and my eyes and look to Heaven for guidance, for temptation is sin and, in straying from the path, I succumbed to sin. For if one as beautiful, virtuous and faithful as she could not save me from the error of my ways in life as in death, in truth who, or what, could?

As sage as Virgil is, I know that Beatrice too has wisdom and she comes to me direct from God in Heaven, but she castigates me and now I am full of guilt, for I weakened and squandered when I should have resisted. But it has happened and I cannot change what has already occurred, and for this I feel nothing but shame, remorse and disgrace. Again, tears prick in my eyes and, overcome with emotion, pressure and humiliation, for in truth I did not expect such a tirade from my beloved and, bereft of the steadfast love of my father Virgil, not for the first time, I disintegrate into a faint.

I am roused from this collapse, for I unexpectedly find myself being pulled through the waters of the Lethe to the dulcet strains of *Asperges me: cleanse me*. Indeed, Matilda has hold of my neck and as I waken, she immerses my head beneath the surface as a baptism, such that I succumb to a mouthful of water which I have cause to swallow. In doing so, memory of my past sins is erased and I am thus free of the weight of shame, for from this point on, I have no means to access them in my mind and I have broken with my past.

The four cardinal virtues from the Pageant of the Sacrament help me alight into a gondola and, with their purple robes, dry off some of the water. They begin to sing and their gentle song informs me they are handmaidens, astral beings, as stars, for I will need the light they emit forth to see into Beatrice's eyes where she will reveal a second beauty. Indeed, cleansed, purified and free of shame, I am being sculled back to Beatrice by this virginal quartet and she waits on the shore, regal, serene, holy; standing face to face with the magnificent griffin. I collapse at her feet but she commands me to stand and lift my head, for she wishes me to look into her eyes.

I am reminded of her beauty and am full of remorse that tears well again but I cannot tear my eyes from hers, for they are green as emeralds and within are flames, dancing. I am transfixed but confused, for where I expect to see the griffin reflected, for her gaze is direct upon him, I see in one eye an eagle, whole, and in the other a lion, whole. For as she looks at the griffin before her, as she gazes upon him, she understands that here stands the power, the glory, the single entity; the Divine. And something within me stirs, for a mystical union takes place such that in this moment, with the prayer of the theological virtues echoing in my soul, with Beatrice gazing upon Jesus Christ and, through his reflection in her eyes, I too, she and I are connected, conjoined, reunited. As one.

And now I am reminded this journey of repentance is indeed painful, for it stings as a nettle and it takes time, such that I endure it until Beatrice is satisfied my remorse is genuine. For it is no hardship to believe that remorse may be dictated by a man's misdirected belief that he cannot endure the torment of the inferno and thus convinces himself he cannot endure the loss of Heaven when, in reality, his remorse should be driven by repentance for his sins. Because he has transgressed, he has deviated from the path of Truth and in doing so, has upset God. And to upset God is to sin. To offend God is to sin. To stray from God is to sin. To abandon God is to sin and we are thus driven to repent, for as we seek eternal life in the kingdom of Heaven, God saves us and releases us unto Paradise.

THE TREE OF KNOWLEDGE

Yet, I cannot blame her. For a decade I have not set eyes upon her and confess I feel as though I am already in Heaven as I gaze lovingly at my Beatrice, intent to savour every inch. Indeed, I am so entranced that her nymphs scold me for staring but they do not know that in her I see Christ in all his glory, triumphant over evil, for he shows mercy unbound. Beatrice speaks unto me, for the procession makes preparations to travel north and we are to follow. Thus myself, Statius and Matilda join the group to the right of the chariot wherein Beatrice is seated, again drawn by the griffin who takes the prominent position in the pageant, followed by the seven candles. He is a noble creature indeed; majestic, serene, strong yet gentle. His control is such that even when he moves, his feathers remain quite unruffled. Matilda whispers devotedly that, in witnessing the griffin, I witness the son of God in all his glory. I believe her.

We continue onwards for a distance of three arrows flights and stop at a tree. All around me murmur the name *Adam*, for this is the Tree of Knowledge of Good and Evil where Eve succumbed to temptation and stole the forbidden fruit; ripe, succulent, plump, enticing. But today it is barren, for it is dead, dry, devoid of blossom or scent, stripped bare of branch and leaf, denied any bounty. Beatrice alights from the chariot, whereupon the griffin ties it to the tree. Immediately, flowers and leaves and fruits blossom forth, the tree newly created in reds and violets, as humanity, as Christ's rebirth. A beatification is delivered to the griffin, for he has not succumbed to temptation despite the dazzling display he beholds. Overcome with rapture at this glorious demonstration of resurrection, intoxicated by the sweet scent of blossom and lulled by the heavenly choral anthem as honey to my ear, I close my eyes and sleep takes over.

With a gentle shake I am awoken by Matilda into bright sunlight. Disappearing into the sky I see the procession leaving, all members ascending, following the griffin eastwards to the sunrise, unto Heaven. I am alarmed and cry out after my Beatrice but am reassured by Matilda that she remains and she points to the Tree of Knowledge. It is here she rests at the root of the trunk, guarding the chariot, surrounded by her seven handmaidens, each cupping a star protecting it from the winds of the north and the south. As ever, I am beguiled, blinded by her beauty, for which there is no comparison. Not the glistening dewdrop on a buttercup, nor a new born babe at her mother's breast, not even the sparkling crystal of the enigmatic snowflake on a winter's day. I am blessed, for as I gaze into her eyes, she gazes into mine.

I make to approach her and she holds out her hand in invitation. She declares that I shall stay with her but for a short while, which rests surprisingly easy with me, for I know that upon the Last Judgement we shall be reunited as lovers to enjoy eternal life as Paolo and Francesca endure eternal death, but with a peace and tranquility such as they do not. In this moment she tasks me, for approaching is a Pageant of the Church and I am to record details that I may accurately describe my observations upon my return to

Earth. I believe she wishes me to write poetry, for she tells me her fervent desire is that my work profits the world which lives badly. This is a challenge indeed, but I am happy to serve my queen and shall attend with all the focus and concentration of a cheetah eyeing his prey in the tall grasses of the African landscape, yet I fear meagre words from the earthly lexicon will not suffice.

As when the sky split in two with the crack of thunder, from nowhere a lightning bolt flashes and an eagle plummets from the heavens, ripping into the boughs and branches of the tree under which Beatrice sits, snapping them off and scattering the blossom therein. With the power of one thousand hammers it attacks the chariot, leaving it a desecrated, mangled mess. Immediately, and before I have had time to process what I am seeing, a malnourished fox jumps into the remains of the chariot and, despite its weakened state, yet with the sly, devious wiliness for which it is known, sets to tearing at the seat to devour it. Within moments, Beatrice leaps up and sends it running, rebuking it for its barefaced audacity.

Next, the eagle reappears and swoops down, scattering its feathers across the chariot as a blanket of the softest nap. An ethereal voice from the Heavens cries down that the chariot carries a consignment of depravity and wickedness, that it is laden with calamity but I confess I am much confused, for it is empty. As if this spectacle is not sufficient, the ground opens up beneath the chariot from where a terrifying dragon rears up and thrashes violently, spiking part of the chariot with its tail as a wasp readying her sting, as a scorpion's barb, which it carries down with it as it submerges back to the earth whereupon the ground closes up and rich, fertile soil and grass burst forth.

The bold eagle returns, plummeting down and scattering its feathers once more, this time as a veil such that the chariot's remains are now cloaked in plumes; a blanket of down. Then, the chariot begins to shift into human form, for seven monstrous heads appear, horned, some single some dual, strange, bizarre, such like I have never seen before. I watch transfixed as a figure takes shape within, that of a woman, of a naked whore in fact, whose guardian is a green-eyed giant. They embrace and kiss in a display of shameful, wanton, lustful disregard and depravity but suddenly her eyes are averted to me and, in this moment, her cunning and guile and seductive glance are aimed in my direction. I am appalled, for the giant rises up in a jealous rage and chastises and beats her in a manner most violent and unrepentant yet I am rooted, unable to intercede. Finally, the giant unties the chariot and whore from the tree and hauls them both to the forest whereupon they disappear and are lost to the woodland within.

I am aghast and at a loss to understand what I have just witnessed, for this entire Pageant of the Church is most certainly greatly symbolic but I confess I have no clue as to what it represents. I turn to Beatrice, for she is wisdom, and I am in need of her teaching such that she wishes me to convey my observations to the earthly souls who race to a death of eternal life and bliss, for her desire is that I divert mankind away from the path of spiritual destruction. Yet to do this, indeed to do justice to this onerous task, I must better understand what I have seen. She tells me that she will explain later, but in this moment we are to make haste, for we need to travel into the forest. Thus, she, Matilda, Statius, the seven handmaidens and myself set off on foot, after the giant, for the glorious chariot is no more. It is for the demise of the chariot the septet of nymphs weep and moan as we walk on, and they sob the hymn *Deus, venerunt genes: O God, the heathen are come.*

In truth, I find their sorrow somewhat over-zealous but Beatrice, swept up in this tide of grief and compassion, is also dejected and wretched, such as I envision Mary knelt at the cross. We halt suddenly, whereupon the handmaidens continue their psalm to the end. Beatrice's face changes hue so it is quite red, as if aflame, and she speaks to say that she will vanish but for a short while and then resurface. She gazes earnestly upon her crying nymphs (who weep at the symbolic desecration of their beloved Church) yet nods to myself, Statius and Matilda and bids us to follow. Indeed, she looks upon me and speaks for she wishes me to walk with her so I can more easily hear her words. In truth, in that moment I am transfixed on her feet, for they do not appear to touch the ground, even.

She expresses surprise, possibly disappointment, that I do not use my time with her to probe and inquire, for she assumes I have many questions upon my lips such that I should delve into her mind for answers. In truth, I stumble and cannot form the words, such is the reverence in which I hold her, but she gently scolds me and tells me to rid myself of shame and fear and to speak up, open and honest, for she is wisdom and has an endless capacity for teaching. I begin to talk of my arduous hike up the mountain but she smiles as she tells me that my ascension upon the rock was not due to any climb for, in truth, I have been drawn by the will of God's grace, guided to attain moral righteousness. It is His light and mercy that has pulled me up, for He invites me to the kingdom of Heaven, home of angels, whereupon He wishes me, as all mankind, to rejoice in eternal life. I yearn to say more but manage only to shrug my shoulders weakly, for in this moment my mouth cannot form any more words and I am mute.

She talks instead of the Pageant of the Church, that which she wishes me to relay to mankind in verse upon my return to Earth. She instructs me, once more, to accurately record the events, for my prose will inform the living. Indeed, I am to save mankind from ruination, for she feels my language will be more suited as her own words are not comprehensible to the earthly human intellect. I make to protest at this colossal commission but she hushes me, for she has not finished. She despairs somewhat that the indecipherability of her words is testament to the distance between man's reasoning and God's. Sadly, she fears that mankind cannot hope to understand God, therefore I am to recall the Tree of Knowledge, the griffin, the eagle, the chariot, the fox, the serpent, the whore and the giant, for these reference God and the teachings of the Divine subjects. Indeed, she begins to describe the meaning behind the sacramental procession, for what I have witnessed prophesies the glorious arrival of the one who shall avenge the attempted destruction of Christendom.

She explains thus: The Tree of Knowledge was created by God for his sole use. Those that tear the fruits offend God and He shall cast them aside, for they have blasphemed. Thus, to ensure no more may trespass against Him, for He shall show no mercy unto them, He has created it too tall, too inverted that none shall climb to reach the pickings. For when the serpent destroyed the chariot it is to be told that none can escape God's vengeance, that the serpent shall be punished. Indeed, the eagle shows of the Roman Empire and the persecution of the Church by its heathen emperors. The fox, the same, but of heresies that, too, troubled the Church. The dragon is Satan himself, the split in the earth synonymous with the split in the Church. The eagle's downy feathers represent the corruption and riches of the Church which in turn lead to its day of reckoning, thus shown by the monster with seven heads. The whore, the harlot, shows of the papacy, committing carnal acts with the Kings of the Earth, for the giant is France, the place whereupon the Pope committed the Papal See prior to Rome. It is a lot to take in and I confess I fear I am much confused and unlikely to unravel the tale with any element of accuracy.

The sun shows it is noon or thereabouts and we come to a second stream, for the Lethe now veers to the left and, forking to the right, so I am informed, is the Eunoë. The handmaidens stop and look to Beatrice who orders Matilda to repeat the cleansing ritual that she first performed in the Lethe where all memory of past sins was banished, for she now wishes that my fading virtue is restored. Fittingly, the four cardinal virtues lead me to the river's edge whereupon

Matilda takes my hand and leads me into the stream, Statius observing from the bank. And now, in drinking the Eunoë's water of Good Remembrance, I am reminded that a restoration of good acts, deeds and memories shall be accomplished. Within an instant I feel myself renewed, remade, restored, as the Tree of Knowledge whence the touch of the chariot charged the resurrection and new life blossomed forth, for I am cleansed. I am free of the reeds of humility which have been washed away in the river of virtue. I am prepared to perfection and my entry to the Heavenly Paradise is assured. I am purged, reborn and pure and I wish now to climb; to rise and ascend to the celestial realms, for I wish to meet my maker.

PARADISE

Death is not the end, for the natural progression is resurrection. And our natural home is the celestial Paradise, which is Heaven above.

ASCENSION

As the penitent Slothful upon the rock I am overwhelmed with fervour, yet Beatrice is keen to tame my zeal for we are to remain in this terrestrial dreamland a little longer to make final preparations to navigate the heavens. We will need to make haste, she warns, for we shall have less than one day to journey through the golden globes that will bring us closer to Divine consciousness and we are already of midday. She wishes to calm me so explains the topography that I may expect to find within the gilded Paradise and reminds me that Heaven is a world of bliss, of perfect delight and joy. It is made up of stars, planets and other celestial bodies and consists of nine concentric spheres, each guarded by an angel of the Intelligencia.

She informs me that there, in God's eyes, every man is equal, for He denies none the fullness of His love. Indeed, all those in the celestial realms reside within the Empyrean, the highest heaven, with Him. There are no physical souls in existence just empty spirits but, for the purposes of my journey and that I may better understand the beauty of celestial joy, they will be presented to me as ethereal visions with pearlized faces and specifically sited within different spheres in relation to the degree of righteousness attained in their earthly life.

She tells me that the structure of the celestial Paradise, an angelic hierarchy of planets, is centred around both the three theological virtues that are faith, hope and love and also the four cardinal virtues, those of temperance, justice, fortitude and prudence. The first three spheres focus on deficient forms of the virtues, namely fortitude, justice and temperance and we shall presently make our way to the first, the Moon, whereupon we shall find the souls who were inconsistent in vows and were thus deficient in the virtue of fortitude. It becomes clear to me then, that whilst the foundations of Hell and Purgatory were based on the various classifications of sin, within Paradise they centre around virtues and all that is good.

The sun is high, for it is just past noon. Beatrice stares intently at the flaming orb, gazing directly within, unswerving in her focus for in this moment she invokes all the powers of Apollo. I watch in awe, for she holds her concentration and her eyes seem unaffected by its dazzling brilliance. I try to do the same, for in being this close to Heaven and spiritually purified, I am certain I may perform this task as easily as she, yet the glare is so bright I am quite blinded. I turn to Beatrice that I may see the sun reflected in her eyes, as the griffin at the Lethe, and again I am much moved, such is the might of our spiritual union. In that moment we ascend, journeying upwards from the Earthly Paradise as arrows in flight towards the celestial realm, whilst a melodic harmony infiltrates my ears as nectar to a hummingbird. Beatrice, who is clasped to me, whispers that this is the Music of the Spheres, created by the revolution of the planets, each of which produces a different musical note which sounds in all perpetuity.

We are enveloped in a shaft of light such that I wonder if I am real, still of mortal man or if I am of spirit, quite separate from my physical body, for indeed my solid mass could surely not rise with such ease. We soar, ascending into the atmosphere, for Beatrice guides my soul and its ascension unto God. I know that my beloved Virgil could not have delivered me thus, for he is reason and knowledge, and what I need to reach the heavens is unending faith and a trust in God, and what is my Beatrice if not virtue, faith, constancy and love? I am a man of immense privilege, for she placed Virgil to release me safely unto her and now she delivers me safely unto God. She can see I am amazed that I fly as a bird on the wing and she explains that human souls have a natural ability to rise towards God when they embrace His spirit in their hearts, for they are converted. Now that my sins have been purged, for I am purified and cleansed, I am open to receive His embrace, thus God draws me upwards through the celestial spheres as an infant to his mother's breast.

I look down upon the Mountain of Purgatory we leave far behind. I search upwards and to the flanks and bear witness to sights so remarkable that, as Jason's Argonauts when he tamed the fire-breathing bull, man would be forgiven his disbelief at their description. In earnest I wonder how mortal man may remember such spectacles with any degree of accuracy, yet am reminded that Beatrice expects me to do exactly thus. For she wishes me to record my journey and through the poetic words of my prose, relay the wonders of the celestial afterlife to earthly man that he may renounce sin. Yet how may I use mere mortal words to express what is Divine? I fear I may not do the realm of Paradise justice, for we have not even reached it and already I know it to be more beautiful than perfection.

We rise higher, ascending and reaching heights inaccessible by earthly might, for we are guided by Apollo and the Muses. Suddenly the light is as one thousand flaming torches and in this instant I know we approach a ring of fire, for we travel to an upper thermosphere. Upwards we fly, into which heavenly atmosphere or dimension I am unsure, clasped together, through the soaring heat of flames yet I find myself quite unharmed. There is no gravity, for I climb as a feather blowing in the breeze and Beatrice tells me that without the burden of sin, a spiritually cleansed soul is lighter than air itself. I am embraced by God, lifted by His arms to this celestial palace because, finally, we are here. We are arrived at our stellar destination. For this is the First Heaven, the sphere of the Moon; the first star of Paradise.

1ST STAR OF PARADISE
THE HEAVEN OF THE MOON

It is a beautiful sight indeed, as a polished diamond, sunlight bouncing off its million facets, sparkling and glistening as the sun's rays upon the oceans. Yet Beatrice tells me to look closer, for it is far from thus. She explains that the Moon is the furthest sphere from the Empyrean, the home of God, and thus does not benefit from the full quality of light as other planets, for those in closest proximity to the highest Heaven collect more power, resonate louder, spin faster and are thus more perfect. The spheres are informed by a blessed mover within, an angel of the celestial Intelligencia who commands it to revolve, navigating its journey through the cosmic planes, outwardly radiating the pure joy he feels for God within. Upon closer inspection I can see the lustre is due to the craters and mottled surface which attract and reflect the sunlight unevenly. Beatrice says that such waxing and waning accurately demonstrate inconsistency for it is these souls who reside upon this sphere; those deficient in the virtue of fortitude. For, in abandoning their vows, they are not entirely trusted to be true or consistent to their word. And, in exerting free will, they strayed from the path of Truth.

But what is this that happens now? For we are transported, as if sitting on a cumulus cloud, carried by feathers to the internal depths of the planet. There is no ground as such, for we float as ethereal bodies, the dulcet melody of the Music of the Spheres echoing around the chamber. My eye catches some movement to the west. I see a light travelling towards us, yet as it approaches I realise it is a group of souls, their faces faint and pearly; almost indistinct, as a reflection in a misted mirror or the blurred pebble that sleeps beneath a bubbling brook. Amongst them is the face of a woman I can just recognise and truly this is most glorious, for she is known unto me! She is Piccarda Donati whose brother, Forese, is the emaciated soul I met upon Mount Purgatory. Indeed, we spoke of her only yesterday and I now recall he told me she was already in Heaven! I know her to be pure and virtuous for she was a nun, married to God, so am surprised to find her cast so far from the Empyrean light in this slowest of the spinning planets.

We enter into discourse, for I am most puzzled by her placement in the outermost sphere furthest from the higher Heavens and she tells me her story thus; that another brother removed her from the nunnery and forced her into a marriage against her will. Her death occurred soon after yet she was deemed guilty of abandoning her vow of chastity and had thus been denied ascension to the higher Heaven. I am shocked, for how can this possibly be deemed just? That she was taken under duress, away from her sanctuary, the House of her Lord God, only for her virtue, her chastity and purity to be ruined? And with no recourse! Yet, she remains unduly serene with her lowly placement in Heaven, as are the other thousands of souls who share this modest status upon the first sphere.

Piccarda gestures to another face, the Empress

212

Constance of Sicily, who suffered a similar fate for she, too, was a nun, removed from her convent and forced into matrimony against her will. I offer my earnest condolences, for this was an act of supreme betrayal towards these righteous and blessed virgins but she says they accept their lowly status with grace and dignity for they recognise that God has assigned them to this place and in doing so afforded Himself a level of bliss. His will, therefore, comforts and delivers them unto peace. She smiles at me, for I can see indeed that she does have a balance and contentment about her, as do all the souls in her group. She announces her parting with a smile and the ensemble moves onward singing *Ave Maria: Hail Mary* fading into the distance as a ship vanishing unto the deep sea, all the while the melodious harmonies of the Music of the Spheres resounding in my ear.

I turn again to Beatrice, for it seems to me a great injustice has occurred and I wish for more clarification, but in the moment I catch a glimpse, I am overwhelmed at her radiance which shines forth in all its celestial magnificence and am quite unable to speak. She has already pre-empted my question, for she declares that despite their devotion to God, in having broken their vows these female shades have been judged to have failed in their endeavours, for even victims such as they have a level of responsibility to resist and show courageous endurance to honour their oaths. She sees I am still not convinced but reminds me that I am shown the faces of the Inconstant hereupon the first sphere, those who showed deficiency of fortitude, only so that their less illustrious state be indicated to me. For in actuality, all souls in the celestial Paradise live in the Empyrean, for although not equal in degrees of blessedness and grace, all are deemed worthy of occupying the celestial palace in God's eyes.

I ask what these souls may do to redeem themselves such that they may be exalted to a higher sphere or level of purity but Beatrice tells me atonement is not an option, for this is

God's will. She says that in breaking one's vows, a soul shows that they lack the faith, courage or fortitude to remain faithful. God recognises they have failed to demonstrate man's greatest spiritual strength which is his enactment of His power of free will to follow the path of truth and light. However, once a soul aligns their own individual will to God's will, as had Piccarda, they may reach a state of bliss and eternal blessedness and this alone may be better than redemption.

We continue our discourse on vows, for I remain perturbed at the idea that even though one may endeavour to maintain them, in forcing their transgression another may cause their ruination. For these pure, blessed women had denied themselves in order to attain the closest proximity to God, such was their love for Him, yet He now denies them. Beatrice reassures me that all those in the celestial Paradise reside with God in His house of angels and that just for the purpose of better understanding the degrees of virtue, ethereal souls are placed upon different spheres to show as much in relation to God.

She seems pleased that I earnestly consider the subject and wishes to expand on the theme for she feels my mind points to the light of truth and whilst I continue to ponder, interjects with further conversation. She is keen to stress that God's most precious gift to man is free will. To make a vow unto God is to present Him with a gift, an oath, a promise; for in doing so, one bequeaths his own free will. God recognises this surrender and treasures it. Therefore, to proffer one's will though a vow and then make light of it by breaking the promise, is to thieve from God that which you have given unto Him. Thus, every endeavour must be made to honour one's vow by maintaining the path of light, righteousness and faith.

She wishes me to understand that the mere act of pronouncing an oath or promise is not enough to erase or exonerate a sin, for there is no redemption in a spoken promise alone. Nor is it enough to proclaim a vow to praise

God. One must follow doctrine, be virtuous, find the path of Truth and remain upon it. For just as easily as a lamb may stray from his shepherd, man can stray from his God. Just as easily as man may abandon his promise, he can abandon his God.

I confess that although I understand her explanation, for in truth she is most eloquent and her reasoning and interpretation is as enlightening as it is convincing, I remain a little uncomfortable that another may intercede and affect one's spiritual destiny. Still, I am reassured that all souls here reside with God in the highest Heaven and it gives me much comfort to know Piccarda takes her rightful place in the home of angels. I look to Beatrice, for I wish to remove any frustration she may feel towards me and, not for the first time does her radiance and beauty intensify, quite taking my breath away. Indeed, her countenance is most altered, for it seems she is at contemplation, gazing into the brightness of the heavens above, reflecting back the Divine light she attracts. In that moment I gaze into her eyes, for they shine as a beacon of hope and suddenly we ascend, bathed in glorious light, soaring as a falcon to the snow tipped mountains, rising to the second star of Paradise.

2ND STAR OF PARADISE
THE HEAVEN OF MERCURY

We reach the heaven of Mercury although, in truth, I find it difficult to see here for the glare of the sun, only two planets away, is most bright and I am quite blinded. As we land, I see the glow of a thousand souls approach, for each radiates a shimmering lustre which reflects in the rays of the sun and, indeed, from us, as Beatrice and I too, are bathed in light. I am unable to make out their faces, for the light gleams too white for me to allow for definition. It is clear they do not take human form, rather they exist as streaks of light, as sunbeams, for it seems they assume every piece of shimmering light which glows throughout all the spheres.

Beatrice tells me we are now at the second sphere of Heaven, the planet Mercury, which houses the righteous ambitious, mercurial souls who coveted human glory and were thus lacking in the virtue of Justice. For although they were righteous upon Earth and chose to follow the path of Truth, their good and kindly acts were tainted by a desire for glory and recognition. Indeed, in loving themselves they denied true love for God, for their prime motivation was to gain personal glory. Thus, they were deficient in their devotion to the Almighty. Beatrice puts it most eloquently when she says that just as Mercury cannot compare to the magnificence of the sun, so does the earthly glory of the souls within pale into insignificance next to the glory of God.

I hear the words *Ecco chi crescerà li nostri amori: Behold someone who will increase our love* and I observe the glowing souls increasing in brightness as each gathers to greet me, for they seem quite overjoyed that I am here. They jostle to acquaint themselves with me and a soul steps forward. In his excitement and joyous state, he is shimmering extra bright. He is breathless and tells me that I am indeed a most fortunate and honoured mortal, for to visit Heaven before I am even dead, to witness the thrones of the eternal triumphant as a living man is a rare privilege. He is mesmerised, for he tells me the light of charity, that which imbues all the heavenly souls upon the spheres, shines within me also. He collects himself and enters into discourse, for he has a hint I may wish to converse and invites me to reveal any issues I ponder upon. Beatrice prompts me to parlay with this gentleman and so I clear my throat.

Naturally I ask his name and the nature of his deficient virtue, for is this not my favourite gambit? He tells me he was Caesar, past Emperor of Rome but is now Justinian for, indeed, in the afterlife all earthly status is foregone, as honours and titles have no effect. He explains the history of Rome from the earliest of days through to the crucifixion, the Redemption and the fall of Jerusalem. He concedes his downfall was a lust for triumph and political dominance. However, his spiritual instructor, Bishop Agapetus, encouraged him to seek the path of Truth and also address the light of the error in his belief that Christ was not a true man but entirely Divine. Having purged himself of this fault, he continued an earthly life proclaiming God and performing wonderous deeds in His name and hence he resides upon the second sphere, the heaven of Mercury.

As with his fellow souls here, noble and virtuous actions were accomplished during earthly life but these were tarnished by ambition, a lust for glory and rapacious desire for good repute. Much like Piccarda who accepts her placement within the Moon as God's will, these souls too rejoice in the blessing placed upon them, for God has considered them worthy of the celestial Paradise. Indeed, they reside here upon the second sphere under the guardianship of the chorus of Archangels, those whom God has tasked with protecting the souls in this celestial orb, bearing tidings of His bounty. The Music of the Spheres plays on, a symphony of melodious nectar and the planet continues to revolve in harmony and balance whilst its souls rejoice in living justice.

With the celestial opus sounding in his ears, Justinian and the other mercurial spirits sing in ecclesiastical praise by crying out *Hosannah!* and twirl off into the distance, dancing in joyous delight. I look to Beatrice such that I wish to further converse on the Redemption but am too overcome by her beauty to engage. She reads my face as a book and relays my perplexity as she suspects it thus: Why did God sacrifice His own son that humankind could attain salvation? Indeed, she has again eloquently described my thoughts, for my dilemma is that surely God could have used alternate means to save humanity and thus deliver us unto redemption? For He had the power to merely forgive the sin of Adam or indeed, he could accept mankind's offerings of penance and atonement.

She explains that such was the magnitude of Adam's sin when he disobeyed God and succumbed to temptation, he damned all men and prevented them from ever atoning sufficiently. Thus, all of humankind was condemned to a path of sin with no route to Heaven. God had to consider a means of salvation, for this would restore mankind's dignity and also reveal His own benevolence and humility.

Therefore, after many generations, in allowing His son to die in crucifixion as both God and man, for Christ is the essence of purity, innocence and light, the debt that mankind had sustained due to Adam's sin was settled. God was gratified, for man's redemption meant He could welcome him back to Heaven once more. Thus, in the act of sacrificing His son and, through Christ, Himself, God had shown the ultimate mercy, for He atoned for mankind's sins and this redress would be of infinite value.

Beatrice has such spiritual understanding and appears at one with the Lord, so she has managed to allay my confusion on this most complex and confounding matter. I exclaim thus but she scoffs and retorts that humankind cannot fully comprehend God and His laws. She further tells me that everything created by God which includes only the angels, the heavenly planets and man, that which derives from Him direct, is eternal, for that conceived by God's intervention holds His goodness and cannot be permanently destroyed. As such, death is not the end, for the natural progression is resurrection and our natural home is the celestial Paradise, which is Heaven above. As a spiritual force, she truly is most impressive.

3RD STAR OF PARADISE
THE HEAVEN OF VENUS

I am not aware of a physical energy that has redirected us from Mercury, but as I look upon Beatrice's face, I see her glow with an abundance of radiance and beauty and know, instinctively, that spiritually I have attained another level. And it is thus, for with the speed of Cupid's arrow, we have ascended to the Morning Star, the heaven of Venus; the third sphere of the celestial Paradise. It is here the souls of the Lovers reside, for in succumbing to the temptations of love through passion and obsession, they were deficient in the virtue of temperance. Now that they are chastened and restrained, their love of God and humanity is invoked. Indeed, such is their delight in being here in Heaven, they rejoice by singing a hymn so mesmerising and dulcet in tone I am quite haunted, such that I almost cannot bear to live without knowing I am to hear it again.

Towards us they come, swirling orbs that birth as sparks in a flame and crescendo into twirling, glowing lights, dancing and singing, for here the loving are in abject bliss.

Indeed, a light stops in front and declares himself so full of love that he is happy to share his pleasure just that I may experience it. Indeed I shall, for I see he glows brighter just at the thought he may please me. He does not introduce himself formally, but from his description of the landscape and timings, I know him to be Charles Martel of Anjou; the young Hungarian prince who was to die of the plague in Naples.

We talk animatedly of his life, which although brief, secured two sons, both of whom would have been kings of Sicily had its unpopular ruler not caused a revolution. He talks of his brother Robert, a greedy man who used mercenaries to accumulate substantial wealth and, from this, conversation progresses to the diversity of men and their natural attributes and how this affects order in society. For, to his mind, it is not just heredity which influences a man's character or his qualities and virtues. Martel's belief is that God directs us all to the path of Truth through providence, for His ultimate goal is the wellbeing and succession of mankind. Without providence there would be chaos, for each man has his own destiny to fulfil, which is to realise his potential and follow the light towards Him, free from obstruction. If there was no sense of predestination, there would be pandemonium and the Creator would be deemed lacking in perfection.

I ask after the angels and stars and he concedes that these do influence earthly man but do not induce him to be different. Man has free will and, as such, if Nature alone directed man, sons would emulate their fathers in every way. Thus, the combination of providence and free will allows mankind every means to achieve his Heavenly purpose. Indeed, such an arrangement permits the creation of a diverse society, for it allows different roles to be fulfilled such that mankind varies in his skills and temperaments. In straying from His path of providence and using free will to direct their own destinies away from the light and truth, they show a disregard to trust God's plan when His only intention is to provide for and protect us.

We are approached by another soul, glowing brightly, signifying that it wishes to converse. I look to Beatrice who nods her approval. The lady is Cunizza da Romano, lover and mistress of the troubadour poet Sordello (whom I met upon the mount) and sister of the oppressor Ezzelino. I exclaim I am surprised she glows so bright given she resides only on the third sphere but she tells me that far from being resentful of her placement here, she has cause to rejoice, for she has surrendered to the light of Venus and directed her love towards God, gratified that He has shown her mercy. I believe her, for her countenance is free and she is indeed united as one, in perfect harmony with God. Her light moves with the Music of the Spheres and she re-joins the dance of the spirits, twirling and laughing.

A third radiance approaches shining brightly and I note it is Foulquet de Marseillae, a poet famed for his amorous liaisons as much as his prose! However, it is not love of which he wishes to discourse, rather the corruption of the Church led by the greed of the clergy who focused more on money and treasure than the scriptures, gospels and ecclesiastical writings. He reserves his greatest criticism for the vainglorious and wanton popes and cardinals, and I am reminded of the large number I encountered within the inferno. I ask how he finds himself to be here, at the heaven of Venus, and he tells me that upon Earth he was a prolific lover, burning with lust and lasciviousness until he repented, took Holy Orders and became a monk. He understood that his early earthly life was misguided, but rejoices that God shows mercy and, in placing him on the third sphere, provides a life free of remorse and recrimination.

The next shining soul to approach is a lady named Rahab. I confess I am most happy to remain and parlay for Venus is as perfection; joyous and blissful and, indeed, we are here for three hours or more. This heaven revolves for there is a blessed mover within from the angelic Intelligencia and, being closer to the Empyrean, it spins faster than the Moon and Mercury. Indeed, the souls here glow bright with radiant brilliance such is the joy and delight within fuelling their energies. In truth, they are so exultant I am compelled to not call them souls, rather darlings or happinesses, for they rejoice in the joint workings of love, justice and mercy and their spirits are exalted. Here, joy is triumphant. It is extreme, intensified, absorbing; exquisite. It is contagious and I am lifted because of it!

My awe for this glorious planet is interrupted as Foulquet gestures to Rahab. He informs me she is the highest ranking of all lights here, for although her life upon Earth occurred before Christ so upon death she was thus sent to Limbo, her soul was the first which ascended to Heaven upon the Harrowing of Hell. I know the story of Rahab from the Book of Joshua and find myself reminded she was a prostitute. This act did not preclude her from Heaven, says Foulquet, for she showed mercy upon two messengers sent by Joshua to spy on the city of Jericho and endangered herself by hiding them then abetting their escape. Thus, in demonstrating virtue and courage, she proved her sympathy and support for Christ, before his existence even, for in securing the Promised Land, the Israelites achieved God's will.

This is a remarkable tale indeed and I am much impressed with the integrity and mettle of the Whore of Jericho, so am delighted to hear she reached ascension upon the triumphant Harrowing of Hell. I move to speak with Beatrice, for I wish her to know that I do not judge Rahab in any way other than with respect and admiration but her eyes are directed towards the Empyrean, beyond the shadows of the Earth below, up into the light, for the next celestial sphere is the heaven of the Sun and we are to journey there. Without effort or, indeed, realization - and in only the time a lightning bolt takes to flash - we are upon that very planet!

4TH STAR OF PARADISE
THE HEAVEN OF THE SUN

Beatrice commands me to express my gratitude to God for He has drawn me unto the Sun, the brightest of all planets. I comply, gladly, for this heaven is God's best creation, His artistic masterpiece. As I look around, below to planets in the Sun's shadow, above to those of the Empyrean, to the stars, the orbiting spheres, to the illuminations; as I listen to the symphonies of the Music of the Spheres and the angelic choir of the Podestà, I am transported to bliss. Indeed, in this precise moment I am ashamed to say my love for Beatrice is obscured by the intensity of that which I feel for God, eclipsing Apollo himself, even. But she does not complain, for in this instant she sees my utter devotion and commitment to God and knows that its degree shall never be surpassed by mortal man.

Residing upon this heavenly, glistening sphere are the souls who, in their earthly lives, displayed positive examples of the cardinal virtue of Prudence. Indeed, the souls here are so wise and judicious they illuminate the spheres on an intellectual level. In truth they are not as the souls of other celestial planets, for their sagacity far exceeds typical humankind. Rather, those of the fourth sphere are saints, theologians and philosophers such that their wisdom lights the way for the remaining virtues.

We have been drifting in bliss and are now at the centre point of the dazzling orb. We are approached by a light glowing so radiant that I have seldom seen beauty like it. Indeed, I confess I am without the words to adequately describe the exquisite and magnificent loveliness this glow emits but fear I must, for Beatrice has tasked me with such a duty. He stops in front of me and declares in song that as I radiate with Godly light, whomever does not satisfy any desire of mine should thus be punished!

He flatters me for I am not aware that I am of any particular brightness but, within moments, we are besieged by a further eleven souls who surround us as a halo, performing a dance of light as they circle around us three times in succession. I am overcome, for all are as beautiful as he; charming, radiant, enchanting and their song is as church bells; dulcet, heavenly, celestial. Again, I am transported to bliss and am quite without the linguistic skills to effectively express the sights and sounds presented to me here.

As the dancing circle of light stops, the soul stands level with me. He introduces himself as Saint Thomas Aquinas and gestures to each of the lights in the crown, for they glow as jewels decorating a coronet as they surround us. Amongst them are Peter Lombard, the scholastic theologian who donated his substantial wealth to the Church, King Solomon, St Francis of Assisi and St Dominic, both of whom founded new orders of spiritual fraternity. Indeed, St Thomas Aquinas was a Dominican friar himself as well as a prominent theologian and philosopher. Albeit King Solomon of the bible was not recognised as a scholar, he was famed for his noble mind, bestowed with so profound a wisdom, his brilliance almost outshone that of the sun.

St Thomas is keen to relay the tale of St Francis and his wife, Lady Poverty. I know him to tease for Francis took a vow of poverty and lived a holy life, denying himself that the needy may benefit. He willingly fed himself at the teat of hardship but in taking poverty as his bride, made the declaration that there was beauty to be found in suffering. Indeed, he was to convince many to join him in his endeavours of deprivation and thus the Franciscan monks were founded. So virtuous was he considered, that he received two ecclesiastical honours; one from the Pope and one from Christ. The first, a canonising papal bull and the second, the wounds of stigmata to his palms.

We are joined by another dozen lights who encircle the original twelve, so we are now of two constellations of 24 illuminous, radiant lights, glistening and shining as golden halos. As before, they revolve around us three times, each in opposite directions as a double rainbow, rejoicing, for they sing melodiously of the Trinity and Incarnation. It is an exquisite sight and I am reminded this is indeed the heaven of the wise for, unified, the wisdom and sagacity of these thinkers quite eclipses the iridescent light of Apollo and his fiery planet.

One of the new twelve steps out of the ring to introduce himself to me. He is St Bonaventur, the Franciscan mystic, and wishes to relay the story of St Dominic, one of the lights in his group. I confess I am unfamiliar with his tale although I know him to be the founder of the Dominican Order, so welcome a chance to learn more. St Bonaventur tells me Dominic was a brilliant student of law and medicine but decided to eschew these studies to become a scholar of theology. Indeed, he considered the pursuit of careers such as business, law and politics to be ungodly, such that they only serve to secure power and wealth. He thus chose the Lady Faith as a wife, zealously fighting for truth, a soldier of God, a warrior for the Church. Thus, armed with this new way of religious thinking, tended to God's flock as a gardener, for he compared mankind to a tree in the orchard who, with the right cultivating by way of learning and espousing, would bear fruit and become better lovers of God. As such, he pruned and weeded out the troubles and pains of the Church. It is told that upon his death, God threw down a golden ladder on which to draw him up to the heavens, so pleased was He with Dominic's ecclesiastical contribution. It is clear to me then, that both these saints and founders of the fraternities are heavenly creatures of seraphic proportions, what with their passionate predisposition to do God's work promoting the path of light and truth and guarding the throne of God with zeal and passion.

I ask why King Solomon of the Bible shares a sphere with the learned scholars and theologians for he was neither. St Thomas tells me that in asking God for wisdom to allow him to intelligently govern his people, to exchange his worldly riches that he could better discern between right and wrong, he showed excellent judgement and is here for his regal wisdom rather than for any scientific or philosophical merits. He became a paragon of sagacity and his prevailing message was to warn others not to judge hastily but to consider, show caution and be diligent about decision making.

I confess I am confused, for I know that Adam and Christ were created directly by God, infused with His light and knowledge so am at a loss to understand how Solomon could possess more wisdom than they, for it is said Solomon is the brightest light in the smallest circle. St Thomas nods in appreciation of my question and explains thus: that he did not say Solomon was the wisest *person* that ever lived, nor the wisest person in all ways, merely that he was the wisest King. For when negotiating with God he could have requested significantly more than just wisdom, yet wished to govern fairly and judiciously. In as much, his wisdom was not absolute, nor infinite or perfect and this is because he was not created directly by God, as were Jesus and Adam,

227

who were considered exceptional examples of humankind.

I ask St Thomas if he believes, as I, that in making a decision, man is inclined to uphold it, despite any misgivings, and to whatever cost. He says that man should exert wisdom in decisions and judgement but if he cannot, then ultimate truth and rectitude should be upheld rather than the desire to appear right. These are words most sage and I will carry them with me upon my return to Earth. I am much reminded of my friend Virgil in this place and am certain that had he lived to know Christ, he too would reside upon this heavenly realm. There is harmony and reconciliation on this planet of the Sun, for in accepting limitations, casting aside their riches and earthly matters to embrace a stricter life, the souls here emit a gay abandon, a sense of joyful liberation and, as I have said before, their light is contagious.

I have a question but Beatrice pre-empts it and gestures to Solomon, for she decrees that he is the best soul herein the sphere to answer it. My query relates to the radiant light the souls upon the Sun emit and how its intensity may be affected upon the day of the Last Judgement for, at the point of resurrection, a faithful soul will be reunited with his physical body. Shall the brilliant light within be preserved, will it shine brighter or will it be depleted when the blessed reclaim their flesh? For the reality is they already shine so bright, glistening with iridescent radiance, it is hard to conceive they may burn brighter still, for one cannot imagine how the eyes of the faithful may bear it.

The light of Solomon moves forward and he speaks in a voice so ethereal and melodious that it is as magic, as the Archangel Gabriel when he conversed with Mary at the Annunciation, for I am certain he has conjured these dulcet tones from God's messenger himself. He answers thus: that immediately man dies, he submits to a heavenly judgement and, according to the state of his soul, is cast to Hell or Purgatory. For the blessed and the faithful, their spiritual glow is eternal, for they radiate the glory and magnificence of God to the degree of the love for Him that burns within. Upon resurrection and reunion with the flesh upon the day of the Last Judgement, such radiance is enhanced as they reach closer to Heaven, and not only will the blessed and faithful endure it, they shall rejoice and delight in it.

He talks of love and glory, vision and grace, for all affect a blessed soul's radiance. The intensity of love within a saint's heart is determined by the level of grace God has blessed him with at the point of death which, in turn, influences the strength of his glory and therefore vision of Him. Thus, grace primes for vision, vision blooms into love and love directs to the path of light. I know that upon the Final Judgement a resurrected soul is reunited with his flesh. Solomon confirms the union with its body will not obstruct the path to glory, rather it will intensify it. For man will be complete, thus all aspects will be enhanced - love, grace and glory - for God will recognise perfection and love us more for it. Indeed, the flesh of the faithful will be imbued with the light of Heaven. Around us we hear cries of *Amen!* for the souls of the Prudent rejoice at the thought of reunion with their resurrected bodies. Immediately, there is animated talk of loved ones so they rejoice, not just for themselves, but all those who were cherished by them.

A third group of souls moves to join us, gleaming brightly, radiating joy and the glory of God they feel within. They form a third circle, surrounding the two already in place and thus, a trinity of golden rings is formed. I look to Beatrice who herself radiates beauty and happiness, for her smile is beguiling and I am entranced. As I gaze into her sparkling eyes the purity of my love for her intensifies and we are lifted, raised up, soaring to the next sphere, a burning orb of red. For we ascend to the heaven of Mars, the home of holy warriors who, in sacrificing their lives for God, demonstrated the virtue of fortitude.

5TH STAR OF PARADISE
THE HEAVEN OF MARS

I am transfixed, for immediately we arrive I am presented with a sign from God. I spot two thick bands of gleaming light formed into a cross, for I humbly observe Christ at his crucifixion. Upon closer inspection I see not Jesus upon the glowing white bars, but thousands of souls, alight, dashing up and down, left and right with cheery, energetic vim, causing it to glisten and glimmer as ten thousand rubies. At the same moment a melodious tune echoes in the sphere, and the souls upon the cross rejoice in a hymn of praise accompanied by the angelic chorus of the Virtues. I have only just gazed upon the grace that is Beatrice, but even her beauty is eclipsed by the harmonious symphony I hear in this heaven such that I am again lost for words, for I am bewitched, enamoured, entranced by the sweet notes of this celestial composition. Within the hymn, I hear the words *Et ortum livorem superem: Rise and conquer*, for indeed the warriors within this sphere, nay the crusaders, prevailed over sin through acts of moral courage as they battled for God and

His supreme Church, surrendering their lives for the love of Him in the slaughterhouse of the Holy Wars.

Beatrice tells me there is nothing more sweet for these warrior saints than the reward of the glory of God who radiates through them and the giant cross whereupon they receive redemption. For these souls are indeed heroes of the faith, devoted to God and the Church and battling in His name whilst proudly wearing the robes of the martyr, adorned with the red cross of the military saint of the Third Crusade; St George. They died for the cross in their earthly lives and here in Paradise, they live upon it, basking in the light that is God's love and, for these Knights Templar, there is no greater honour.

The warrior souls upon the cross are singing in harmonious verse and I am compelled to look again to my beloved Beatrice. I find myself quite stunned by her beauty; more radiant, hypnotic and pure such that I believe myself to have already reached the Empyrean. It is clear to me she grows more graceful, more beautiful and majestic with each moment upon this celestial plane and that as we ascend through Paradise, so her magnificence and radiance increases. My admiring gaze is interrupted, for a spirit dashes down along the cross, as a shooting star, and cries out 'O blood of mine!' I suspect he is an ancestor but in his exuberance, he discourses in a dialect that a mere mortal such as I is unable to decipher. Seeing my confusion, he abruptly stops and continues in a language such that I may better understand him, all the while, glowing brightly. He praises God, for I am bestowed with great privilege such that He allows me to visit Paradise, and he hails Beatrice for fulfilling His providence by granting me wings such that I may more easily ascend through the celestial spheres.

I remain silent, for in my mind I know that souls here may interpret thoughts and he is primed to respond. He tells me he is my root; the spirit of my great grandfather, Cacciaguida, the holy warrior whose ardour in serving Emperor Conrad during the Crusades was rewarded with a knighthood. His death came at the hands of the Saracens during the second crusade but it was valiant, glorious and triumphant and his martyrdom was recognised by God, such that he was placed upon the celestial Paradise to live in eternal peace. I confess that finding myself in such ecclesiastical heights, in these upper realms of Heaven, in the presence of kin of such spiritual and military standing induces much gratification and delight. I feel pride too, but shall call it honour in an effort not to chastise Beatrice into thinking me arrogant, although she does not rebuke me for it, rather she enjoys that I glory in Cacciaguida's success.

We engage in easy conversation and he talks of Florence new and old, reminiscing about the halcyon years of peace and tranquillity, free of improper lust and general deviance, when families were happy and marriages were celebrated. He mourns the demise of his beloved city for, today, chastity and virtue have been supplanted by corruption, decay and avarice, whoring and lechery, such that I am now witness to during my lifetime.

Since Cacciaguida has already mentioned God's providence, I ask if he knows of my destiny, the path that God has directed for me, for I am interested to know if I shall experience joy or misfortune on my return to earthly life. Indeed, he says he is able to state it with much accuracy although warns that the news will be bittersweet for me. To my mind, the only confirmation I seek is that upon Judgement Day I will join Beatrice within the Empyrean. But, as Farinata back at Hell's fiery tombs of the Heretics, he tells me I am to be exiled from Florence and experience all the harshness of penury because of it! For I shall be destitute and impoverished, relying only on the benevolence of strangers. In truth I cannot imagine one reason for banishment from my precious homestead, but Cacciaguida states it is recognised as unjust and unwarranted and will occur after the Black Guelphs, those in support of the Papacy, take control of Florence from my beloved Whites.

I am in utter despair upon hearing news of this tragedy,

for I know not where I shall go or what I shall do! Cacciaguida reminds me that I have an important task to complete, that set by Beatrice, and such a time should be used wisely to accomplish it, for it shall bring unto me the sweetness of attainment and contentment. For, he reminds me, I am to fulfil a poetic mission to record all that I have witnessed and experienced during my time in the three realms of the afterlife, to produce an epic vision of the Divine, such that earthly souls may better understand that to remain on the path of Truth will deliver them to salvation. Indeed, to stray from it will condemn them to damnation and eternal separation from God within the sewer of the inferno. It is thus, then. That I am tasked with saving mankind from spiritual destruction.

Cacciaguida sees that my mind is in disarray and comforts me as a father. He tells me that although I will undergo suffering and deprivation, exile may bring forth liberation and self-awareness for, through reflection, I may come to better understand myself. Indeed, I may act as a pen wielding crusader, for what is fortitude if not the courage to make declarations against injustice and wrong-doings? And, he reminds me, I am obliged to speak the truth of what I have witnessed within the funnel, the mountain and these orbiting spheres, for this is my spiritual calling. He tells me I am to consider my journey through the afterlife as a personal pilgrimage and one in which I will find my true voice, for if I speak boldly through my writings, thus will I fulfil my obligations to Beatrice. Indeed, he says, in knowing that I am called by God to speak the truth, I shall know mercy even in the depths of my despair and dislocation.

There is a disorder and confusion to my mind, albeit I am less anxious than before, for Cacciaguida has been able to placate me somewhat that despite the hardship and suffering I am set to endure upon my return to earthly life, I shall attain salvation and enjoy eternal bliss with my beloved in the kingdom of Heaven. In this moment, Beatrice, who knows me so well, takes my arm, for she wishes to console me. She reminds that God heals every unjust hurt, that He lightens every unjust darkness. I know she means to bolster me, to reassure me that God is with me, but I confess my mind whirls as a spinning top when I consider my earthly fate, yet I am grateful that she tries to distract me from this tumultuous news I am pondering. I gaze into her eyes from whence all love and light and radiance is emitted and I am spellbound. She offers solace and hope, and my troubles vanish into the celestial atmosphere. She chastises me gently for staring so, and points to Cacciaguida as he has not quite ended his speech about the spirits hereupon the fifth sphere, and I must focus a little longer.

He too, reads me as a book and knows therefore I am uneasy about the enormity of the task placed upon me, for I alone am one man and although *a* son of God, not *the* son of God. I confess to overflowing with doubt and misgiving, for how may I persuade mankind, convince mankind to revert to the path of righteousness in order that he may attain salvation? The sights I have seen upon this celestial Paradise, the melodies I have heard, the orbiting lights and stars I have borne witness to are so ethereal, too beautiful, I agonise that I do not possess adequate language to do them justice. For mortal words alone are not sufficient to convince earthly souls of the iridescence and splendour that abounds herein the celestial realms. In truth, I fear it is the same of the realm at the inferno, for the torture, depravity and unbearable brutality of suffering is an obscene horror I know I may never accurately convey, such that my earthly linguistic skills are woefully deficient. Indeed, the words colossus, titan and gargantuan are no accurate reflection of the sheer size and scale, the magnitude and magnificence of the volcano that is the Mountain of Purgatory and already I am despairing at my depressingly paltry, feeble, nay trifling linguistic inadequacies.

Cacciaguida gestures to the cross whereupon the spirits of the saints reside and as he calls their names, they light up and twirl and dance their way to the base, just as shooting stars, that they may converse with us. He tells me these spirits are epic heroes; warriors and champions of such great renown that any mention of them and their gallant feats would enrich my prose and elevate it. Indeed, here are William of Orange, the medieval warrior, the Duke of Bouillon, hero of the First Crusade and first Christian king of Jerusalem, also Robert Guisard, a prominent Norman warrior. I am most obliged to him, for already forming in my mind are rich themes of sacrifice, holy wars, martyrdom and triumph. The saintly spirits on the cross begin to sing and glow brighter with each canto. Cacciaguida moves towards them disappearing within the lights and he is gone. I look to Beatrice and already she radiates with a purity, light and beauty unsurpassed on any heaven here. I know this to be the sign that we are to ascend for the sixth sphere is above us, that of the heaven of Jupiter.

6TH STAR OF PARADISE
THE HEAVEN OF JUPITER

We travel up and away from the blood red planet of Mars
to the silvery white celestial star where gather spirits of the
Just, those showing fairness and composure, the souls who
valued and practiced the virtue of Justice. Indeed, they are
as balletic dancers, for I am not fully arrived and already I
see their lights twirling and diving, as a flock of swallows in
the sky, using their glowing bodies to form letters in the air.
No sooner has one letter been shaped the souls fly off,
sparking as a stoked fire, then immediately return to fashion
another. In truth, such is their speed I cannot keep up with
the sequence of letters and thus invoke a Muse, the diva
Pegasea, for she is the inspiration for verse and can help me
construct order from this chaotic alphabet that I may know
its message.

She watches momentarily and informs me the words
articulate the Call to Justice - *Diligite iustitiam qui iudicatis
terram: Cherish justice, you who judge the earth*, that sage and wise
verse spoken by King Solomon himself. Immediately the

last letter is formed, thousands more spirits descend and the dance of light begins in earnest, for in the air, as a fading fire reborn with the bellows, the glowing souls of five thousand spirits shape the letter into an eagle's head. Moments later, the five thousand lights become ten and the eagle's head is contorted until the complete bird emerges in front of me. The Eagle of Justice.

I do not need the wisdom of a scholar to know that God is with me now, for He has shown me that justice appears in the Heavens such that he has presented me with the emblem of that greatest of virtues. I am moved to tears, rejoicing in this wonder and thank God for His blessing and ask that justice be served upon Earth. For I know, too, that the eagle symbolises the imperial power of Rome but I do not wish to contemplate further on it such that corruption and greed, indulgence and pretence reside upon Earth because of it. I pray to God that justice may prevail and that when I return, it is a kinder, better, more moral and just place.

Oh, that I was blessed with the language of the Muses, of the celestial stars, of the Gods of the Heavens, for what I must relate has never before been written or spoken in the words of mortal man! Nor is it possible to conceive in one's imagination, for it is quite beyond description. For the lights of the souls within the eagle's head transform to flowers and, as they blossom, a beak is formed and it opens, for the eagle speaks! The Eagle of Justice speaks unto me upon this sixth sphere, the Heaven of the Just, and as he does, the exquisite scent of every flower of the heavens is released. He commands me to abandon my despair, for justice is not denied upon Earth, merely hidden, like a shipwreck relinquishing at the sea bed. For, upon Judgement Day, the sins of the unjust rulers upon the earth shall be revealed, for this is God's will; His Divine justice. It is not therefore for me, mortal man, to criticise God and the apparent unjust nature of His plan. It is for me to trust in Him, to have faith that He will ensure that Divine justice prevails.

I am much relieved but, confess, a little ashamed that I am rebuked so. For I have a question for the eagle and in truth it regards a matter that has irked me since the very beginning of my pilgrimage, for it concerns my brother and guide, Virgil. For just as we talk of Divine justice, so must I question unjust damnation. For what else can I call it that Virgil, this paragon of virtue and wisdom, of serenity and steadfastness is estranged from God, denied salvation to spend eternity in Hell, in the oblivion that is Limbo, for it is of that vile place. For there are many virtuous pagans, those who, only by the timing of their births or geography of their birthplace were unaware of Christ or denied knowledge of him and his teachings so are thus denounced as unbelievers. For if God is truly just, surely a virtuous soul, irrespective of these disadvantages should not be condemned, damned to spend eternity furthest from His love and light because they were denied the knowledge of Christ that leads to salvation? Is there not one in good grace with God, that may intercede on their behalf?

Suddenly, the eagle quivers. Its entire being is shaking and it claps its wings in a display of will, beauty and glory. It speaks again but this time with two voices; those of the Just rulers which is judiciousness and wisdom and those of the angelic chorus of the Dominations, which is sweetness and honey. For this is the voice of Justice. It booms a declaration that no one entered Heaven who did not believe in Christ, for virtue alone does not elevate human reasoning to the pinnacles of the Divine viewpoint. He reminds me that Virgil, full of human reason but lacking the benefits of Divine revelation, was not considered spiritually worthy enough to guide me through the spheres of the celestial Paradise. For it is through the theological virtues of faith, hope and love that mankind will be exalted to the heavens. Indeed, if human knowledge were to be recognised as Divine truth, this would be considered wanton idolatry. Faith alone will elevate man to the heavens and this is why Beatrice leads me unto the kingdom of Paradise, not Virgil, for she is nothing if not faith, love, truth and light.

The eagle ceases his address that I may contemplate and reflect upon his words. In that moment, the souls within his image raise their voices in heavenly song, for they rejoice and delight as ten thousand stars lighting the sky at the sun's rest. Within a moment, the song is over and replaced with a hum that rises as a crescendo within the throat of the imperial bird, for he speaks again. I am commanded with a thunderous roar to look upon his all-seeing eye, specifically the pupil and crease above, whereupon sit the six premier souls within this sphere. Placed directly within its pupil is King David, the brightest soul here, author of the Psalms and a biblical king, who radiates with light, purity and judiciousness.

Within the crease sit five others including, unbelievably, Trajan and Ripheus, both of whom are known by me to be pagans! I am indeed flummoxed that nonbeliever souls such as these have secured a treasured spot amidst the spiritually faithful in the Heavens when my precious Virgil has been denied. The eagle has spotted my confusion - in truth I am incredulous - and explains that these two souls died as Christians for they were saved by Divine intervention, such was God's will. Trajan, cast to Hell upon his death was brought back to life through the fervent prayers of Pope Gregory such was his justness perceived in life. Upon his brief resurrection, his baptism was secured and thus his conversion to Christianity recognised, such that at the moment of his second death, he was declared a true follower of the faith and drawn up to the celestial heavens.

Ripheus, deemed the most just of all Trojans, born before the coming of Christ and therefore ignorant of his existence and teachings, could not be of faith. For reasons no man may fathom, God bestowed upon him a prophecy, a vision of Christ, the future saviour of Christianity and he was persuaded to convert, even undertaking a baptism (indeed the trio of Theological Virtues descended from Heaven above to perform the ceremony), all before the birth of the saviour, and his path to Heaven was secured. Thus, explains the eagle, the providence and mercy of God will always triumph, such that His Divine will is not reliant upon the opinion or criticism of mankind.

I find the unpredictability of God's providence mightily confusing and somewhat frustrating. I concede, nonetheless, that in allowing for free will, man is forced to take responsibility and accountability for his actions. Without knowing the exact nature of God's plans, the incompleteness of our knowledge allows us to strive to be virtuous, to show our love of Him by invoking the theological virtues of faith, hope and love in the hope God shows us mercy on the day of the Last Judgement and draws us too, flesh and soul, unto the spheres of Heaven. I shall pray it is thus for Virgil.

I am fortunate that I have around me shades and celestial beings who hold such insight that they may inform and enlighten me, for some matters are too complex for mortal man alone to reason. I look to Beatrice for she is loveliness, grace and beauty but am perplexed that she does not return my smile. She speaks to me in earnest and reminds me that upon each ascension through the heavens, her beauty burns brighter and with more intent for she reflects the brilliance of God's love, such that my mortal senses are incapable of tolerating her growing luminosity. If she were not to moderate it, the radiance of her smile would ignite a fire and I would burn to ash as Semele when she aimed her adulterous gaze upon Zeus. So, it is thus and in an instant we are in the seventh celestial sphere, the mesmerising heaven of Saturn.

7TH STAR OF PARADISE
THE HEAVEN OF SATURN

It is of crystal and we are within, deep inside, dazzled by the sun's rays that reflect off the surface as gold, albeit the Music of the Spheres is strangely absent here. Housed within are souls of the Contemplative, for they exemplify the virtue of temperance such that they devoted their lives to the reading of the scriptures and prayer. I gaze into Beatrice's eyes, for the sight here is one of brilliance, of glistening jewels and treasure and I confess I can barely tolerate such sweetness. As with the griffin at the River Lethe, her eyes reflect what I did not see for myself. They reveal an extraordinary image such that I am compelled to swing round to see if it is real and, indeed, sited within the depths of the planet is a golden ladder, a celestial staircase leading upwards to the heavenly heights. As with the mountain of Purgatory, I am unable to locate its summit, for it extends beyond my mortal vision but I suspect it leads to the Empyrean. Yet I am intrigued and, as with the great rock, wonder if I am expected to climb it.

I see the ladder glistening, sparkling, glowing and marvel as I realise that upon it are thousands of spirits; radiant souls of the Temperate who dart about, glimmering brightly, running up and down, back and forth, across the rungs in assembly, as a murmuration of starlings flitting and swooping in the sky. One breaks away and races to the bottom rung, glowing brightly, radiating brilliance such that his light takes over my thoughts and I cry out in delight for the love that he sends my way. He stops such that he believes I wish to discourse with him and indeed, I do. For I wish to know why there is silence upon this magical seventh heaven when all others bask in the glory of the Music of the Spheres and why he, specifically, has stopped to speak with me.

He speaks of the symphony of the spheres, for upon Saturn it plays too sweet, song is sung too glorious, with a tone too exquisite and melodious such that mortal man may not tolerate its perfect beauty as it would inflict damage to his delicate ear. He talks of Beatrice for her lack of smile belies the same mystery; that mortal man may not tolerate increasing perfection as he ascends through the spheres so he is protected by experiencing the glory, the light and love of the higher spheres in moderation.

Moving straight to my second question he agrees that he was compelled to stop and converse with me, but not for any personal inclination to do so. I must look confused, or wounded, for he clarifies that his spirit is directed by God's will and he thus obliged merely for God's governance instructed him to reposition himself upon the golden ladder such that he might enter into discourse and answer my questions. I press him, for I feel God must have sensed something within him specifically to preordain our meeting, for this is God's providence at work, surely? Immediately, he begins to spin, twirling and whirling at speed, burning brightly and radiating light and joy. He tells me that God has graced me with His blessings and I do not need to know why, for only God knows His own mind. For not even a

242

favoured angel nor the most enlightened soul within the heavenly spheres may know God's law and it is not for me to demand it. He suggests this would be a suitable message for earthly man and I am to convey it to him upon my return.

At the sound of his voice and the bright glow of light that his spinning radiates, the other brilliances from the celestial ladder hurtle down and form a dazzling spectacle of light at the base. Finally, he introduces himself as St Peter Damiano and talks briefly of the corruption of the Church and the moral wickedness of the clerics within. I concur, for as I have said before, the Church has a canker growing, although I am much reassured that the prelates will meet their justice upon Judgement Day, as God's will dictates.

St Peter mourns the demise of morality at his own monastery and mentions the greed and excesses there, such that whilst the prelates ate as gluttons at a feast, only he and St Paul moderated their intake. As he speaks his last word the souls nearby cry out in support, in joyous delight and agreement. Their voices combined, as nectar and honey but so thunderously loud I have never heard the like upon Earth, causes such intense wonderment upon my senses that I am quite overcome and feel myself falling into another faint.

Beatrice arouses me with words of comfort, as a mother to her troubled infant, and I confess I am much in need of them, for that celestial roar has quite terrified me such that never before have my ears known such tumultuous volume. To compound my terror, I could not even understand the meaning of their words for, to my mind, they may have been accusatory against me, for they were most passionately executed. She bids me gaze again upon the souls within this sphere who, she reminds me, shine brightly, radiating only in the glory and light of God, for this is Heaven where all is sacred. The cries I heard, she says, were nothing more than a zealous prayer for vengeance against those clergy responsible for the corruption of the Church, of whom St

Peter spoke. Indeed, she tells me those prayers shall be answered during my lifetime.

A crowd gathers, as a hundred little suns, and she pushes me forward that I may converse. I confess to shyness but a glistening spirit moves forward and tells me not to be afraid, that if I was aware of the love in their hearts for me I would gladly offer my question. He is St Benedict of the first religious fraternity in Europe, named after him, one who openly despairs at the moral decaying of monastic life. Indeed, he motions to the golden ladder with sadness for he says what I see are the glowing lights of the Contemplatives as they ascend, for they seek to attain a true knowledge of God. Since the prelates have ruined the modern church with their corruption, avarice and degeneracy, earthly man has lost his desire to pursue and improve his knowledge of God and, thereto, the inclination to climb the celestial stairway to Heaven to attain meditative glory. In part, he concedes, mortal man is not worthy of stepping onto the lowest of rungs even, whereas Jacob, patriarch of the Bible, could see to the very top whereto the celestial angels gather.

Much invigorated by his kind discourse, for he has given me confidence such that I feel I open as a rose to the golden rays of the summer sun, I ask that I may see his human face, for I wish to know him in the flesh rather than as a light, radiant as it may be. He gently rebukes me and declines although, most tantalisingly, he says that upon my arrival at the final heavenly sphere, my wish shall be granted. This is immense indeed, for St Benedict suggests to me that his soul shall be reunited with his body and that it is to take place in the Empyrean itself, although he does not say if it is upon today's travels or Earth's last day of reckoning. He sends himself into raptures at the very mention of the *Regnum Caelorum*, the Kingdom of Heaven, and, with that, erupts into an iridescent radiance and disappears up the golden ladder followed by the glowing souls of the Contemplatives. I find myself clinging to Beatrice for, in a burst of radiant light, we follow him up the celestial stairwell and make an unnaturally speedy ascent to the eighth sphere of Heaven, that of the Fixed Stars, the twelve Zodiac constellations where we arrive at the realm of Gemini, the arrangement under which I was born one May day 34 years ago.

8TH STAR OF PARADISE
THE FIXED STARS OF THE ZODIAC

We are within the core of this celestial heaven, where five thousand lights glisten in triumphant glory of the righteous faithful. For here reside the heavenly choir of angels who rise in a chorus of beatific exultation, for they sing the anthem of the holy queen of the Empyrean, she who is the Virgin Mary. Beatrice tells me to sharpen my vision, which I confess seems remarkably clear in this sphere, for I am to gaze down upon the seven planets we leave behind as she wishes me to acknowledge the magnificence of the world she has presented to me in this celestial Paradise.

I am reminded of the stark warning given to me at the Gates of Purgatory before my ascent up the seven terraces; *qui respicit exterius redit: he that looks back returns outside* for I have no wish to jeopardise my ascent to the Empyrean which, I sense, is tantalisingly close. My beloved knows I hesitate such that she issues a contrary instruction but she says there is no danger in Paradise, for here there is only love and bliss. She tells me that I should look back upon the planets as a purification ritual; a shedding of all that is evil in my world. I may therefore consider the celestial heavens to be obstacles over which I have triumphed and when I look down in contemplation, (for my journey soon comes to an end), my heart shall be full and joyous and I may be judged worthy of entering the kingdom of Heaven. I breathe deeply and do as instructed, for I am not Orpheus and she is not Hades thus a backward glance will not condemn me to eternal separation from my beloved.

It is an exceptionally long way down and my eyes make a dizzying descent through the heavenly spheres whereupon I spy Earth at the cavernous depths. It looks small, depleted and insignificant in comparison with the splendour and majesty of the celestial orbs but Beatrice says this is only to demonstrate that Earth's hardships in relation to the glory of Heaven are not as insurmountable as I may feel. She is all that is wisdom, purity and light and I find myself once more transfixed by her radiance as I gaze into her eyes, knowing that she prepares me for my final destination, that which has been the purpose of my ecclesiastical pilgrimage.

She looks up and I follow her eyes to the heavenly heights eager to know what stirs her interest. She stares east into the distance so I suspect it is the dawn sun she seeks and indeed she lingers, as a mother bird awaiting the sunrise that she may hunt for worms for her precious fledglings. But already there is light; bright and resplendent. This increases to a dazzling radiance, for she tells me I am to witness another procession, the Light of the Saints of the Church Triumphant, for these beatific souls, cleansed of all sin, embracing the theological and cardinal virtues of Heaven, exemplify the total perfection of humanity. Basking in the stunning luminescence of the souls he has redeemed, yet surpassing all with his glittering, iridescent lustre, for in truth he shines brighter than the Sun of the heavens, she says it is Christ himself, the glory of God.

Her face, shimmering and holding more beauty than I have ever seen in that place before, exudes joy such that no mortal words may adequately convey. I could eulogise thus: that not the moon nor ten million twinkling stars in that moonlit sky could compare, but this language is insufficient, shamefully inadequate, for her beauty radiates to a degree such that I may not look directly into her eyes. Instead I look to the light of the Church Triumphant. I am blinded by the effulgence, for it is as the blazing sun in this celestial sphere of the Fixed Stars yet I cannot resist the light. It is the most exceptional sight my eyes have ever beheld and I am overcome with emotion, love, awe and, indeed, faith. Beatrice tells me again I see Jesus, the irresistible power created by God, whose sacrifice unlocked the gates of Heaven for earthly man which, since Adam's sin, had been firmly locked.

I am momentarily blinded by his brightness, for my eyes are quite incapable of tolerating the glare of his glory and in this moment I know not if I am of the living or dead; if my body and spirit are as one or if they have parted. She invites me to look upon her once more, for now that I have seen Christ in his glory I may endure the magnificence of her smile. I turn to her, brightness personified, face lit by love, eyes radiating joy such that again, earthly words do not suffice description although I find the realms of her perfection etched within my memory. Praise be that I find I may at last endure the gleam of her smile, for I have quite missed it.

I return my eyes to the pageant which is now a meadow of ten thousand flowers, the glistening souls of the redeemed Virtuous basking in its ethereal beauty. But above, sitting high in the heavens is a rose, a living star, for it is our blessed mother, Mary, and she is enveloped within a glowing halo. I see now the lights in the halo are the souls of Christ's troops and they sing in rapturous exultation as they revolve around her, the most dulcet of melodies, the most exquisite of sounds, as crystals tinkling in the breeze such that no other tune may compare, outshining the symphonic Music of the Spheres even. Their words promise they shall glisten and spin, rejoicing and rotating around Mary until she has risen again, ascended to the heavenly heights whereupon Divine perfection shall be attained. To the right of her are four shining lights whom Beatrice tells me are the three Apostles, who radiate light in rapture of the Virgin and, with them, stands Adam.

In the precise moment the dazzling souls within the revolving garland triumphantly cry *Mary!* in loud and glorious unison, her ascension begins, as she follows Christ to the ninth heaven. This is the uppermost sphere, but I am in despair, for she disappears into the glorious realm that is the Primum Mobile without me! I am left thus, watching the virtuous souls of Christ's army, led by the angelic love of Gabriel of the Annunciation as they cry *Regina Coeli!* in adoration and desire; their hands stretched upwards in reverence of the Queen of Heaven and her son. For they have risen.

Beatrice entreaties the many souls herein, the thousands of lights still assembled at the point of Gemini, for she wishes me to partake in their rejoicing such that I may delight in the privilege of tasting a slice of Heaven; the supper of Christ. At this, they spin and conjoin, creating spheres of holy redemption, arms flailing so they resemble golden comets swirling through a midnight sky. She addresses those chosen by Jesus, the Apostles, who stand in the distance and one steps forward, spinning and dancing around Beatrice in three complete circles, as the Trinity. He sings in such dulcet, intoxicating tones as he twirls around her that I am quite transfixed. Beatrice tells me this is St Peter, holder of the keys to the gates of Heaven, triumphant in the upper celestial spheres. Gesturing at me, Beatrice asks him to test me on one of the theological virtues that I may travel upwards into the heavenly realm.

So, I am to be examined. Do I need to satisfy St Peter I have sufficient knowledge of God that I may attain meditative glory? It appears so. Indeed, he asks of me 'What is Faith?'. I am anxious to persuade and feel compelled to exude academic reasoning, to assume scholastic tone, for I fear I have only one chance to impress upon him a coherent argument on this simple, yet complex question. To my mind one cannot talk of faith without examining logic, for the fundamental essence of faith is that man believes in the existence of God in the absence of such logic, without evidence. Indeed, in the total absence of proof. Faith allows mortal man to partake in the mystique of Heaven, for although he may not witness the splendour of it in actuality, by studying the Bible he may believe the miracles presented within as evidence of the existence of that place. Therefore, to have faith is to unlock the doorway to Heaven.

St Peter, clasping the gold and silver keys in his hand, ponders upon my words. He praises me on the quality of my response and thus affirms my faith. He blesses me by dancing and whirling around me, singing with the angelic chorus of the Cherubim who erupt into a celebratory song of *Te deum laudamus: Thee, O God, we praise*. I am overcome at this beatitude and, in this moment, wonder if my prose relating to this epic journey through the afterlife, to be completed upon my return to Earth, will bring me such honour as St Peter, that I shall return to my beloved Florence. For, in truth, it is the place where my journey to God began and I yearn to be received there again as a lamb returning to his flock, to be crowned with the laurel leaf as my precious Virgil.

I am distracted from my thoughts, for I notice a bright light approaching. It makes for St Peter and they are reunited, as a dove with his mate, calling and cooing in delight. Beatrice tells me this is the martyr saint, the teacher of the gospels in Spain so I know him to be St James. He is to examine me on the theological virtue of Hope albeit he suspects I already have much awareness, for he acknowledges I am blessed that God has allowed me to journey through the celestial spheres ahead of my time that I may instil hope in earthly man. He requests of me that I answer on what Hope is, whether I am in possession of it and from where I think it comes.

Beatrice steps forward and proclaims I have no need to answer the second question, for it is clear that by virtue of my presence within the kingdom of God prior to any judgement, that no Christian man may possess it more than I. St James concurs and I am invited to speak further. In answer to his first I declare that hope is an expectation that salvation will be attained, that soul will be reunited with flesh and that, like St Peter, man shall receive the keys to the kingdom of Heaven. The question of where Hope comes from is, I feel, a more personal one and I answer thus: that David first placed light in my heart through his psalms and then, he, James through his epistles. He seems much pleased at this answer for his flame burns bright from within, iridescent and luminous. He has one final test for me and I am to tell him what it is that I hope for. This is no hardship for, upon the Last Judgement, I seek resurrection of the flesh and through this, an eternal attachment to God. The chorus of the angels of the Cherubim herald that my task is complete, for they erupt into voice singing the hymn of praise *Sperent in te: Let them hope in you.*

As they reach their crescendo, a bright glare flashes as lightening and we are joined by another soul who shines as radiant as a new bride rejoicing in love. He makes for St Peter and St James and, reunited, the trio delight in song and dance, gleaming brighter, lighter with each beat of the Music of the Spheres. Beatrice tells me this new soul, burning far brighter than the others, is the apostle loved by Christ. I know him, then, to be John the Evangelist, he whom Jesus bequeathed with the care of his mother, Mary, as he died upon the cross. As they whirl and dance, twirl and spin, their light becomes so bright my mortal eyes cannot tolerate the magnificent glare. I look to Beatrice but all is dark for, in this moment, I am quite blind!

Panicked, I shout out, for all around me, with no warning, is blackness. St John calms me for he tells me that soon enough my sight will return and it shall be thanks to my beloved Beatrice's own healing eyes. Before that happens, he wishes to speak to me of Love, the third theological virtue. He asks what love it is that I wish for. I have only one, for all my heart desires is God's love, for He exemplifies all that is virtue and goodness. St John asks me to expand further for he wishes to know the source of my understanding that God is the paragon of goodness and thus the embodiment of love. I tell him of three things that have directed me towards God; my personal study of Aristotle and his meaningful writings on philosophy, revelations through scripture including Christ's death and the resurrection and, finally, my love of the Christian faith, for upon Earth, I endeavour to travel on the path of Truth such that it may lead me to God. For, in death, I seek eternal life.

He bids we continue our discourse and asks if there are any other reasons for my love and trust in God. I suspect he wishes to hear that I know my scriptures so I tell him thus: that God created the Earth, that God created then sacrificed Jesus that man may live and, that in striving to demonstrate the theological virtues of faith, hope and love, He may take mercy upon me and draw my spirit unto Heaven. Upon hearing this the redeemed souls burst into song, for they rejoice in a hymn of praise. I notice a glimmer of light, nay a flicker, then a sunbeam, now a radiant lustre, shining as bright as Apollo himself, for a miracle has occurred and my sight is restored! Indeed, I see a fourth figure clearly now, standing in front of me.

THE FATHER OF HUMANKIND

Beatrice steps forward and gestures to him, for it is Adam, God's own creation, the first man, the first soul. Indeed, he is the father of humankind. My mind is awhirl for I have many questions but it seems that Adam knows already the nature of my thoughts, for he tells me that he sees my mind reflected in the untarnished mirror that is God's mind, for He is the mirror of all things. He pre-empts my first question which relates to his age. He confirms he has seen 6,498 years which he calculates from the time elapsed since God placed him in the Garden of Eden. For he spent 930 years upon Earth before he was exiled to Limbo whereupon he spent 4,302 years waiting for the resurrection of Christ before he was released during the Harrowing of Hell. He has spent a further 1,266 years in his current home, which is Heaven.

I confess to absolute fascination, for he is most exact in his mathematics. My fascination is overtaken by shock at his next revelation, for I wish to know how long he remained in the Garden. He tells me it was a mere seven hours from his creation to the moment of his disgrace when his virtuous soul transgressed and he was cast into exile by God. I ask for the reasons behind God's wrath and he says it was not that he took a bite of the apple, rather that he succumbed to the temptation to sin by trespassing beyond the boundaries set by God thereby disobeying His law. I am captivated by Adam's answers, for he is being honest and truthful and I learn much during this lengthy discourse.

My final question is one that has perplexed me for many a year, for it relates to the language spoken by Adam, one which, as first man, I assume he conceived. He speaks in riddles, for he says it became extinct before the giant Nimrod built the tower at Babel. For language, as man, is mortal and condemned to change such that it shifts on the moving tides, changes with the breeze and re-forms as the clouds in the skies, for it is a human creation. Nature determined that man must speak and Heaven bestowed speech upon man, yet human taste causes it to reshape and reform as deemed most fitting at any given time. Thus, the language of Eden is long dead as he suspects will today's language be tomorrow. His eloquence is sublime and we five are enraptured by his words; me, the Apostles and my beloved, graceful, most favoured lady, Beatrice.

Indeed, as Adam finishes his enlightening description of his time upon the universe, the celestial chorus of the Cherubim erupt into such enthusiastic singing, it is as if the heavens smile upon us, such that they rejoice in the celebration of the Holy Trinity, for they sing *Gloria in excelsis, Deo!* We are all uplifted. Indeed, I am intoxicated, drunk on the bliss of the rapturous sweetness and nectar herein for, in this moment, we all experience a taste of Heaven where all is pure and beauty and grace. As we bask in the glory of love, light and happiness, I gaze upon the four torches burning brightly in front of me when, suddenly, the celestial choir is silenced, as if their maestro has angrily swiped down his baton, violently concluding a fortissimo coda.

St Peter, luminous with an iridescent flame, burns yet brighter still, close to combusting, glowing from Jupiter white to Mars red, for it seems he is set to do battle. And indeed, he does thus for he begins another tirade against the prelates who have sought ecclesiastical office only for personal gain, to amass great fortunes, for their corruption and greed sinks his Church to the depths of the cesspit, a sewer now lying in place of his own burial ground. For these disgraced clergy there is no sacrifice, no martyrdom, no surrender and he is furious they deny themselves nothing.

I confess his fierce outburst shakes and unnerves me somewhat, yet I sympathise with his predicament for we must not forget St Peter was the first Bishop of Rome and he despairingly witnesses the downfall of his beloved Church; the soiling, decaying and corruption of the sanctity of the Papal See his spiritual descendants leave as their legacy. As his rage roars into a final crescendo, the entire sphere glows blood red, including my beloved Beatrice, blushing as a chaste maiden upon hearing of another's fallen virtue. I am certain she fears that the sanctity of Paradise itself may be tarnished such that holy figures within seek retribution on the failing throngs upon Earth.

St Peter cries out in anguish, for he wishes God to be more swift in His vengeance. Yet he knows as I, that God's providence will mete out Divine justice for He sees the wrongdoings by dishonest popes and their prelates and, upon Judgement Day, shall set them right. St Peter tells me, nay urges me, to be truthful in my writing, to ensure that my earthly prose is formed of honest words which he concedes should be frank and candid, for this will help mankind understand that the Church must be protected from ruination at all costs. He falls silent and gazes hard upon me and I am aware of the magnitude of the task I am assigned; for it is vital that mortal man respects the sanctity of the Church, praises the glory of God and His Divine providence, for in life, he must follow the path of Truth in order to attain salvation in death.

I feel the heavy weights of burden and anxiety upon my shoulders yet, as I look up, I am lifted, for I witness a succession of beautiful, sparkling iridescent snowflakes rise aloft from the realm of the Fixed Stars to that of the highest heaven. As I look upon the snow flurries in earnest, I realise they are not flakes, but the illustrious souls of the blessed, rising upwards, for they climb in their own ascension. Indeed, my mortal eyes may not follow their entire journey as they drift, ascending to the heights of the Primum Mobile, for they cannot yet behold the wonder that is the Empyrean although I confess I am utterly transfixed and my neck cranes to track their progress.

Beatrice sees me straining and commands me to gaze down once more upon the heavens below to see how far I have orbited. My vision is clear such that although I am risen higher than the last time I looked back, the clarity allows me to see in intricate detail the planets and the heavens, the stars and the sun and the moon I have left behind. Indeed, there is the island of Crete and the sea across which Ulysses traversed! I note from the placement of the sun that my time in the Fixed Stars under the constellation of Gemini has been seven hours and I am reminded of Adam and the time he spent in the heavenly garden before he was cast into exile. God does not intend to do thus with me I am certain of it, for lo, the light and the beauty and splendour of the pageant of the Saints of the Church Triumphant descend from the Empyrean and are upon us.

PRIMUM MOBILE - HOME OF ANGELS

I look to Beatrice, for she must share in the glory of the magnificence of the procession but already she gazes into my eyes with a love, beauty and radiance so pure it is as unique as the snowflakc itself. As I search for her smile, my heart flutters, for I am quite dazzled by her beauty such that in this moment His light is reflected in her face. In this instant we are united as one soul and we ascend, spinning as the wheels on the griffin's chariot for we, too, have become orbs of holy redemption and mimic the comets firing across the midnight sky. She laughs, rejoicing in celestial delight and takes me with her, for I imbibe the pleasure, joy and rapture radiating from the depths of her heart and soul, and I am intoxicated. We rise thus, ascending to the ninth celestial orb, the crystalline outermost sphere of Heaven. For we enter the core of the Primum Mobile; home of angels.

Beatrice looks about this invisible sphere and sighs in contentment, for we are in the core of the heavens, the prime mover of the spheres below, for this celestial heaven is the origin of the universe. From here derives the motion which informs all the orbital planets beneath, the stars and the sun and the moon, the seas and the tides and mankind, for it moves by God's will alone. She tells me that, here, we move beyond the realms of space and time, for this heaven is God's Mind. It is called the Swiftest Sphere, for it revolves faster than all other heavens for it radiates light and love, is surrounded by love and light and is the place where time began. Unlike the moon, the surface is smooth, for there are no blemishes, no craters, no shadows; no landmarks. More impressive even than the planet Saturn of crystal, it is a place of celestial supremacy and vitality. Perfection.

She stands sublime in her serenity as she inhales the glory of God in this place, for she has come home. I am surprised then, that as quickly as St Peter when his glow turned from Jupiter white to Mars red, my beloved, graceful, blessed Beatrice begins a ferocious outburst against the sins of humankind. She vilifies mortal man for his avarice, for in eschewing the virtue of temperance he risks losing the ultimate honour and rapture of rejoicing in the salvation of Heaven. She castigates man for his ineptitude at managing free will for, she says, as he leaves the innocence of his childhood behind, he uses free will deficiently and imperfectly, thus he loses his spiritual sight. I ask how this may be righted and she tells me mankind lacks leadership and this is the root of his issue, for he needs guidance.

In this moment she prophesises a tempest of the seas leaving ships rudderless and directionless but, she assures me, Divine intervention in the form of God's providence will set the prows firmly back on course so the fleet may resume their journey on the path of Truth. I know then, when she talks after, of the blossom and ripe, succulent fruits these mariners will enjoy as they reach dry land, that she talks of man's redemption. That through God's intervention, humankind shall attain salvation, as it did when He showed the ultimate mercy and sacrificed His son, that man could rejoice once more in the glory of Heaven.

I am transfixed, for she stands as a goddess. I am

captivated by her strength and her unwavering devotion to God, for her stance is that of a warrior, fighting to keep God's troops secure, that they may be delivered safely unto the bosom of their mother, Mary. Again, my gaze is fixed upon her eyes for they sparkle with the intense light of purity. Upon closer inspection I realise that what I see is a reflection so I turn to know its source. My eyes rest upon a tiny point, yet it glares white with a dazzling radiance, a brightness such as my mortal eyes have never seen before, not even when I witnessed Christ in the pageant of the Church Triumphant.

Surrounding this miniscule flashpoint of blazing, overpowering light are nine enormous concentric rings; luminous, glowing, glittering as halos. It is astonishing. The smallest ring, that closest to the source, spins fastest and brightest, the remaining eight rotating at an ever-slower pace as each radiates out, the intensity of light diminishing until the ninth, at the furthest distance from the source, is seen to revolve slowest and dimmest. Beatrice sees the wonder in my face, for indeed, this is a sight most glorious which I know to be not earthly, rather, celestial. She informs me that I look upon the nine orders of angels; the three hierarchies, so called as they are placed in accordance with their nearness to God. And so it proves, for as I focus my sight, I see that indeed the rings are formed of dancing angels, those beings unblemished by original sin, radiating their love and light as they rejoice in the glory of God.

As I wonder if I have the linguistic capacity to convey such a beautiful vision to earthly man, she asks me of the central light; the source. I speculate it is Christ himself for it burns bright and fierce but she reminds me we are in the kingdom of Heaven and thus my mortal eyes look upon the light of God. I am transfixed. Hypnotised. Spellbound. For, truly, He is magical. And so, with intellectual reasoning, one may deduce that the ring closest to Him radiates light brighter, whiter, purer and revolves more intensely than any other, because it radiates the greatest love, the most fervent desire and deepest faith in Him. It rejoices in the glory of God with such intensity, for it has the clearest sight of Him, is closest to Him and His Divine love for, indeed, these are the Seraphim, the highest ranking of all angelic orders in the heavens.

Beatrice tells me the angelic rings in the spiritual realm are as the heavenly spheres in the physical universe such that they both follow the concentric arrangement. God is at the centre of the spiritual realm and, the planet Earth, of the physical. Yet they share a converse relationship in that the heavenly spheres get larger and spin faster as they radiate away from Earth while the gleam of the angelic rings dim and rotate slower the more remote they are from God's source. The formation of the spheres and the angels thus correspond, for the outermost sphere of the physical universe, the Primum Mobile, and the innermost circle of angels are both situated closest to God and, as such, revolve faster and burn brighter than their partners.

I must look confused, for Beatrice attempts to untie the knot I have created in my mind by introducing the idea of Nature and its influence on the situation. She says it is usual in the natural world that size and power are linked - the larger a being the more power it has and, therefore, the more blessed it is. Thus, the largest sphere of the celestial heavens, the Primum Mobile, is closest to God and therefore radiates more light and revolves faster than all other spheres. Yet, when we consider the angelic rings in the spiritual realm, size is irrelevant, for power - the intensity of vision and love for God - is of the greater importance. Thus, the Seraphims, the most powerful angels in Heaven, are placed nearest to God in the smallest ring, for they love Him with a complete passion, in glorious exultation. Their love for Him is perfect, she says, because their sight of him, by virtue of their proximity to Him, is perfect.

At this, the angelic halos begin to vibrate, gleaming with intense brightness and lustre as they radiate light and love into the universe. They burst into a chorus of *Gloria,*

Hosannah in excelsis! for they sing in triumphant delight, rejoicing in God's love as they praise His glorious light at the source. I am transfixed and feel an urgent compulsion to study them in earnest, for this scene is as a celestial theatre and I need to know more of the troupe, such that I may be fortunate enough to converse with one.

Beatrice tells me the Order of the Angels takes the structure of a hierarchy formed into three triads. The innermost rings contain the most powerful and devoted of all angels including the Seraphim and Cherubim, whilst the outermost include the Archangels and angels. This is not to say those angels furthest from God's source possess less love or devotion for Him, nor Him for they, rather they radiate with the intensity of grace and blessing they possess, which is determined by their sight of Him. The closer in proximity an angel is to God, the more blessed he is and thus he radiates love and joy in abundance. I see this now, for the central source shines brighter than a thousand suns, the powerful angelic order of the Seraphims at the first ring blaze as a million stars, whilst the halo of Archangels at the outermost ninth ring glow as softly as a hundred moons.

Have I not claimed my beloved reads me as a book? She can see I have tied another knot in my mind which needs untangling. Already she knows my thoughts as I consider the universe and heavens within, the angels and their connexion to the universe and, indeed God and also the Fall. For, in truth, I ponder upon the Creation. She looks to the source of light at the centre of the nine glistening rings and it seems to inform her thoughts, such that she clarifies that the mind of God has revealed itself unto her for the specific purpose of addressing me. She takes on a scholastic tone and lectures me in earnest. The Creation of the universe, she says, denoted the beginning of time. Nothing pre-dates it as there is no 'before'. It was performed in an act of supreme munificence as an expression of love and triumph, nothing more. There was no motive for glory such that His only desire was to see a reflection of Himself in his own Creation. It is a timeless, Divine concept, for it is untouched and unaffected by human action, communication or movement.

This is a lot of information to absorb but she is eloquent in a way I am not and I am confident her staccato delivery helps me to understand. So, she tells me of the reasoning behind the Creation, but not the physicality of it. She takes a breath and continues. In one fiery eruption of light, three elements were conceived, instantly yet concurrently. These were pure matter, pure form and a blend of the two. They were apportioned into a hierarchical formation with pure form at the head, pure matter at the base and the blend sitting in the middle. Pure form, she says, refers to the angels. Pure matter, to the planet Earth and the blend, to the celestial heavens. She talks of the creation of angels and says this occurred at the same instant God created the universe, for in needing to keep the heavens revolving, he needed primary movers.

One cannot talk of the Creation without discussing the Fall whereupon Lucifer and his unruly mob of angels rose up and rebelled against the higher power that is God. We know his punishment for this vile demonstration of the sin of Pride was to be cast down to the depths of Hell on Earth with his demonic crew, the Damned; all fallen angels exiled to the furthermost and lowest realm of the inferno, the weight of the entire universe upon them. But what of the angels remaining in the highest heavens? Those purest in form who displayed humility, loyalty and obedience to their benefactor? Beatrice tells me He gifted these holy ones grace and intelligence, the latter of which they use to ensure the universe and all the planets and spheres within maintain a perpetual motion, for he named them the Intelligencia, the Angelic Movers.

She tells me that angels, as humankind, have free will. They have intelligence also but no memory, for there is no need, such that their love for God is so perfect and all-encompassing their gaze is always upon Him, free from distraction. Mankind has divided thought but angels have no such requirement to record events, thoughts or deeds to memory for they enjoy permanent contemplation of God and His glory. Their love of God is pure, such that they perpetually radiate His love and light. Their loyalty is eternal and their vision of Him clear for He is within their sights as they reside with Him in the kingdom of Heaven rejoicing in his warm embrace.

She changes stance and I believe she prepares for another battle. Indeed she does and, again, the prelates of the Church are to endure a further tirade! For she castigates them and their deliberate attempts to silence the Gospels by misrepresenting the beauty of the Holy Scriptures, continuing to present inaccuracies as ecclesiastic fact. They philosophise for vanity's sake, preaching elaborate tales, mystical fables, rather than adhering to the words of the Bible, she accuses. As shepherds, she says, they neglect the needs of their flock such that they fail to nourish them with spiritual and moral counsel.

I know Beatrice to be nothing if not grace, elegance, truth and humility and, as such, for her to be rebuking the clergy in this manner does indeed suggest that her frustrations have merit. I wish to divert her from this exasperation so return to the subject of the angels. I ask after their number, for the halos encircling the source of light are immense such that there must be thousands contained within each ring. She welcomes the distraction and tells me it is impossible to calculate, for the number is infinite such that God's love is infinite and angels reflect His glory. His love is endless, the ways He communicates His love are endless and thus, there is no end to the number of angelic souls sharing in the celestial spheres and radiating light and love in His name.

As I turn to look upon the glorious halos of the angelic choirs to acknowledge their magnitude and enormity, their light weakens and they disappear from view, vanishing upwards as they are drawn into the highest heaven, one by one, scaling heights beyond my earthly vision. In the moment the immense glare of the source point fades into oblivion, I turn to Beatrice and am overcome, struck by such inordinate beauty, a loveliness, a vivacity and ethereal glow so perfect that, again, mortal words may not capture the very essence of her radiance. Indeed, I truly believe such exquisiteness is beyond the reach of mortal man, for surely only the creator of such beauty may rest His eyes upon her face and relish the joy?

She tells me that in this instant we have reached the magical tenth and highest heaven, that of the Empyrean, a place beyond physical existence, beyond space and time. Here, I will find everything that is the purest form of love, light and intellect as this is the abode of the angels, the home of the flesh of the blessed souls. For it is the house of God. She speaks in earnest, showing grace and humility as she declares that here too, I shall witness the flesh of the Virgin Mary, Queen of the Heavens, and she shall present herself to me complete; as body and soul reunited upon that final day of judgement.

THE EMPYREAN
THE CELESTIAL ROSE

I am overwhelmed, utterly joyous at this wondrous news yet filled with trepidation. I do not have the words to convey such a heavenly tale to earthly man, for surely the language does not exist to do it justice. I have humility enough to know I do not possess it. In this moment, a lightning bolt flashes and I am enveloped by the pure living light of this highest heaven which blazes with a brilliance unseen by me before. Once more I find myself almost blinded. Once more Beatrice soothes me, for she informs I partake in a ritual of welcome, for a man's soul must be prepared that he may tolerate the ultimate light of God in the Empyrean.

I attempt to gaze upon my surroundings and my weakened eyes are drawn to a winding river of light, emitting live, fiery sparks onto the banks either side, whereupon they blossom into glistening rubies, then jump back in to replenish themselves so that others may leap out and take root in the fertile soil. Beatrice tells me I look upon the Fountain of Grace and that even displaying the beauty it does, what I see is not the true joy of Heaven, for I still have limited mortal mind and vision. However, I shall know bliss. I will rejoice in the complete experience of the celestial Paradise soon enough, for I need to make only one final preparation. I feel compelled to move forward to the river, drawn to taste its nectar.

I realise in that moment it is not nourishment I seek, although I am pulled to it as an infant to its mother's breast, for instead, I plunge my face into it such that I may bathe my eyes. She instructs me to open them and look, for I now possess vision so powerful that I may set my gaze upon even the brightest of radiances and know that my mortal eyesight may bear it. Indeed, there is a light here, dazzling in its form and I rest my eyes upon it with ease. I am astounded, for I realise this beam is of God himself! It bounces off the very top surface of the Primum Mobile, reflecting upon the entire universe, for this single source of light from God illuminates the earth, the moon, the stars and the sun, the celestial heavens and the Primum Mobile. I am shocked, for the clarity of my vision is exalted to such levels it seems I may visualise beyond infinity, for my sight is no longer of mortal man. It is of the celestial heavens. In that instant, the river changes from a long, winding path to a circle. Another ring of light. Another halo.

Immediately, my eyes rest upon it, for the ring is formed of a series of thrones, seated upon which are all the saints in Heaven. Behind are yet more thrones where sit evermore blessed souls radiating back in tiers of concentric circles as petals on an open flower imbibing the sun. Behind the thrones of the saints sit all the angels in Heaven, again, as soft, perfumed petals. As I take in this majestic sight, I realise I look at the form of a celestial rose and radiating from the centre, as the stamen, is a blazing white effulgence, a light so brilliant I know it may only be the love of God. In truth I am mesmerised by the entire apparition, for it is enormous, quite magnificent, with thousands upon thousands of snow-white petals teaming down from the uppermost tier to the centre. Beatrice tells me that with my perfect vision I look at Heaven's Court wherein sit the two heavenly hosts; the blessed saints and the holy angels.

We move closer to the rose which is in full bloom, rejoicing in the love, light and warmth of the sunbeams it attracts. She turns to smile at me and quietly tells me that I, too, shall enjoy this glory when God's will bids it. She points to an empty throne. Is this mine? Am I to know beatification and reside on a tier with the blessed saints? It seems not, for this is reserved for Emperor Henry VII for he, not I, shall be the spiritual saviour of Italy. As we continue our approach, I recognise some faces that I have seen within the celestial spheres. Beatrice tells me all blessed souls, those of the faithful reside here in the Empyrean with God, for she reminds me I encountered them upon the seven heavenly orbs only that I should know their strength of grace.

I watch entranced while angels, as pollinating bees, gently fly around inside the rose, dipping into the stamen that they may share the love and peace within their hive. I marvel at the size of the flower and wonder how I may accurately convey its sheer height and breadth, for there are many truths within Heaven I will struggle to find the language to precisely describe if I am limited to the lexicon of mortal man. And now, all souls within the shimmering rose direct their faces upwards to the beaming glare, this single star which radiates the pure light and love of God.

I am at a loss for words, such as the Barbarian hordes when they first set eyes upon the glory that was Rome, for this is a beauty and purity that I am privileged to behold. I turn again to Beatrice, for this celestial wonder is a miracle, a phenomenon, an absolute sensation and I wish to share in my sense of wonderment but she is gone, for she resumes her place in the unreachable heights without a parting embrace or a backwards glance. In her place stands an old contemplative, a mystical soul, but I yearn for my Beatrice who, in this moment, has abandoned me. I am forsaken.

Indeed, I am bereft, for she is my life, my love, my joy; for she is the very essence of beauty and purity. I know not why she has deserted me when the light of God shines down upon us both and the heavens rejoice in rapturous bliss, for I know she loves me. I am liberated because of her, for she has reset me on the path of Truth that I may begin again my journey to salvation. For in casting me to the vile, torturous cesspit of the inferno, I now know to reject sin and seek only the light of goodness. She has presented me with a gift that is priceless in its worth and more than that even, she has already told me we shall be reunited as Divine providence wills that we spend eternity as one in the celestial heavens. I fear I am lost without her, for my journey is near completion so I cannot fathom why she is not at my side that we may triumph in my success, in this glory, together.

Sensing my despair, the elder shuffles forward and declares that he is to guide me the remainder of the way for Beatrice specifically asked it of him, for my day's journey through the celestial Paradise is almost complete. He tells me that my ecclesiastical quest, to understand one must attain salvation through redemption, that which has lasted the duration of Easter week, too, is almost over. He bids me to look upon Beatrice in the celestial rose and I locate her in the dizzying heights of the third tier from the top, seated upon her throne. It is an immeasurable distance away from where I stand yet with my vision exalted since my eyes were purged in the Fountain of Grace I may see in intricate detail the beautiful features of her precious face; from her tender lips to her sparkling eyes, to her soft lashes and luminous skin as the light of God radiates upon her. I am compelled to offer a spontaneous prayer of thanksgiving, for without her, I am nothing. I entreat her to continue to offer me her prayers, her guidance and protection, for my soul is hers in life on Earth and upon death in the heavenly spheres. She gazes upon me with a sweet smile and then returns to her contemplation of God above. She is gone, then. Mine no more until we meet upon my Judgement Day.

The elder enters into discourse and introduces himself as St Bernard. I am impressed to make his acquaintance for I know him to be the French abbot responsible for creating the rules of the Knights Templar, the fearless warriors of God whom I met upon the sphere of Mars. He is to be my chaperone to the end of my quest and, I confess, I am nervous and full of wonder for he is most inspiring such that Pope Pius VIII granted him the honour 'Doctor of the Church'. He suggests that I take a further look upon the rose for it will help prepare my vision for the ultimate light that I am soon to meet. Through the living light of God from above, I search the thrones and look at the faces of the holy angels and blessed faithful souls, for these are God's chosen in the realm of His creation.

St Bernard tells me that as a strict Benedictine monk he is a devotee of Mary although, in truth, he has no need to dispense with this information, for he is famed for his utter dedication to her, for his writings promote her as a paragon of Divine wisdom and the Mother of all humankind. He tells me he was thus specifically chosen by Beatrice such that he may entreaty the Virgin direct to intercede, in order that God may reveal Himself unto me so I may eulogise appropriately upon my return to Earth. He bids me return my gaze to the rose and seek the furthest edge of the top tier whereupon there is one light burning brighter than the infinite thousands. It is encircled by floating angels; singing, rejoicing, triumphant as they herald the sitter upon the throne. For it is Mary herself, the Queen of Heaven. The Mother of God.

She smiles her thanks at the angels who radiate in exultation and I find myself utterly entranced. I look to St Bernard but he stares at her so intently, with such pure love and devotion that he seems as adoring as the host of all heralding angels herein combined. Indeed, I am compelled to look upon her again and this time more ardently, for his face reflects the glory of her and I, too, am intoxicated. Again I am confused, for this spectacle, this sight I behold, is so glorious, so elaborate, so beguiling, I do not know how I am expected to accurately convey its celestial perfection using only mortal words, for I see the blessed Mother in all her triumphant glory. For I see her in the flesh. Yet I confess to heartbreak for I am undeserving and, in this moment, am tempted to omit all reference to this theological masterpiece, this supreme vision, for I bow to the grace that is Mary and fear I shall prove unworthy.

We breathe in this magnificent spectacle a few minutes more for, truly, it is wondrous. St Bernard says he wishes me to explore the heavenly court in finer detail to better understand it, for it is split into various sections, hemispheres and tiers. I am therefore bid to look upon the rose again, specifically to the petals where I shall find the key spirits installed upon their celestial thrones. To the middle of the uppermost and outer tier sits the ethereal Virgin, our mother, Mary. She is flanked by Adam and Moses to one side and St Peter of the Keys and St John the Evangelist on the other. Directly opposite on a lower tier is John the Baptist. At her feet kneels Eve for, in truth, they are both mothers to all humankind; one earthly, one spiritual and thus they reside here together, in perpetuity.

I am mystified to find Eve so welcome here, but St Bernard explains that despite executing the first ever sin, that which inflicted such pain and injury to God, the blessed Mary, Queen of Heaven, showed mercy, for she closed the wound and, in doing so, provided salvation to Eve such that she may reside alongside her in the celestial rose. This will be a revelation to earthly man, I am sure, that the first sinners, both of whom were cast into exile for four centuries, responsible for the banishment of mankind from Heaven, for whom God sacrificed His blessed son, reside upon thrones in the celestial Paradise to enjoy heavenly glory.

The rose flares white for St Bernard speaks of the innocent infants, those babes who reside upon the midline, watched over by Mary, for who is she if not the essence of purity and chastity? The Virgin Mother. He has pre-empted my question, for he can see I am confused. Indeed, I am certain that a number of these children would have died before the coming of Christ and as such, like the virtuous pagans as my brother Virgil, would be expected to reside in Limbo. I am at a loss then, to understand why they are here. St Bernard concurs that this would be the case if children followed the same path as their adult counterparts, but they did not. He explains thus: that before the birth of Christ, children of the faithful attained salvation as a matter of course and were placed within the celestial heavens irrespective of their virtue or grace. Since the resurrection, only those souls who had undergone baptism could expect to attain salvation, for this was a holy requirement to enter the kingdom of Heaven.

Those children therefore, fortunate enough to have been born unto the time of Jesus yet unfortunate enough to have died unbaptised, would find themselves exiled to the painless borders of Hell in Limbo. He concurs that children have free will but by virtue of their innocence they do not exert it. I thus see, that still, the components of beatitude that are grace and merit may only apply when they are conjoined. For whilst a virtuous pagan may possess an estimable and worthy soul, he lacks grace. A saved child, conversely, lacks merit yet possesses grace in abundance. He is quick to clarify that no soul resides in the celestial heavens by chance. For it is God's will, His Divine providence that directs their final dwelling such that it is preordained. Mortal man has no influence over Divine destiny, he reminds me, and therefore he should not attempt to scrutinise it or unravel the mystery that is God's mind.

Despite my frustrations at the finality of his answer, it seems this is the limit of his discourse upon the subject, for he now gazes intently upon Mary and instructs me to do the same. She remains surrounded by angels who rejoice in a hymn of praise, but one hovers with intent, resplendent, with magnificent wings fluttering gently such that he consumes her entire vision and it is he St Bernard wishes to observe. For this is Gabriel, he of the Annunciation; the Archangel. He cries out *Ave Maria gratia plena: Hail Mary full of grace* and the celestial chorus erupts into a triumphant herald, for he asks that she opens her heart that she may show mercy and favour.

St Bernard tells me that we are now ready to pray to Mary, for she alone can intercept God's mind such that she may persuade Him to reveal Himself unto me. For mortal matter alone is not sufficient to take me beyond the celestial heights and it is here I am expected to navigate if it is the Divine light of God I seek. He tells me the wings Beatrice bestowed upon me are unlikely to suffice as we aim for the summit, so it is to the Virgin Mary we look to make final preparations for this propitious encounter. And in this moment, I understand why St Bernard was sent to me. For Beatrice is my love and, as such, too great a distraction when my gaze needs to turn to the Virgin intercessor and then, if I am to understand it, the Deity himself. For the face of my lady is too radiant, too beautiful and pure such that I may not tear myself away from the light of her smile to witness the light of the Mother and Father of Heaven.

St Bernard raises his eyes, his heart, his soul to his saving grace, the Holy Mother. He begins the prayer of intercession, for he knows that without her intervention I will not be granted the grace to allow me to behold the Almighty. He pleads with her to purify my sight, to remove all earthly clouds that obscure my vision such that I may experience the supreme joy of the final bliss; the beatific image. He appeals to the tenderness, love and generosity within her heart that she may offer hope to the humble pilgrim I am, that grace and virtue enough will be mine that I may ascend further into the heavenly realms, that I may look upon the face of God. Finally, he prays that she may grant me the memory that I may succeed in my mission to save mankind, to spread the word of God for, through her charity, earthly man may believe that he too, as I, should she grant it, have Hope.

At this moment Beatrice places her palms together in reverence, as do all hosts within the heavenly court and they join in the prayer of intercession until it rises to a crescendo, the angelic choirs and Music of the Spheres deploying their best and most fervent entreaties. The Virgin has listened. Our Mother has heard. The Queen of Heaven accedes. For Mary consents. A triumphant heralding rouses from within the rose and Mary looks up, to the highest heights. St Bernard bids me to follow her gaze but he tarries, for my eyes are already there as the Light of Truth burns brighter than five thousand suns and all the descendants of Apollo within.

The Mother has blessed me indeed and her intercession has triumphed, for I look upon the True Light, an effulgence of supreme clarity and it is dazzling; astonishing. Indeed, I gaze upon perfection and fear to look at another thing, another being, another soul, an angel, my Beatrice even, would be to look upon inadequacy, deficiency, imperfection. I am transfixed, for I know now that from this light all other is mere radiance or reflection.

THE LIGHT SUPREME

I gaze upon the Eternal Light in earnest, for by the grace of Mary, my eyes were prepared specifically for this moment such that they were charged and may thus penetrate the glare. It remains a constant, yet as I stare deep within, I observe a transformation, for one light becomes two, then three. Three lights become three glares. Three glares become three luminous orbs. And within the Eternal Light, the luminous orbs of the Divine, I witness a harmony; the unity of all creation and all time. For I gaze upon the Divine trinity. The Father, the Son and the Holy Spirit.

I know in this precise moment I am spiritually moved as never before, yet have a deep stillness and, through this, know that I have attained total peace. I am compelled to contemplate the incarnation I witness, this physical embodiment of the Deity, for upon sight, overcome, overawed and overjoyed, I have surrendered the entirety of my love and my will unto Him. Immediately, a flash of white cracks as lightning and I am acknowledged for, finally, my soul is at one with the Almighty, the Heavenly Father, the King of Heaven. And in this moment of rapture I ask of

Him to reveal the true meaning of this incarnation that I may take the message back to earthly man. He, as Mary, accedes and He deigns to inform me for, momentarily, within the Light of Truth and by His Divine grace I glimpse it. For I am shown the Godhead, the true being of God; His divinity. His substance. And in this precise moment, my soul is aligned with God's love, for I have gazed upon His face.

And now that I have seen the True Light, the Holy Trinity, the very face of God, the Godhead, all memory fails me! And this, despite St Bernard's entreaty! Yet I am certain it was of supreme significance, for although I do not recall the specifics, I have an impression of it and my heart knows a peace and stillness, a bliss and contentment as if I have risen from a perfect dream. Indeed, it fades as a perfect snowflake melts in the sun such that I may evoke only the sweetness of the memory, yet not the memory itself. So how may I convince humankind of the glory of God, of the triumph of the heavens, of the Holy Trinity and the Godhead if I have no memory, for it has disappeared as autumn leaves caught by a mischievous wind. And without recollection I am lost. For with memory only of the sweetness, yet reliance solely upon mortal words, I am undone, for these are woefully lacking, as inept and insufficient as those on the tongue of a newly born babe.

I must pray to God. I must ask for the power to express these celestial truths and visions, to retain memory of these heavenly miracles and wonders, for the bestowal of words and language such that I may do justice to His creation, such that I may shine a celestial light upon the darkness that is earthly life. For now that I have seen God's truth, now that my eyes have been opened in the heavens, I see clearly that temptation is a trap, to ensnare mankind to deviate from the path of Truth. For if one is not on the path of Truth, how may he see the light of Truth? And if he may not see the light, he must stumble through the blackness, staggering through The Dark Wood, as I, alone and frightened, obstructed by the vicious she-wolf and all the horrors, inhumanities and brutal agonies of the inferno.

I therefore beseech Him, to arm me with a spark, just a glimpse, a glimmer of what I witnessed in the Eternal Light, that I may remember and relay His Glory unto the world, for it is my human failing, a mortal weakness that I have not the language to adequately convey the beauty of the pure light and love that is Heaven. I believe I retain free will and although feel it now synchronises in perfect harmony with God's will, with His providence, such that my mind explodes with joy because of it, it is not enough to carry the miracle of Creation to earthly man in the words of my poetry.

I need memory of it to do it justice, not the sensation of the memory. For how else may I inform humankind of the joys of Heaven, of the bliss of the spheres, of the love that God has in His heart for the faithful? For through love of Him, we may ascend to the celestial realms of the highest heavens and know that the rotating planets spin at the providence of His will, to the dulcet melodies of the Music of the Spheres, for God is the eternal force that informs the moon and the sun and the heavens and angels, the light and the love and the stars.

The End

Beyond The Inferno

Beyond The Inferno Audiobook

Beyond The Inferno Collection

Inferno

Purgatory

Paradise

www.alexlmoretti.com

Printed in Great Britain
by Amazon